The Abusive Wager

First Edition

Christopher Trevor

The Abusive Wager

First Edition

Published by The Nazca Plains Corporation
Las Vegas, Nevada
2007

ISBN: 978-1-887895-04-0

Published by

The Nazca Plains Corporation ®
4640 Paradise Rd, Suite 141
Las Vegas NV 89109-8000

PUBLISHER'S NOTE
The Abusive Wager is a work of fiction created wholly by
Christopher Trevor's imagination. All characters are fictional and
any resemblance to any persons living or deceased is purely
by accident. No portion of this book reflects any real person or
events.

Cover, © Vladislav Gansovsky - FOTOLIA
Art Director, Blake Stephens

Acknowledgements

To my buddy Adam H. for his ticklish sense of humor.

Timmy- thank you for inspiration for some many tickle tales and for being such a (un)willing tickle hero...

Vince- you fiendish tickler you, thank you for helping to bring the tribute story to life...and for a most sinister ending...

Craig- We met briefly and your inspiration was awesome. Keep up the great hi-jinx and shenanigans buddy...

Daniel- one of the handsomest Wall Street executive's I have ever had the pleasure of meeting.

Tom Shaw- (author of "That Day at The Quarry) Thank you for setting me on the road to writing with "games of chance" as the instigator for harrowing tales.

The Abusive Wager

Christopher Trevor

Contents

Introduction

I love games of chance. I love seeing just how far a guy will agree to stretch himself in an agreed upon game of chance. Most guys won't admit to it but they love putting themselves in situations where their machismo is put to the test. I love cruel irony wherein a situation with an intended goal goes totally awry. I love seeing the tables turned on an unsuspecting guy. And I especially love when an ordinary evening spent sipping beer in a bar can turn into a festive and watered-down occasion. I suppose it can be said that I am drawn to darkness and the more sinister side of game playing. The book that so inspired me nearly a decade ago ("That Day at The Quarry" written by Tom Shaw) still haunts me (in a good way) when I write stories of games of chance and cunning. In this latest book I explore the facets of what I am describing herein...to a point of exaggeration of course. In "A Tribute to Timmy and Vince (they are my two buddies that I dedicated my book "Don't!! Stop!! That Tickles" too) I bring to fictional life Vince's ongoing fantasy of nabbing and finally tickle torturing the handsome Southern gentleman, Timmy Backman. (Timmy Backman, as most of my readers now know was introduced in my novel "Timmy's Ticklish Trials" and "Timmy and The Hong Kong Tailor".) This story (A Tribute to Timmy and Vince) revolves around the fact that Timmy has just acted as an usher in a buddies wedding and the tables suddenly turn and the tuxedoed guy finds himself in the clutches of Tickle Master Vince. What could be more ordinary than being an usher in a friend's wedding? What could be more unordinary than winding up as a tickle victim after being an usher in a friend's wedding? Just for some campy fun I put myself into the story as well. "Timmy confronts his Brother Bruce" and "Timmy Tickled by Santa Claus" (a twisted holiday story if ever there was one) both show what can happen when the most ordinary situations go totally hairy...or when the rug is suddenly pulled out from under one's feet. Timmy knows that it was his brother who set him up to fall tickle victim in the stories "Timmy at the Leather Bar" and "Timmy and The Hong Kong Tailor" so it seems only fitting that the handsome guy would confront his brother on this. What does not seem fitting is the guy having the tables turned yet again and winding up tickled by his own flesh and blood. I wrote Piss Fried (Literally) after an internet chat with a buddy who is somewhat into water sports. When he told me in our chat that he cannot piss, no matter how filled up he is, if his nipples are being squeezed I nearly went crazy. I had never heard of such a thing. So, by using Craig's quirk and my fetish for handsome guys in suits I concocted this story. The first thing I thought about was, "Why someone would be squeezing a guy's nipples when he's pissing?" That was when I decided to have the story take place in the sleazy bar known in some of my stories as "The Local." It's a place where anything goes and most men cum to fulfill some of their most twisted fantasies. It's a most erotic place of ill repute and of having tables turned that any man could possibly venture into…

I decided to round out the book with the story "The Abusive Wager", the title of the entire book as well, for various reasons. First and foremost it contains the element I love of what I stated earlier, "cruel irony." In the story a handsome and exotic looking Asian gentleman agrees to a game of cards with sinister and still unknown consequences for the loser. Daniel finds himself in over his head and in up to his nipples when his new train buddy Christopher challenges him to such a card game. Another reason I left this story for last in this book is it contains the fetishism of dress socks and business attire that is truly my signature as an author of this genre. Daniel is a well dressed masculine office worker who finds himself made vulnerable and sexy when he loses at the ill fated card game… Like in "Piss Fried (Literally), like Craig's, Daniel's nipples become two of the star attractions for this tale of irony…

A Tribute to Timmy and Vince

"I have to tell you Tim, it sure was cool of your friends Leonard and Kathy to invite me to their wedding, I had a great time," Chris said as he drove along the nearly empty road on the outskirts of Atlanta Georgia, his handsome buddy Tim seated in the passenger seat next to him.

"I'm glad you enjoyed yourself buddy, when I told Len and Kathy that you were going to be down here in Atlanta on book business they immediately told me to extend the invitation," Tim said, sounding totally and regally Southern, clad in a black Armani tuxedo complete with bowtie, cummerbund and patent leather slip-on slipper style shoes. "They said it was great to have a published author at their wedding..."

"Well, I'm truly flattered... I'll make sure to send you a thank you e-mail when I get back to New York so that you can forward it to them...or better yet, you can just give me their e-mail address and I'll send it myself..." Chris said, smiling from ear to ear. "Man, the food, the music, everything was awesome. And the place they picked was magnificent!"

"Yeah, the Tajmahal down here in Georgia isn't half bad eh?" Tim asked, giving his bowtie a squeeze.

"Nope, not half bad at all..." Chris said and veered off the main road and onto another more secluded one.

"Why'd you switch roads buddy?" Tim asked, pressing his feet against the plush floor of the car. "If you'd have stayed on that other road we would have been back at my house within the hour..."

"Yeah, but I saw a sign back there that said there's a "Rest Stop" along this road that I just turned onto and I really can't wait an hour before I have to take a monster-sized leak..." Chris said with a grin. "I'll just scoot into the rest stop and use the facilities and then we'll be back on our way to your place..."

"Okay, no problem..." Tim said. "Anyway, I can't complain...you are driving me home after all... Stephanie had to stay at the wedding hall for the last of the picture taking with the other bridesmaids...I'm glad the ushers were given leave...I really cannot wait to get out of this monkey suit..."

"What monkey suit?" Chris chuckled, reached over with one hand and tugged on Tim's suspenders under his tuxedo jacket. "I for one thought that you looked very handsome up there in your tux. It was an honor for you to have been asked by Leonard to be an usher in his wedding."

"Yeah, I suppose you're right at that," Tim said. "But it sure was an honor to have to spend the rental fee too for this monkey suit..."

The two men laughed good naturedly as Chris drove toward the rest stop that he so urgently needed.

"God, where is this place?" Chris asked no one in particular, his hands gripping the steering wheel tightly as he drove. "I have to piss like a god-damned racehorse. I feel like I could float away. That sign back there said the rest stop was only a half mile down this road..."

"Well, you've only gone a bit less than that..." Tim said. "Besides, you said that you didn't drink at the wedding, being that you would be driving today... I don't understand why you suddenly have to piss so badly..."

"I didn't drink beer or any other alcohol," Chris explained. "I did however drink a lot of diet Coke."

"Ah, that caffeine will do it to you every time," Tim laughed.

"Damn, if we don't find that place soon I'm just going to pull over and piss on the road," Chris said, starting to sound exasperated. "There's no one around anyway so no one will care..."

"Water the weeds a bit eh?" Tim asked with a grin.

"Yeah, I suppose you could say that...the weeds out there sure do look dry and undernourished..." Chris replied and gripped the steering wheel tighter yet.

"Man, you know, I've lived out here for years and I've never driven down this way at all..." Tim said, looking out the window of the car. "It's utterly and totally deserted around here..."

"It sure seems to be, I'm beginning to think that that was an old sign back there, maybe there is no rest stop here anymore," Chris said, his teeth clenched now.

"Well, at least it's still light out," Tim said, glancing at the digital display clock on the car's console. "Six PM, I'm glad Leonard and Kathy decided on a daytime wedding. Those evening affairs never seem to end. At least with a daytime wedding most people have to get home to the kids and whatnot..."

"Yeah, whatnot..." Chris said. "Okay, we have now driven half a mile on this horrid road and still no rest stop..."

"And what a horrid road it is at that buddy," Tim said, loosening his bowtie. "I swear, if I didn't know better I would think this was a scene out of one our tickle stories where Timmy Backman is abducted into tickle torment hell..."

Chris glanced over at Tim, rolled his eyes in his head and drove on...

"And I thought my imagination was really out there buddy..." Chris said. "I think we've worked on too many stories together Tim..."

"Oh really?" Tim asked with a wide ear to ear smile now on his face, his charming Southern accent really pronounced now as he spoke. "And who was it that when he heard I was going to be an usher in a wedding bought me the danged silk sheer black socks I'm wearin' right now, *right now*, silky sheer socks on my danged big feet? My word; never thought I would see the day that my feet, my danged own feet would be dressed up like my story's namesake! Sent them to me all wrapped up in frilly paper at that..."

Chris grinned fiendishly and said, "Sorry buddy, I couldn't resist. In my opinion you and black socks, no matter what the style just go hand in hand, or foot in hand in my book, no pun intended, depending on how you look at it. Besides, in a wedding the groomsmen should all wear sheer black socks with their tuxedos, its proper etiquette after all..."

"Wrong buddy, wrongo," Tim laughed. "According to proper etiquette the groom is to wear sheer silk socks with his tuxedo while the groomsmen all wear solid black nylon socks. You had me in reverse back there at that wedding. I for one noted that when I and my buddies lifted Leonard onto our shoulders for some friend's pictures he was most definitely wearing solid black nylon socks."

"I cannot believe I have to piss like there's no tomorrow and we're debating the styles of guy's socks..." Chris said, looking straight ahead, wishing that the rest stop would magically appear at that point.

"You had to see the expression on Stephanie's face when your package with the silk socks arrived in the mail," Tim went on. "She could not believe that a buddy would send another guy silky socks..."

As Tim chuckled again and loosened his bowtie a tad more Chris suddenly called out, "There it is, oh thank God!" as the rest stop set along the road all by itself came into view.

A sign which read "Restrooms, telephones, food and beverages" came into view also as they drove up...

"Sure is a lonely looking sort of place," Tim said, rolling his window down as Chris brought the car to a halt along the road. "I don't see any other cars around here whatsoever."

"Who cares what it looks like?" Chris asked. "The main thing is that they have a bathroom there..."

That said, Chris stopped the car and turned off the ignition.

"Do you need to go too?" Chris asked, reaching for the door handle.

"Nah, I'll just wait here while you go take care of business," Tim said, pressing the back of his head against the headrest behind him.

"Okay, I'll be back as quick as I can..." Chris said, sounding apologetic. "Then I'll drive you home lad-er-buddy."

In the next moment Chris was out of the car and hurrying toward the entrance of the rest stop. Tim smiled at his friend who was clad in a navy blue Brooks Brothers suit as he hurriedly entered the rest stop.

"Sure glad he made it..." Tim said to himself, loosened his bowtie the rest of the way till its ends dangled around his neck and over his tuxedo shirt.

The handsome tuxedo clad Southern gentleman then closed his eyes as he sat with his head pressed against the headrest.

"Ah, now I can breathe without that danged bowtie choking off my air…" Tim mused.

A few moments passed and Tim heard the sound of another car pulling up behind Chris's.

"Looks like this area isn't so deserted after all," Tim said softly to himself.

With his eyes still closed and resting Tim heard the sound of a car door being opened and then slammed shut. He figured that his buddy Chris wasn't the only one who needed to make a piss stop along the lonely road…

Suddenly, Tim heard, "HEY TIMMY, TIMMY BACKMAN!!!" and his blood ran ice cold in his veins. *TICKLISH* TIMMY BACKMAN!!! MY TIMYBE!!!"

"H-huh???????" Tim said and his eyes popped open as wide as saucers. "TICKLISH TIMMY BACKMAN???"

Then, just as suddenly, a huge ham-sized hand reached into the open window of the passenger side of the car and a white chloroform soaked cloth was pressed hard over Tim's nose and mouth.

"GGGRRRMMMFFFFFF!!!" Tim blurted in total fear, his slip-on shoed feet suddenly quivering and quaking against the plush floor of the car. "WH-what the fu….MMFFFFFF!!!! HOLY FRUUUCCC…RRRRMMMMFFFF!!!"

The back of Tim's head was pressed hard against the headrest and he was abruptly powerless to stop the onslaught…

"TIMMY BACKMAN," the voice outside the car cackled and the handsome tuxedoed guy felt the fingers around the chloroform soaked gag tighten against his cheek bones. "Timmy Backman, the ticklish laddy, about to be *my* *ticklish* laddy for a while…"

"T-ticklish???" Tim murmured and tried to raise his hands to swat away the hand pressing the sickly scented cloth against his handsome face.

But the vapors of the chloroform had already done their job in weakening him and he was only able to raise his hands part of the way before they fell back down in his lap.

"That's it laddy, just breathe, breathe baby…" the voice said. "Hee, hee, hee…"

The second Tim heard that "Hee, hee, hee" he knew who the culprit outside the car was…

"V-Vince…" Tim swooned as the cloth was taken away from his face…momentarily.

"Glad you recognized my trademark sinister laugh laddy," Vince drawled, sounding comically sinister. "God knows I've hee, hee, heed at you long enough on the internet and during our IM chats…hee, hee, hee buddy…"

Tim glanced out the rolled down window of the car and through slightly hazy vision saw the angularly tall handsome bald black man standing there. His eyes were gleaming in triumph at his capture of his special laddy and his smile was from ear to ear, stretching his goatee wide, the whiskers looking awfully tickly and prickly. When Tim imagined those whiskers pressed and trailing against his bare feet a shiver went up his spine, starting at the bottom of his feet. The black man's bald head shined in the sun and even though Tim was in tickle fear of the man there was no doubt he was one of the handsomest looking scoundrels he had ever seen.

"L-laddy, y-you called me laddy, that's in fiction, th-this is reality…" Tim said and his body pitched forward halfway in the car as his head spun from the chloroform effects. "And you know my name's not really Backman… SHIT! Y-you can't do this to a guy…"

"Ah, but I beg to differ buddy," Vince said, soaking the cloth again with chloroform, looking around at the same time to make sure no one saw what he was up to. "Because you see, I am doing it to a guy…I am doing it to a very, very ticklish guy…a ticklish laddy to be exact…I'm doing it to *you* Timmy my laddy, my TICKLISH laddy… Didn't I tell you that Big Brother was watching? Didn't I tell you how it's so easy to nab a tickle victim on these secluded roads here in the outskirts of Atlanta? Didn't I tell you that you had me beguiled to the point that I would, *I would* somehow, someday snatch you for myself? And let's face it Ticklish Timybe, you are the ultimate tickle victim! I mean Ronald, Valerie, the Hong Kong tailor, Bull, and so many others have had their tickle fun with you! So it's only fitting that now it's my turn laddy! I'm Christopher Trevor's biggest fan and talk about the irony of ironies, that I've captured one of his major ticklish stars! I guess you really *weren't* paying attention to me in those e-mails or in our internet chats buddy boy."

Cackling and hee, hee, heeing again Vince reached into the car and once more pressed the chloroform soaked cloth against Tim's nose and mouth.

"HHHRRRRRMMMFFFFFF!!!" Tim squealed fearfully and involuntarily inhaled the chloroform.

Vince pushed hard with the cloth against Tim's face till the back of his head was again pressed against the headrest. The handsome tuxedoed executive struggled to no avail…his eyes squeezed shut as he inhaled the nasty vapors… At his sides Tim's arms tremored and his hands and fingers shook and waved like the ocean.

"Oh man, this is delicious laddy; I'll give it to you in small doses so you conk out slowly, a little at a time, in little tasty smidgens, just like Ronald did in the story…" Vince said, leering at his quest. "God man, you're fuckin' beautiful Tim…you have the kind of beauty that could make me cry while I make you laugh…and Chris is so right, *so right*, that Senator John Edwards Southern accent of yours sends chills down my spine."

He pressed the cloth harder against Tim's face. Tim's arms shook some more at his sides, his head reeled against the headrest, his eyes rolled in his head and his feet quivered and twitched against the floor of the car. With his head then slightly bent he whimpered miserably.

"R-Ronald???" Tim asked when Vince had taken the rag away the second time. "B-but, he's a fictional character...j-just like all those others you mentioned, Valerie, Bull, th-the tailor...ooooooooooo gawd...oh my word..."

"Ronald a fictional character?" Vince squawked, laughing fiendishly at the same time. "Fuck me man, Ronald ain't no damned fictional character... Maybe the other ones are, but not good old Ronald! Ronald is me and Chris all wrapped up in your tickle nemesis...buddy..."

Tim's head lolled back, his mouth hung open as tears welled up in his eyes and then Vince reached a huge muscular arm into the window of the car and hooked it around Tim's upper torso.

"C'mon muh laddy, time for you and me to make like magicians and disappear..." Vince said.

Suddenly, Tim felt himself hefted up and off the passenger seat of Chris's car. Vince's arm was like a huge iron vise clamped around his upper body. The next thing the handsome tuxedoed guy realized was that he seemed to be gliding out the car window...

"AW jeez man," Tim grunted and failed in his quest to reach for the car horn as he was lifted bodily out of the car.

His feet slapped against the bottom part of the rolled down window, causing his patent leather slip-on slipper style shoes to peel away from his heels and dangle on his feet.

"Time to make like trees and leave," Vince laughed as he hoisted his prey into his arms.

"V-Vince, p-put me down man," Tim said hazily. "Th-this doesn't make sense..."

"And don't you look so pretty all decked out in your tux," Vince said lecherously, propping Tim against the side of the car while quickly soaking the cloth a third time with chloroform.

"I-I was in a wedding..." Timmy said as his head spun into orbit and his vision blurred. "I- I was a- an ush-usher...Th-that's why I, I, I'm wearin' a danged tux..."

Smiling meanly Vince gripped Tim by the back of his neck with one hand and pressed the once again chloroform soaked cloth over the guy's nose and mouth...

"HHRRRRRMMMFFFFF!!!!" Tim moaned and doubled over next to the car as Vince held him tight and fast.

"That's it buddy, just go with it..." Vince said softly and yanked Tim against his muscular body, holding the cloth tightly over the weakening guy's face. "God almighty, you have no idea how long I've waited for this Timmy my laddy, my *beautiful* laddy…"

Tim felt Vince's lips peck the side of his neck…

"RRRRRRMMMFFFFF!!!!" Tim bantered helplessly, tears of fear filling his eyes now.

"I told you to be careful my laddy," Vince whispered in Tim's ear, his lips grazing the regally handsome guy's earlobe as he spoke. "I told you that someone might come along and snatch you away from your family for some tickle time…"

Then, Vince took the rag away from Tim's face…

"Wh-where's Chris?" Tim said in a stupor now, trying to balance himself by holding onto the side of the car while looking toward the rest stop building. "Wh-where's Chris? What in the hell is t-takin' him so danged long in that rest stop bathroom???"

"Never you mind about Chris Timmy my laddy," Vince said and grabbed Tim from behind by his upper arms. "So you were an usher in a wedding eh?"

As he spoke Vince whirled Tim around facing him, Tim trying desperately to balance himself with his shoes half on and half off his feet and his head seeming to spin at a hundred miles per hour from the chloroform doses.

"OHHHHHHHH, GAWD, I-I-yeah, I was an usher, m-my friends, Leonard and Kathy got m-married…" Tim groaned miserably as Vince pulled him a few wobbly steps forward with the ends of his undone bowtie.

Tim's arms flailed out at his sides…

"Did you do a lot of dancing at the wedding Timmy muh laddy?" Vince teased the nearly unconscious guy.

"Y-you might say that…" Tim replied.

"Like this maybe?" Vince asked Tim and then holding Tim's upper arms real tight began whirling him round and round and round.

"HUUUUHHHHHHHH, n-no, I wasn't the one being spun on the dance floor!!" Tim said loudly as he wobbled and spun and even slammed against Chris's car a few times. "UUUHHHHHFFFFF!!! For heaven's sake Vince, s-stop this! Stop this now man! Oh my word!"

"Hee, hee, hee," Vince chuckled sadistically into Tim's ear. "But you sure as all hell are the one being spun now eh my laddy?"

Vince grabbed hold of one of Tim's hands, raised his arm straight up and pirouetted the dazed and confused guy around and around and around. The world spun in Tim's hazy vision.

"Ch-Chris…g-get me out of this…" Tim moaned when Vince stopped spinning him and balanced him again against the car.

"I told you to never mind about Chris Timmy my laddy," Vince said while soaking the cloth a fourth time. "I think this dose should do it…"

Tim looked toward the rest stop and the building seemed to be moving up and down...

"Ch-Chris...help me..." Tim bantered almost pitifully, stretching an arm out in desperation toward the rest stop.

Vince chuckled and Tim murmured the words, "Oh no," as he was whirled around again facing Vince and he saw the cloth once more headed for his face.

"MMMMMMMMFFFFFFFF!!!!" Tim screamed as Vince pushed him down atop the trunk of the car.

"I think this dose should do it..." Tim heard Vince say as if from far away as he again held the chloroform soaked rag against his face, right over his nose and mouth.

Tim's arms thrashed helplessly at his sides and his long muscular legs thrashed wildly as well, causing his expensive slipper style slip-on patent leather shoes to fall off his feet, them landing on the ground next to the car...

"MMM, this is just like the ending scene in that book by Anne Rice, The Tale of The Body Thief, where Lestat slowly turns David into a vampire by taking nips from him, rather than bighting him all at once..." Vince said merrily. "I'm enjoying dosing you slowly my laddy, it gives us time to talk before you go to La La land...and then to Tickle City...Hee, hee, hee..."

A few moments later Vince took the cloth away from Tim's face again. Vince looked adoringly at the sleeping Southern hunk atop the trunk of the car. Tim was truly a vision of male beauty that he'd waited a lifetime for it seemed. With his dark gray hair, his piercing green eyes, those chiseled handsome looks and muscular well toned body Timmy the ticklish laddy was Vince's dream come true...and how regal and dapper he looked in his tuxedo, complete with those damned sheer black socks, a Christopher Trevor signature mark if Vince ever saw one. It was when Christopher had told Vince that he had been invited to a wedding that Tim was to be an usher in that Vince had started making his plans to capture the handsome Southern gentleman. Vince had read the short stories starring Timmy Backman, the fictional incarnation of Christopher Trevor's real-life buddy Tim (real last name withheld) and of course the novel, "Timmy's Ticklish Trials" that had started it all. Tim had met Christopher after reading some of his tickle stories on a now defunct website called ROPEJOCK.com. After reading Christopher's stories Tim contacted Christopher through the website and the two became instant tickle buddies, in fantasy land only however. That was not enough for Vince though. As Christopher and Tim became friendlier they worked on tickle stories together, stories that were enough to send the most heartened tickle fetishists to Erotic City and the land of Fever, stories that they posted on the internet, stories that many tickle fans out there enjoyed, tickle fans and tickle fanatics like Vince. When Chris introduced Vince to the real Tim on line he instantly began teasing and tormenting the handsome laddy by e-mailing and IMing him about all the ways that he would, *he would* someday visit upon his tied up muscular body. The real Tim took all of it in good stride, even enjoying the e-mailed teasing torments that Vince would send him. Tim secretly enjoyed how Vince would threaten to somehow nab him someday for some real-time tickle fun. Tim, being a married guy with a family figured that the handsome and rugged Vince was only teasing him. But on this day, on the day of his friend's Kathy and Leonard's wedding the real-life Tim found out just how serious Vince had been all along...all along the African American tickle fetishist had been simply awaiting the right opportunity to present itself...and now it had...woefully for Tim it had...

Smiling fiendishly Vince then took in the sight of the wedding band adorning Tim's ring finger on his left hand...

"Stephanie is sure going to miss you for a while eh laddy?" Vince asked the sleeping handsome as a prince guy.

He lifted Tim's hand to his mouth and sucked the ring finger into it, dribbling and drooling on it liberally. Tim stirred slightly in his stupor, the sucking sensations on his finger sending chills through him as he lay atop the trunk of the car. With his eyes closed in ecstasy Vince sucked and suckled Tim's finger, moistening it enough to slip his ring off him...for the time being that is. Vince was sadistically ecstatic beyond words. He had actually pulled it off. He had captured the model for one of Christopher Trevor's fictional characters; it was Timmy Backman in the flesh...or at the least he would be in the flesh soon enough Vince mused to himself as he thought about stripping the handsome laddy slowly of his classy looking tux. Vince had to wonder if Tim was wearing his ever-present kangaroo style white briefs under his tuxedo. The laddy had told him several times in their e-mail exchanges how his cock was of the Grade A, extra large size and the briefs with the kangaroo style pouch held his oversized equipment quite comfortably. Moments passed as Vince sucked Tim's ring finger and then he had Tim's wedding band in his mouth. Smiling he sucked on the ring in his mouth like it was the sweetest tasting candy. He ran the ring over his gums, letting his tongue be its guide. He thought of the day when Stephanie must have slipped the ring on handsome Tim's finger, their wedding day. And how fitting that Stephanie's handsome groom should be captured on their friend's wedding day. Vince wondered if Tim's friend Leonard, his friend who had gotten married that day was ticklish as well. As he slid the ring under his tongue and tasted the gold mixed with Tim's scent he thought of how Stephanie must have adored this man from the moment she saw him, dreaming of the day when she and he would both slide wedding bands onto each other's ring fingers. How she must have looked at him adoringly the first time they made love Vince thought as he then held Tim's wedding band between his front lower and upper teeth, trailing the tip of his tongue over the back part of it. All these thoughts came to Vince as he chewed, sucked and drooled on Tim's wedding band. He then took the ring out of his mouth and quickly hung it on a gold chain that was around his neck…

"And off we go laddy…" Vince whispered and lifted Tim off the car and up across his strong broad shoulders.

He looked down at the ground where Tim's tuxedo slipper style shoes had landed and said, "I'll leave those there as a clue for your buddy Chris…"

When Chris came out of the rest stop building he sauntered over to the car and was mystified when he did not see Tim. His heart thundered in his chest and the beginning of an erection began in his suit pants when he saw Tim's shoes on the ground next to the car…

"Holy fucking shit, my word…" Chris whispered and his cock twitched in his suit pants. "Vince…"

A short while later Tim came to in Vince's car as the handsome African American guy drove along the lonely and deserted road that Chris had veered onto in order to use the facilities at a rest stop.

"AAAAAWWWHHH, man, oh my word," Tim groaned miserably as his head lolled downward in blindfolded darkness, his hands securely roped behind him as he sat now in the passenger seat of Vince's car. "Wh-where are you takin' me Vince??? This is horrific man!!"

"Ah, my beautiful and special laddy, that is for me to know and for you to find out…but not just yet…" Vince laughed meanly.

"Vince, listen to me man, fiction is one thing, its fun, its fantasy, but this isn't fiction," Tim said pleadingly. "This is reality and you've kidnapped me man! I'm a married guy, for real, with kids, for real, not just a son named Tim Junior like in that godforsaken story! My wife will wonder where the hell I am Vince…please… And just for the record I'm not ticklish like Timmy in the story… For heaven's sake man, I am not Timmy Backman! I'm Tim, but you know as well as Chris knows that Backman isn't my danged last name, oh my word, this can't be happening, it just can't be!"

"Well Timmy my laddy I suppose we're going to find out whether or not that's true, about your being ticklish that is…" Vince said threateningly.

"Aw no man, no…" Tim grunted and looked through the windshield stupidly with his blindfolded eyes. "Let me go Vince, you must let me go!!"

Vince quickly pulled over along the side of the road, soaked the cloth with chloroform yet again as his captive looked around in blindfolded darkness.

"Nitey nites again my laddy," Vince snarled and pressed the cloth hard over Tim's nose and mouth.

"HHHRRRRRMMMFFFFF!!!" Tim ranted, his sheer socked toes quivering involuntarily as he was dosed for what seemed like the umpteenth time.

As Tim drifted back into the arms of sleep he could have sworn he heard Vince whisper the words "handsome as a prince" and Tim felt thick lips pressed against his…then he again slumped forward in the passenger seat...

An hour or so later, along with a few chloroform doses later as well Tim slowly came to in Vince's basement turned gym, turned massage room, turned tickle torture chamber.

"PWAHHHHHHHHH HA, HA, HA, HA, HA, HA, HA, HA, HA, HA, HA!!!!" was the sound that filled Vince's basement as he had wasted no time in putting the tickle screws to his handsome blindfolded captive. "V-VINCE, s-stop, stop this now!!! I-I'm laughing, you got me laughing for sure here, but this isn't funny... oh woe is me, not funny at all, HAHAHAHAHAHAHAHAHA HAHAHAHAHAHA!!!!!"

"Oh Timmy and you said you weren't ticklish my laddy..." Vince chuckled.

"WH-what did you expect me to say man???" Tim shrilled loudly. "That I was indeed ticklish to the point of madness??? OH MY WORD, stop Vince, please STOP!!! HAR, HAR, HAR, HAR, HAR, HAR, HAR, HAR, HAR!!!!!!"

The handsome guy found himself tied to a straight backed wooden chair in the most unusual of positions. The wooden chair was actually more of a "short-back" wooden framed chair that was housed in front of a short wooden cabinet with a wooden chopping block surface. Like a kitchen piece, sturdy, but flexible to fit with other furniture. The chair that Tim was on was secured to that table and had a wide base so that the laddy's knees could be separated and Tim could be laid over the table surface. Vince had a sinister imagination; Tim had to give the man that... Even though he was blindfolded he was clever enough to feel from the position he was tied in how Vince's contraption was situated. Tim was kneeling on the straight backed chair, his stomach area pressed against the front-most part of the chair. His hands were still of course securely roped behind him. A leather strap was wound around his upper stomach area and around the front of the chair as well, pinning the laddy tight and forcing him to stay in the kneeling position for the time being. His semi erect cock and balls had been slipped out of the fly opening in his tuxedo trousers and squeezed through one of the wider openings in the rungs in the chair-back. A length of rope had been wound and snugly tied around the base of Tim's juicy and sweaty balls...no way of pulling his manhood out from between the chair rungs. A long white cloth blindfold was wrapped twice over Tim's eyes and knotted behind his head. His tuxedo jacket had been taken off him and his tuxedo shirt was splayed open, exposing the handsome laddy's semi hairy muscular chest and fat nipples. Sharp teethed tit clamps had been snapped onto Tim's already very erect nipples, the clamps keeping them good and jutted up and very sensitized. Lastly, Tim's bare feet dangled off the end of the chair. Vince had slowly and ceremoniously taken Tim's sheer socks off him, wallowing in the pleas and begging's as Tim said, "Aw no man, no, don't take my danged silky socks off me Vince!" as Vince had slid his hands up and under the laddy's pants legs and inch by inch removed his socks. Tim's knees were resting on thick cushion material. Vince wanted to make the laddy's position as comfortable as possible. This also raised Tim's hips up to allow his torso to bend over the table surface without difficulty. Oh yes, Vince wanted his captured laddy as flexible and mobile as possible, even though he was tied tighter than a drum that is. Tim's bare ankles were secured to the edge of each "chair arm" in order to separate his knees and calves properly. The captured Tim's thighs were aptly secured to the back of the chair. His arms were secured to each end of the table surface and to a chain that led to the base of the table legs, opposite from the chair that supported his knees. As the laddy knelt on the chair it was what Vince was doing to Tim's feet that had the poor captured guy in huge stitches of laughter.

"V-Vince, HAHAHAHAHAHAHAHAHAHAHAHAHA!!!!!! Ch-Chris, Chris will get you for this!!" Tim screamed in between laughing and hooting. "HOO HOO, HOO, HOO, HOO, HOO, HOO, HOO!!!!"

"Ah my special laddy, the real question here is will Chris get you?" Vince countered and sent poor Tim on another laugh brigade.

"HARHARHARHARHARHARHARHARHAR!!!!!!" Tim cackled.

"The only things left behind at the rest stop were your pretty slip-on tuxedo shoes," Vince said mockingly. "Fucking things fell right off your feet as I carried you off like a sack of laundry, hardy, har and har buddy…"

"HAHAHAHAHAHAHAHAHAHAHAHAHAHA!!!!" was all Tim could say.

"Oh yes, yes, I agree Tim, you should laugh some more…" Vince whispered as he squatted behind the tied up and laughing Southern prince's bare feet.

And it was those de-socked and dangling feet that Vince was presently tickling and warming up at the same time for Tim. Vince was squatting behind the chair that Tim was carefully tethered to. He was holding Tim's feet tightly together as he lick tickled, nuzzled and used his fingertips as well to tickle the tied up guy's soft bare tootsies.

"V-VINCE, you monster!!" Tim then managed to cry out loudly. "HARH ARHARHARHARHARHARHAR!!!! Oh man, we've had oodles of fun with the stories that Christopher writes and I even let you tease me in those e-mails and our IM fantasy sessions! But this is reality, like I said man, this is *reality*!! HAHAHAHAHAHAHAHAHAHAHAHA!!!! And the reality you need to get through your head is that you've kidnapped me, kidnapped me, kidnapped a family man and a real estate broker all in the same danged package…ha, ha, ha, ha, ha, ha, ha, ha, ha, ha, ha, ha!!!! And what a package I am here…all tied up and laughing my fool head off!! HAHAHAHAHAHAHAHAHAHAHAHA HAHAHAHA!!!!"

"Good observations laddy," Vince said and then did the one thing that truly drove ticklish Tim over the edge at that moment.

Vince rubbed his goatee style beard up and down and up and down against the meaty bottom of Tim's feet...

"OOOOOOOHHHHHHRRRRRRR HAHAHAHAHAHAHAHAHAHAH AHA!!!!!" was all Tim was able to say to that.

Tim squirmed miserably on the chair as he laughed and laughed uncontrollably... The ends of Vince's goatee whiskers were sharp and prickly and the way they tickled him sent searing sensations through him from his feet all the way up his shapely legs and into his well toned thighs. The laddy could do nothing but laugh as the sensations became tickle hell...

He felt the tip of Vince's tongue as it snaked up his foot from just below his toes to his heel on his right foot and then down from the heel to his toes on his left foot...

"HEYYYYYYYYYYYYYYY!!!!!! HAHAHAHAHAHAHAHAHAHAHAHAH AHA!!!" Tim screeched as Vince held his feet tight by the toes and slobbered over them and then lick tickled the laddy as he lapped up his saliva.

"V-Vince, STOP, STOP licking my danged feet man!!" Tim bantered. "I am not like Timmy Backman in the story, stories, ha, ha, ha, ha, ha, ha, ha, ha, ha, ha, ha, ha, ha!!!! I do not enjoy what you're doing to me here!! HAHAHAHAHAHAHAHAHAHAHAHAHA!! Tickling does not get me excited!!! PWAHHHHAHAHAHAHAHAHAHAHAHA!!!"

Tim threw his blindfolded head back and reeled madly on the chair...

"Careful there laddy, you want to keep yourself properly balanced on that chair," Vince teased Tim. "The way you're positioned is rather perilous for a guy in your present circumstances..."

"UUUUUUHHHHHHHHHH!!!! HAHAHAHAHAHAHAHAHAHAHAHAH A!!! A poor guy like me shouldn't be balanced in these danged circumstances Vince!!" Tim reeled and faced his blindfolded eyes forward. "I should be home now since the wedding finished up...OOOOOOOOOOO HAHAHAHAHAHAH AHAHAHAHAHAHAHA!!!"

Vince held Tim's parted feet real tight at the toes, squeezed the laddy's twitching and quivering toes and alternately brushed the sides of his captive's arches with his goatee...

"Yeah muh laddy, I can tell that you are definitely enjoying that..." Vince said reflectively. "And oh man do these feeties of yours feel so warm and tender in my grip...sheer heaven buddy boy...I waited too long to have these beautiful feets of yours in my clutches so you can bet your sweet laugh-ter that I'm not going to be letting you go all that easily...or all that soon..."

Then, Vince puckered his lips and pressed them against the bottom of one of Tim's feet. The handsome African American muscular guy hee hee heed as he slid his puckered lips up and down Tim's left foot, followed by doing the same thing to his right foot, and then back again at his left foot. Vince reveled and delighted in the torments he was inflicting on Christopher Trevor's model for a fictional character... He was also delighting in the sounds of Tim's uncontrollable laughter as it burst forth from him like a volcano spewing hundreds of years of pent-up lava...

"Do you think Chris has realized you've gone missing laddy?" Vince asked Tim meanly and then the sound of both men laughing was heard.

One man laughing uncontrollably from being tickled while the other laughed maniacally over his capture and conquest of the laughing guy fettered to the chair...

"HAR, HAR, HAR, HAR, HAR, HAR, HAR, HAR, HAR, HAR, HAR, HAR!!!!!" Tim cackled like a banshee anew as Vince then splayed his lips apart and pressed his front-most teeth against the bottom of his captured prize's left foot.

"Now for some chop tickling muh laddy," Vince murmured softly and poor Tim felt chills travel through his tickled feet and up his spine.

Holding Tim's bare feet now from the fronts of them Vince started moving his front teeth upwards along the bottom of Tim's left foot, making chewing motions as he went.

"HA, HA, HA, HA, HA, HA, HA, HA, HA, HA, HA, HA, HA, HA, oh shit, ha, ha, ha, ha, ha, ha, ha, ha, ha!!!! Oh my fucking word!!!!" Tim screamed as he felt Vince's teeth slithering up and down his foot while at the same time his goatee wreaked havoc on the sides of his foot.

Vince proceeded to do the same thing to Tim's right foot, barely halting in between switching feet and tickle torturing his captured treasure.

"Oh yes, laugh for me, laugh, my angel of comedy," Vince chuckled and made sucking sounds against Tim's feet with his teeth, tongue and lips.

Tim saw bright lights flashing in his blindfolded prison and he was off again on another gale of uncontrollable laughter...

"M-MONSTER!!!! HAHAHAHAHAHAHAHAHAHAHAHAHAHA!!!!" Tim guffawed and balled his tied hands into one big fist.

Finally, Vince stopped lick tickling Tim's bare feet. He soaked his cloth with chloroform and again sent the laddy to dream land... Tim made "MMMMMMFF" sounds as Vince once more put him in a sleepy stupor...

While Vince prepared his ticklish captive for the next session of torments Chris was sitting in the driver's seat of his car, still parked in front of the rest stop where he had stopped to use the bathroom, still not fully aware of Tim's perilous and ticklish plight.

"I don't know where the fuck he is," Chris was saying into his cell phone as he spoke to Valerie, a somewhat good friend of Tim's, but more of a friend to Tim's wife Stephanie. "If what I'm thinking has happened then he's in a shit load of trouble Valerie, a real fucking ticklish situation!"

Chris listened as Valerie spoke, her telling him that she and the rest of the bridesmaids were almost done with the picture taking back at the wedding hall.

"Well, just keep Stephanie there until I find Tim," Chris said, glancing over at the passenger seat where he had placed Tim's tuxedo shoes. "I don't want her going home and finding that he's not there. I don't want her suspecting anything untoward."

Chris listened as Valerie spoke again, licking his lips as she did so...

"I'm sure he'll show up at some point," Chris said. "If what I think has happened has happened then Tim will be back by tonight at the latest. I mean, how much tickling can a guy endure?"

Chris listened again and heard the disbelief of what he had just said in Valerie's voice...

"Yes, you heard me right, tickling!" Chris said and clicked off his cell phone.

He put his cell phone next to one of Tim's tuxedo shoes, leaned back in the driver's seat and a devilish smile played across his lips, lighting up his face...

"Vince, you are a man after my own heart," Chris whispered.

Not all that much later Tim was again awake and Vince had the poor laddy once again laughing his fool head off...

"HAH, HAH, HAH, HAH, HAH, HAH, HAH, HAH, HAH, HAH!!!!! OH my word, oh my word of words, this is awful, HAHAHAHAHAHAHAHAHAHAHA, just fucking awful..." Tim screamed laughingly as Vince did his dirty work.

Tim was still kneeling on the chair, tethered tightly to its front frame as he was earlier, but now his upper muscular body was lying splayed out on the wooden cabinet that the chair was hooked up to. His cock, which had gone totally stalked up was still pulled through the rungs of the chair along with his big juicy tied up balls. Tim's tuxedo shirt had been taken off him and his upper body was strapped to the wooden chopping block, his head lying at a sideways angle, still blindfolded as Vince now tormented him with a stiff, prickly, quilled sharp pointed goose feather. The tit clamps still chewed at Tim's very sensitive, very worked up nipples.

"YAHHHHH!!!!! HAHAHAHAHAHAHAHAHAHAHAHAHA!!!" Tim crowed loudly as Vince trailed the tip of the feather up and down and up and down the tied up laddy's spine. "N-NEVER knew that my danged back was so damned ticklish!!!"

"Oh believe me muh beautiful Southern laddy, during the time you spend here with me today we are going to find out just how many parts of you really are ticklish!" Vince said, leering at his prize as he trailed the tip of the feather slowly up Tim's spine, swishing it a bit as he went.

"AAAAAAAAYYYYYY!!! HAHAHAHAHAHAHAHAHAHAHAHA!!!!!" Tim laughed when the feather was pressed against the very top of his spine.

It felt to Tim as if the feather tip was pressing hard against the top of his spine but Vince was a master at tickling and he knew just how to maneuver the instrument of the laddy's torture to really get him laughing in overdrive; and to make it feel as if the pressure on his spine was immense.

"HAR, HAR, HAR, HAR, HAR, HAR, HAR, HAR, oh fucking fuck!!!" Tim cried out as the feather trailed downward along his spine now, settling on the lower-most section of his back this time.

Vince twirled the feather against Tim's lower spine and the tied up, strapped down blindfolded Southern guy laughed raucously. Tim's muscular back heaved upward as much as the strap would allow and Vince trailed the feather against the laddy's ripped muscles.

"HAHAHAHAHAHAHAHAHAHAHAHAHAHAHAHA!!!!" Tim laughed crazily.

As Vince used one hand to trail his feather over and over Tim's spine, his back and then over to his sides (that really got the Southern prince laughing good and loud) he tugged on Tim's wedding band with his other hand as it hung on the gold chain around his neck. Vince's heart pounded with a feeling of triumph mixed with sadistic ecstasy and real love thrown in there at the same time. Holding tight to Tim's wedding band in his fist he trailed the feather a bit faster up Tim's spine this time.

"HAAAAAAAAAAAAAA, ha, ha, ha, ha, ha, ha, ha, ha, ha, ha, ha, ha, ha, ha!!!!" Tim shrilled. "VINCE, you let me go, you let me go man!!"

Tim's Southern accent sent shockwaves through Vince and it was almost as if he were tickling the handsome Southern senator John Edwards.

"WH-when my wife gets home and finds that I'm not there and the kids won't be able to explain my absence she'll know something has happened to me man!!" Tim pleaded. "HAHAHAHAHAHAHAHAHAHAHAHAHA!!! And that's not funny I might add!"

"Tell me Timmy Backman, my ticklish laddy, tell me, how do you suppose Stephanie would feel seeing her handsome princely husband in the position I have you in at present?" Vince asked Tim teasingly, spine tickling him with the feather at the same time.

"M-my wife, sh-she would not think that it was all that marvelous for her poor hubby to be in the position you got me in Vince!!" Tim drawled. "HAHAHAHAHAHAHAHAHAHAHAHAHAHAHAHAHAHA!!!!! And again man, my name ain't Backman!!! OH MY WORD!!!! HAHAHAHAHAHAHAHAHAHAHH AHA!!!"

"But Timmy my laddy, that's an incorrect assessment me thinks," Vince said fiendishly. "Because if I recall correctly in the story of your trials Stephanie rather enjoys seeing you tickled. As a matter of fact she even enjoys being the one to tickle you."

"AGAIN man, that story is fiction, HAHAHAHAHAHAHAHAHAHAHAH AHAHA OH GAWD, stop ticklin' my danged spine Vince!!! PLEASE!!!!!!!!!"

"Well, fiction or not I doubt that Stephanie will get home to find you missing laddy," Vince said.

"WH-what in tarnation do you mean by that???" Tim asked through clenched teeth as Vince trailed the feather tip from his spine to his sides again.

"HAR, har, har, har, har, har, har, har, har, har, har!!!!!"

"Well, if I know Christopher like I think I do he'll have figured out already that it's me who nabbed you," Vince said. "And I'm pretty sure I know that he'll want you thoroughly tickled before I give you back to him so I'm sure that he'll find some way of keeping Stephanie occupied while I keep you occupied…"

"Th-that's where you're wrong Vince, totally wrongo!!!" Tim cried loudly in between laughing and laughing. "Chris will search for me man!! He'll search for me and rescue me from you!!! HAR, har, har, har, har, har, har, har, har, har, har, har, har!!!!!! He has to drive me home after all!!!"

"Ah my laddy, and tell me, where would Chris begin searching for you pray tell?" Vince asked his ticklish captive. "He doesn't know those back-roads in Georgia like I do. You see, I studied that area and just awaited the right moment to capture you Timmy Backman, Timmy the ticklish laddy…no one would believe where I've brought you…it's so simply sinister and fitting…"

"HAHAHAHAHAHAHAHAHAHAHAHA!!!!!" Tim laughed, sweating now as he lay there splayed out in just his tuxedo pants, his cock dribbling pre seed as he cackled and ranted. "What a twisted and fucked up turn of events…"

"Oh yes laddy, yes indeed and very well said I would think," Vince said, sounding villainous. "I studied those back-roads and found this place just for this occasion. What a real stroke of luck that you should ask your two newly wed friends to invite Chris to their wedding…a wedding that you *just* happened to be ushering in. When Chris told me how he was going to be seeing you this weekend for the wedding I began making my plans to nab you Timmy. Oh man, without even realizing it you signed your capture and tickle warrant."

As Tim laughed Vince trailed his feather up and down and up and down Tim's back as it glistened with sweat…

"And, and, HAHAHAHAHAHAHAHAHAHAHAHA you mean to tell me that Chris was in on all this?" Tim cackled incredulously, wondering if his good buddy had actually participated in the diabolical plan to have him tickle-napped so to speak. "He took that road to the deserted rest stop purposely??? Chris worked with you in snagging me?"

"I didn't need Chris to help me nab you laddy, all I needed was for Chris to tell me that he was coming to Georgia on book business and to see you at the wedding. The rest I left up to fate…and to the fact that our good buddy Chris has the weakest bladder on the planet. Hardy, har, har for you buddy. I counted on the fact that on the drive from the reception to your house Chris would have to go to the bathroom and since I've gotten to know him I know that he would never, ever, under any circumstances piss on an open road. Chris may be a writer of sinister fiction but when it comes to the men's room Chris is a gentleman. So while looking over the maps of this area I found that there was a rest stop that somehow I knew, *I just knew* that Chris would need to use before he drove you the rest of the way home."

"HAW, HAW, HAW, HAW, HAW, HAW, HAW, HAW, HAW!!!!" Tim laughed. "What a sick turn of events!! HAHAHAHAHAHAHAHAHAHAHAHA HA!!!!"

Vince leered down maniacally at his tied up tickle captive as he continued to feather tickle his spine. By now Tim was awash with goose bumps.

"So you see my ticklish laddy, my ticklish Timybe, my ticklish Timmy Backman, fate brought us together online through Christopher Trevor and then fate was kind enough again to bring us together in real time, again through Christopher Trevor," Vince chuckled and tickled the epicenter of Tim's spine. "That author is our link buddy boy…"

"HAH, HAH, HAH, HAH, HAH, HAH, HAH, HAH, HAH, HAH, HAH, oh please, please stop that… OH VINCE, please stop… HAHAHAHAHAHAHAHAHAHA!!!" Tim shrilled and felt Vince's lips pressed lovingly against his cheek. "Oh dang it all, dang, my word…"

A while later Vince pressed the chloroform soaked cloth again against Tim's nose and mouth…

"Coming up, your third tickle session with me laddy," Vince said as soon as Tim was conscious again.

As his head quickly cleared Tim now knew what his namesake in the story was put through when captured by Ronald and how he used chloroform on him. The stuff was volatile. As Tim came to he realized he was able to see. Yay and hooray for small miracles that Vince had taken the damned blindfold off him, but when he tried to raise his head to look around was when Tim realized his latest (tickle) peril, for he could not raise his head. Looking down Tim saw a full-length mirror under the table he was now laying on, facedown. The laddy gulped audibly in sheer (socked) terror and quickly realized why Vince had taken the blindfold off him.

"OH VINCE, what now man???" Tim cried out…

As Tim lay somehow immobilized now atop a cushioned table, back at the reception hall his wife, Stephanie was at that same moment climbing into the passenger seat of Valerie's car.

"Thank God the picture taking is done," Stephanie said as she situated herself comfortably in the seat of the car. "I thought for sure that Kathy would never finish with all of us bridesmaids. I cannot wait to get home."

"Well, before I drop you off at home there's one more stop that you and I have to make Stephanie," Valerie said, trying to hide the snide sound in her tone as she spoke.

That said Valerie opened the glove compartment of her car and took out an envelope, handing it to Tim's wife.

"What's this?" Stephanie asked.

"A gift for you and me from Kathy," Valerie said. "It's actually a bonus gift, something she didn't give the rest of the girls in the bridal party. It's her way of thanking you for having me help with the antique looking decorations from my shop for the reception hall."

Smiling from ear to ear Stephanie peeled the envelope open and was delighted to find a gift certificate valued at more than five hundred dollars for her favorite beauty spa.

"Oh my, this is so nice of Kathy," Stephanie said.

As Stephanie eyed the gift certificate Valerie thought how it was the perfect way to keep Mrs. Backman occupied for a few hours...while her handsome hubby laughed his head off.

"So we'll go there now and then I'll drive you home," Valerie said, starting the car. "I figure we can do the whole nine yards, manicures, pedicures, massage, facials, everything."

"You mean we're going to go there in our bridal gowns Val?" Stephanie asked.

"Well, once we're there we'll change into robes and sandals that they provide," Valerie said.

"Wait, what about Tim? And the kids are still at the sitter," Stephanie said. "Tim must be home by now. He'll wonder where I am..."

"Not to worry," Valerie piped up quickly. "Tim and a few of his buddies went to have a few after wedding drinks and all you have to do is call the sitter and let her know that you'll be a tad late in getting home." As she spoke and drove Valerie handed Stephanie her cell phone, after quickly pushing the "End Call" button on it. Stephanie had no idea that Chris had been listening to their entire conversation. Sitting in his car still at the rest stop where Tim was captured earlier Chris put his cell phone down, ran a hand over Tim's shoes and whispered "Thank you Valerie."

"Okay, I guess I can't turn down an offer like this one," Stephanie said and dialed the number for the sitter. "I'll give her time and a half for the three or four hours that it'll take us to get done at the spa. And knowing that husband of mine I'm sure he's having some kind of ticklish fun with his buddies..."

As Stephanie put the cell phone to her ear and rolled her eyes in her head Valerie looked straight ahead as she drove and smiled a secret smile of her own...

While Stephanie unwittingly sealed her poor husband's latest tickle fate Tim was now taking in his latest form of bondage and how he would be tickled this time by Vince, his so called buddy and master tickler. Laying face down on a cushioned table and looking straight down at and into a full length mirror under that table Tim took in the fact that he was strapped down on his stomach to a genuine massage table. The massage table had thigh and calf straps along with biceps and wrists straps. Each time Tim tried to raise his head from the face cradle he was reminded that the table also had a head strap of some sort on it. As he squirmed helplessly he was able to surmise that Vince had employed the use of all the straps attached to the table. As he wriggled his chest area Tim could feel that the tit clamps had been removed from his nipples. He scanned downward in the full-length mirror under the table as far as his eyes would allow and was astounded when he saw his cock and balls dangling freely through a glory hole that was cut in the table. As always the laddy was hard as a rock in that area and his cum chocked balls were hanging succulently low. Beads of pre cum adorned his cock slit and hard and worked up as he was there was nothing for him (as is always the case in the stories) to rub his erection against to afford him some relief. It seemed as if Vince had gone to great lengths to make the real Tim feel as ticklishly helpless and vulnerable as his fictional namesake.

"Oh my word, my cock and rocks are on display down there," Tim drawled, sounding regally Southern and John Edwards, yet sleazy at the same time as he spoke of his most private parts.

"Ah, so you are awake my ticklish laddy," Tim heard Vince say as he stepped over to the table. "I trust you're comfy there."

"Vince, all this foolery has gone far enough," Tim panted and tried to raise his midsection, to pull his cock and balls out of the glory hole, but to his dismay learned that there was also a strap secured around his stomach area as well. "Oh dang it all and fuck me, Vince if you know what's good for you you'll let me go and pronto at that."

Stepping next to Tim's secured feet Vince moved his captive's bare tootsies by the ankles into a pair of stocks that were secured to the bottom of the table. He locked the stocks around Tim's already tethered feet, thus truly making them immobile now. At this point Vince had stripped his tickle captive totally nude. Tim's kangaroo pouch style underpants stuck out of the back pocket of Vince's jeans.

"Oh my lord, what're you doin' down there at my feet Vince?" Tim asked as he then felt his naked toes being looped up somehow and affixed firmly within the stocks prison, now keeping his feet not only immobilized but also taut. "Aren't you listening to me at all? You have to let me go man!"

In response Tim felt Vince start to slather and slop his naked feet with what felt like handfuls of baby oil.

"Oh no, no," Tim bantered downward, seeing the anguish on his face as it lay trapped in the face cradle. "Fucking guy, right about now I wish you'd kept me blindfolded here."

"Getting the picture my handsome laddy?" Vince asked as he slowly and methodically sluiced Tim's feet with the baby oil. "You're going to watch yourself laugh your head off this time..."

Tim took a deep breath and his cock twitched in the glory hole as he felt the tickle master slathering his feet all oily. Looking at his huge erection under the table Tim saw that a thin length of leather was tied off around the base of his luscious balls.

"You know laddy, I love dripping oil slowly onto a guy's feet, I love watching it drip and trickle down the bottoms of them, just like I'm doing to you right now..." Vince said and Tim felt the oil now being applied to his feet in small drippy trickles. "And having you, Christopher's most famous fictional character brought to life here in my clutches is just too unnerving..."

"I'll second that danged comment Vince," Tim bantered downward, his Southern accent seeming to have intensified somehow. "But like I said, enough of all this, this is real life here, I'm the inspiration for the fictional Timmy, I'm not him, I'm not fiction, I'm real."

"Feel how I'm using my dexterous fingers to make sure to coat every nook and cranny of your beautiful feet laddy, and this time when I tickle them its going to be lots more intense than earlier," Vince went on. "Oh Timmy, my beautiful laddy, how delicious it looks as this oil drips on your gorgeous feet-ies. I will say this, Chris chose well in you buddy."

"Vince, by now Stephanie will be wondering where I am," Tim pleaded, trying to reason with his tickle captor.

"Speaking of your lovely wife Timmy, tell me, does she appreciate your feet as much as Stephanie in the stories does?" Vince asked Tim, sounding sinister and comical at the same time, gripping one of Tim's feet as he asked him.

"Oh dang it all man, I am just not getting through to you here I don't think..." Tim drawled miserably as Vince slathered more of the oil onto his feet and worked it in well.

"Now ticklish Timybe, you make sure to tell me if I'm missing any spots on these hyper-ticklish peds of yours," Vince laughed and pressed his thumbs hard into the balls of Tim's feet as he applied more and more baby oil.

"Leave my danged feet alone here Vince; I've laughed enough for you..." Tim catcalled angrily.

"Me thinks you have not laughed nearly enough laddy, not even halfway enough for me," Vince replied, massaging the oil with his nimble fingers into his tickle victim's tootsies now. And you know that with me you shouldn't say things like that...because the more that I may think you have laughed enough the more I'll start to feel that I must help you release the stress from inside your body. And you know with that in mind that I will have you laughing even more hysterically than I had you cackling the last time."

Tim scrunched his eyes shut momentarily and pursed his lips together as his erection raged in the glory hole. Needless to say but while he wasn't being tickled the feel of what Vince was doing in massaging the baby oil into his feet was amazing and driving him sexually insane. The poor strapped down boy would have done anything to give his throbber some relief.

"Oh wow Timybe, your sweet sexy toes are wriggling and helping me distribute this slick oil lube into all the right places and spaces," Vince chuckled, his long fingers working meticulously between the laddy's toes. "Amazing how you do this upside down with your toes anchored and your feet in my ankle stocks the way I have them, hee, hee, hee."

The sounds of that "Hee, hee, hee," sent shivers of ticklish fear up and down Tim's spine. It reminded him of all the times Vince had hee, hee, heed at him in their internet chats and how the handsome black man had teased him unendingly about someday capturing him and tickle torturing him for real. Unnerving to say the least Tim thought as the tickle master played out his sadistically comical fantasy...

"My toes are wriggling and quivering involuntarily Vince," Tim panted downward in the face cradle. "I'm not doing that."

"OH YES, look at this, totally quivering toes as I take each supple foot digit into my fingers, rubbing this oil like individual tongues to your hyper-ticklish flesh..." Vince mused sadistically.

"When Chris finds out where you have me he'll come and rescue me...you'll see..." Tim said as his harder than hard cock swung in the glory hole and his balls hung down heavy with their pent-up supply of sperm.

"And just how is Chris going to figure out where I've got you laddy?" Vince laughed as he finished oiling Tim's feet. "Although where I have you is so diabolically comical that no one would believe it...hee, hee, hee..."

At that point Tim's feet were glistening...

"If I know my buddy Chris like I think I know him he'll be here to save my poor ticklish ass," Tim drawled his Southern accent beyond paramount now.

"But not before you've laughed your ticklish ass off some more for me buddy boy," Vince said snidely, leaning down and directly into Tim's ear.

Snickering as he wiped the oil off his hands he pecked Tim on the earlobe and said "Now where is that blow-dryer?" Tim had read Chris' story "Tickle Time for Julius" so he didn't need three guesses as to what Vince needed the blow-dryer for. He clenched his teeth in anger as he next felt the warm wind as Vince used a portable hair blow-dryer on his oil slicked feet.

"Oh dang it all man, you've been reading Chris' new books eh Vince?" the laddy panted as his oiled feet were heated up.

"Oh you know it my laddy, Chris is ingenious when it comes to the art of tickling a guy," Vince said as he dried up the oil all over Tim's feet. "After I'm done blow-drying your sexy feeties here I'll apply a second layer of the oil to them, then I'll blow-dry them again. I'll do it three times. By then the skin on your feet will be so soft and sensitive so that when I tickle you with the plastic toothpicks that I have on ice you'll scream your laughter like never before. You'll laugh even harder than the time Ronald had you in his clutches and trapped at his tickle palace."

"Vince, again, that was fiction, that never happened in real time like this is happening," Tim pleaded. "There is no Ronald. There is no tickle palace! Oh my word, how can I get through to you man??? P-plastic toothpicks on ice??? OH MY WORD!!!"

When Vince was done blow-drying the oil on Tim's feet he turned the device off, set the dryer aside and Tim felt Vince's long sinewy fingers applying the second coating of the bay oil...

"Oh my word, oh my fucks," Tim panted.

While Vince oiled and blew-dry his tickle captive's bare feet Chris was now driving along the road where Vince had captured his prey.

"Okay Vince, lets see how well I know you," Chris said softly as he drove Tim's shoes on the passenger seat next to him, along with a Georgia roadmap. "If I know you like I think I know you it'll be some place totally deserted where no one will be able to hear the laddy's laughter."

Chris reached into his suit jacket pocket as he drove with one hand on the wheel and took out his cell phone. He looked up Vince's number...

The sound of the blow-dryer turned up to full force drowned out the sound of Vince's cell phone as it rang in his jeans pocket. With a maniacal looking smile on his face he finished drying the laddy's feet for the second time and began a third time of slathering and slopping Tim's tootsies with baby oil.

"Wow, talk about service here buddy boy, you're getting an oil pedicure for free today," Vince laughed as he worked his hands and fingers strongly over Tim's feet.

Tim tried again in vain to lift his head from the face cradle.

In his car Chris clicked off his cell phone when he got no answer from Vince.

"Okay Vince, looks like you're going to make this even more difficult for me eh?" Chris said softly and pulled over on the road.

He picked up the Georgia roadmap and looked it over...

"Okay Vince, a place totally deserted, and big, yeah, it would have to be big as well," Chris figured. "Now, from reading my books what have I learned about you that you have learned from me?"

As Chris tried to get inside Vince's head as Vince had done with him so many times in the past he started the car again, turned around on the road and started heading back the way he had originally come.

After having slathered Tim's feet three times with the baby oil and blowing them dry with heat from the blow dryer the tickle master stepped over to a small refrigerator and took out a tray of ice cubes. In each ice cube, a dozen in all was a plastic toothpick.

"Ah my laddy of lads, you are going to laugh city now," Vince said and rubbed the cold tray against Tim's creamy white ass cheeks.

"YOWWWWWWW!!!" Tim reeled. "That's cold Vince!!"

"Of course it's cold laddy, I just took it out of the freezer section of a refrigerator," Vince laughed meanly. "Now its time to see how your heated feet react to the ice cold toothpicks I mentioned earlier..."

"AW no, no, come on Vince, give a guy a break already here," Tim pleaded.

With that Vince slid two plastic and frozen cold toothpicks from two of the ice cubes on the tray. He took position at the ticklish guy's fettered feet and pressed the tip of one toothpick against the heel of Tim's right foot and the other toothpick he pressed against the top of Tim's left foot. Up and down and up and down Vince began strumming the cold toothpicks against the bottoms of Tim's bare and oiled sensitive feet.

"PPPPPPWWWWWAAAHHHHHHHHHHHHHHHH!!!!" Tim cackled madly. "OH NO, woe is me and my word; here we go again, me off and laughing like a loon!!"

As he laughed uncontrollably Tim could do nothing but lay there and watch as his face contorted in peals of raucous loud laughter. Looking downward at himself in the full-length mirror under the table as he laughed crazily somehow made the ticklish guy laugh even harder. His cock twitched with a life all its own in the confines of the glory hole and leaked and leaked pre cum, his sperm trickling onto the mirror.

"OH my, look at that would you?" Tim laughed. "Is that how my face gets when I'm cackling away??? HAW, HAW, HAW, HAW, HAW, HAW, HAW, HAW, HAW, HAW, st-stop Vince, please stop!!! HAHAHAHAHAHAHAHAHAH AHAHAHAHAHA!!!!"

As Tim laughed Vince's cell phone rang again…

He stopped strumming Tim's left foot, set the toothpick aside and continued tickling Tim's right foot as he pressed the cell phone to his left ear.

"Hello?" Vince said.

"Vince, its Christopher," Vince and Tim's buddy said as he sat in his car, pulled over on the side of the road, his tie now pulled down, him hearing the sound of Tim's laughter in the background.

"Hey Christopher, good of you to call buddy, how's the author doing?" Vince said merrily.

"Never mind that for now Vince," Chris replied as his cock pounded in his suit pants. "What are you doing Vince, and to whom are you doing it?"

"Ha, ha, good question buddy," Vince replied. "But you have his shoes there, and you know exactly who I'm doing what to. My God Chris, he's beautiful, a true Southern prince if ever there was one. And his feet, oh holy fuck Chris, his feet are so soft and ticklish. I've never seen such exquisite looking feet."

"Vince, I cannot believe you actually did this," Chris said, half angry and half desperate to join in the tickle fun.

"You want to say hello to our laddy?" Vince asked and held the phone out and under the massage table, close to Tim's trembling lips.

As he did so and because he's so tall and long-,limbed Vince was able to continue tickling Tim's right foot at the same time, sliding the long toothpick between the boy's hyper-ticklish toes.

"Hey Timmy my laddy, my ticklish Timybe," Vince laughed and Tim saw the phone near his face in the cradle. "Say hi to our good buddy Chris."

"HAHAHAHAHAHAHAHAHAHAHA, oh my word, Chris, ha, ha, ha, ha, ha, ha, ha, ha, ha, ha, ha, ha!!!!" Tim cried out laughingly. "Come here to where he has me man...I need you to help me!!! HAHAHAHAHAHAHAHAHA HAHAHAHAHA!!! OH GAWD, Vince captured me while I was waiting for you outside the rest area and now, HAHAHAHAHAHAHAHAHAHA he won't stop ticklin' my danged foot, my danged feet, oh woe is me man, woe is me!! HELP ME CHRIS!!!"

"Tim, is that really you?" Chris said, although he knew that his ticklish buddy could not hear him.

"CHRIS, I can't tell you where he has me, HAW, HAW, HAW, HAW, HAW, HAW, HAW, HAW, HAW, he-he, hee, hee, hee, hee, hee, hee, hee, hee, hee," Tim laughed. "He brought me here blindfolded man!! OHHHHHHHHHHHHH HAHAHAHAHAHA!!"

"Tim, can you hear me???" Chris shouted into the phone.

"Y-you have to find me Chris!! HAHAHAHAHAHAHAHAHAHAHAHA HA!!!" Tim screeched. "He, he, hee, hee, hee, hee, hee, hee, hee, hee, hee!!! He's not goin' to stop ticklin' me anytime soon I don't think buddy!!! OH MY FUCKING WORD!!!"

Vince put the phone back to his ear and said "Talk to you soon buddy" and clicked the phone off.

"VINCE!! VINCE???" Chris called loudly into the phone. "Damn!!"

Chris punched the steering wheel, loosened his tie some more and pressed his foot to the pedal...

"Okay, we had a very good signal, which means he's not far from here at all..." Chris said as he drove.

"HAHAHAHAHAHAHAHAHAHAHAHAHAHAHAHAHAHA!!!!" Tim screamed, watching his face contort, twist and screw up in the mirror as he laughed harder and harder, Vince now sliding the toothpicks up and down both his feet yet again.

"Didn't I tell you that if I heated your feet they would be more tickle sensitive with the icy toothpicks bud?" Vince laughed.

"Y-you hung up on Chris, why didn't you tell him where you have me???" Tim screamed. "HAHAHAHAHAHAHAHAHAHAHAHAHAHAHAAAAAAA!!!"

"Oh, Chris has as devilish a mind as I do laddy, trust me, he'll find you, eventually..." Vince snickered.

"TICKLE MONSTER!!!" Tim cackled. "I've been captured by a tickle monster!!"

"Keep talking and complaining like that my super-ticklish laddy and I'll give you a really ticklish assignment, just like Ronald did to you in the book..." Vince said as he slid two new icy cold toothpicks up and down Tim's bare feet.

"And what pray tells is that?" Tim asked. "HAHAHAHAHAHA, seeing as Ronald did a lot to my fictional namesake in the "Trials" book.

"Well, as you recall I'm sure, in order to get some time off from being tickled Ronald forced you to reveal things from your ticklish past..." Vince mused, leaned down at Tim's feet and kissed his heels a few times each as he strummed his toothpicks over the meaty bottoms of the laddy's tootsies.

As Tim felt Vince's lips on his heels his cock stalked up even harder. His eyes scanned downward again and he was actually able to see the thick veins in his hardness in the mirror under the table.

"HAHAHAHAHAHAHAHAHAHAHAHAHAHAHAHAHAHA!!!! But Vince, come on man, I don't have a danged ticklish past to reveal to you!" Tim cried out and clenched his teeth. "PLEASE MAN, oh for heaven's sakes, and mine, please, please stop tickling me!! HEEHEEHEEHEEHEEHEEHEEEEEEEEEE EE I keep trying to make you realize here, I am not Timmy Backman from the novel that Chris and I wrote..."

"Now Timmy my ticklish laddy, have you really forgotten all about our internet chats?" Vince asked and finally stopped tickling Tim's feet with the ice cold toothpicks.

At that question Tim's heart thundered in his chest as his laughter slowly subsided.

"Have you forgotten how you once mentioned that young lady you were dating while you were in the army, and when the lass found out you had cheated on her what she did to you?" Vince asked. "You weren't very detailed in your "Instant Message" response to me because we were states away from each other, so I really couldn't extract the story from you. But here we are now buddy, together at last in real time and tell you will...or else..."

To hammer his point home Vince pressed another ice cold toothpick against one of Tim's feet and glided it upwards...

"YAAAAAHHHHHH HAHAHAHAHAHAHAHA, okay man, okay, oh dear, loose lips really do sink ships, even in the world of internet "Instant Messages..."

Vince smiled triumphantly and undid the strap holding Tim's head down. Tim slowly peeled his sweaty and handsome face from the cradle.

"Thirsty buddy?" Vince asked and grabbed a handful of Tim's hair as he held a bottle of cool mineral water to his trembling lips.

"I want to hear all about what the young lady did to you laddy," Vince snickered as he fed Tim the cooling drink.

"V-Vince it was so long ago," Tim drawled when he was done drinking the water, looking up desperately at his tickle captor. "Please, is it really necessary that you make me tell this?"

In response Vince pushed Tim's head down and his face back into the cradle...

"Tell me what I want to hear or I'll just resume tickling those feeties of yours again," Vince said, holding Tim's head down in the cradle.

"OKAY, okay, I'll tell you...just don't tickle me anymore...PLEASE!!!" Tim pleaded.

"Well now, I wouldn't say that I'm not going to tickle you anymore laddy," Vince chuckled meanly. "I will say though, that by telling me what I want to know will take time off your next tickle session...like maybe five minutes off two hours worth of tickle torture..."

Tim rolled his eyes in disbelief...

A few moments later Vince was undoing the straps holding the laddy to the table, starting by releasing his feet from the stocks. As Tim sat up on the table Vince quickly pressed a chloroform soaked cloth over the laddy's nose and mouth...

"RRRRMMMFFFFFFFF!!!!" Tim panted angrily as he inhaled and his head spun.

"Easy my handsome ticklish prince," Vince said and pecked Tim on the cheek as he dosed him. "Just want you to relax a bit before you tell me your tirade...and this makes it easier for me to get you tethered more comfortably...can't have you struggling can I?"

Timmy relates his army day's tickle tale...

A short while later Tim came slowly awake. He found himself sitting on a couch with his hands tied behind him, blindfolded, his long legs stretched out in front of him and his once again sheer black socked (tied) feet in Vince's lap, who was seated at the other end of the couch.

"OHHHHHHHH..." Tim burred, lifting his head slowly as the spinning sensations cleared.

The laddy's cock was semi hard between his legs as he sat on the couch with Vince...

"It sure took a bit longer for you to come around that time my ticklish Timybe," Vince said and snapped the tight sock elastic around Tim's calf against his skin.

"I- I would suppose that all the laughing you made me do sapped a lot of my strength," Tim replied, licked his lips and felt Vince's fingers toying with his socks. "Put my danged sheer wedding socks back on my feet eh buddy?"

"Well, just like in the novel when Ronald made you tell your past tickle tales he had you wearing them," Vince said and again snapped the elastic in Tim's sock against his leg.

Tim grimaced and his semi hardness began stiffening yet again...

"Seems to me that you and Chris both have this danged fetish for seeing me in my thin black dress socks, what I sometimes refer to as my stinkers..." Tim drawled his eyes scrunched closed behind his blindfold as he felt Vince grip his socked feet tighter.

"Good word for them laddy," Vince mused and sniffed Tim's tied up socked feet.

"You know, Chris sent me those danged black sheer thick and thin stinkers," Tim said, wiggling his toes under the socks, Vince quickly gripping them, loving the feel of the laddy's toes, his feet, his heels... "When I called and told him that I was going to be an usher in my friend's Leonard and Kathy's wedding a few days later the socks arrived in the mail. Chris said that it would be nice if his model for a fictional character was wearing his trademark black socks...so I wore them... and just like my namesake in the novel was wearing black socks when Ronald captured him so was I, the real Tim, when you captured me Vince."

"It would seem that black socks are your curse Laddy," Vince snickered.

"Don't I know it? My word..." Tim said and licked his lips again, feeling Vince grip his sheer socked feet.

His cock built up higher and harder between his legs...

"So did the groom wear sheers?" Vince asked, squeezing Tim's toes.

"Nah, I pointed that out to Chris in the car, how he had me in a reverse tradition where the groom's and my danged socks were concerned," Tim said and managed a smile.

"So Timmy my ticklish prince, are you about ready to relate a past tickle torment event in your life, and I do mean your real life buddy," Vince said sternly, the tip of a finger pressed hard against the bottom of one of Tim's socked feet.

"I-I suppose so Vince," Tim said. "Unless Chris shows up to get me out of this danged mess..."

Vince snickered and trailed his finger upwards against Tim's foot...

"HOO, hoo, hoo, hoo, hoo, no need to spur me on Vince, I'll tell you..." Tim said and composed himself as best he could. "Dang, being blindfolded like you got me I can see her face so clearly...so clearly..."

"Whose face Laddy?" Vince asked and held Tim's feet tight against his stomach.

"Belinda, her name was Belinda," Tim replied. "She had long red flowing hair and the longest sharpest red polished fingernails you ever saw. And oh man was she a piece of ass, a real piece of work, she knew so well how to work me and push my buttons. Just thinking of her used to set my rocks rolling...if you get my drift..."

"I think I do Laddy, I think I do," Vince replied. "Now, why and how did she tickle you?"

"Well, the why of it I can sum up rather quickly, she found out that while I was seeing her on my leave time at home from the army that I was also seeing Stephanie, the woman I wound up marrying," Tim went on. "As you know I spent four and a half years in Uncle Sam's army when I was in my early twenties. Like most young guys I had women all the danged time, all over the danged place, but I was usually very clever about keeping them all secret from each other. Belinda found out about Stephanie through a mutual friend of theirs and I was ratted out you might say..."

"How were you ratted out?" Vince asked.

"It seemed that someone, and I'm guessing it was Valerie saw me with Belinda while I was home on leave one time and told Stephanie about it," Tim said. "You would think that Stephanie would have been the one to teach me a lesson, but oh no, the woman I had asked to marry me simply took her victory in the fact that I married her...whereas Belinda decided I needed some lessons taught to me when it came to being a two timer... So anyway, I was home on leave from the army. I hadn't been with a woman in nearly seven months that time. For some reason I had been restricted to the base for those months so when I arrived at Belinda's apartment that night, before I would go to see Stephanie you can imagine the wood I was sporting in my army issued underpants. Belinda was like my ultimate fantasy woman, long red flowing hair, nice sized tits, a body like a dancer, and a danged sweet tight pussy that would not quit. Well, I wasn't at her place ten minutes and she served me my usual glass of red merlot wine. She kissed me long and hard on the mouth as she undid my tie and I worked at unbuttoning my army uniform jacket. She kissed and kissed me till my lips were coated with her fire-red lipstick. I figured I would have to wash it off before I went to see Stephanie. It was because of that lipstick that I wanted the top portion of my uniform off pronto and real quick. I didn't want to risk lipstick stains on my dress shirt. While I was on my second glass of merlot her and I were sitting on the couch, both of us bare-chested, rubbing our nipples together. We each had very sensitive nips and doing that really sent us over the edge you could say. By then I already had my patent leather lace-up shoes off and Belinda was having a great time squeezing the bejesus out of my nipples, what Chris and I called my man tits in the novel, her long dexterous fingers working them lithely, sending chills through my muscular well-toned military trained body. She even used the tips of those long red polished nails of hers on my danged nipples. She squeezed my nips between her fingers and then ground the tips of her nails against the meaty sides of them. That really sent chills through me and made me reel let me tell you Vince. As Belinda manhandled my nipples I squeezed her jugs and she kissed me hard again and again. She moaned how it was so good to see her handsome soldier boy again. She seemed to really be into pleasuring me that time, even going so far as to feed me a third glass of wine. It was so hot and erotic somehow the way she held that glass to my lips and I slowly sipped the wine down. She kissed me on the cheek numerous times as I drank and drank. By then my head was spinning and the feeling of my wood turning to concrete in my olive colored briefs was becoming overwhelming. I mean, I'm always hard in my danged under shorts as you know Vince, but this time it was different somehow. I felt as if I could diddle and fuck Belinda a few times just as a warm-up for when I got over to Stephanie's. As I was about to tell Belinda that I was harder than solid and feeling real sleazy she wrapped her arms around my big neck and ran her fingers through my short military style haircut. She scraped her nails against my scalp and then my head was really tingling, both my heads were tingling actually, hardy, har and har. She raised herself up on the couch and buried my face in between her cleavage. I inhaled her scent and began lapping her nipples alternately as she squeezed the back of my neck, both of us moaning and groaning now. Somehow we were both working at getting my uniform pants off me, I don't remember who got my pants off me just that at some point I was clad in nothing but my black calf length ribbed cotton dress socks, always danged black socks at these ticklish events in my life and in the novel it seems. My word, looking back on it now I don't even recall who or how we got my underpants off me. The next thing I remember was sitting on the couch, splayed out being more like it. My cock was harder than a rock and throbbing like a thing alive between my muscular legs; my balls were all juicy and filled with ball juice, ball juice that I was ready to unload on Belinda. She toyed with my cock head, using her fingernails as well as the tips of her fingers to sluice the accumulated pre seed that had formed there. As she now held the bottle of merlot to my lips I chugged it down in gulps and watched as she licked my pre seed off her fingertips. Oh dang it Vince, watching that made my balls rustle around in their sac let me tell you. Anyways, after just about all the wine was gone I was ready to pounce Belinda like it was nobody's business. You would have thought that with all that wine sloshing around in me that I would be ready for a nice long relaxing sleep, but hell no buddy, I was raring to get my solidity buried deep inside sexy Belinda. I was all naked but for my black socks and she was still in her under panties, nothing else. Damn but she looked good, what a Southern boy like me would call a beautiful belle. I took the bottle of wine from her, placed it on the coffee table, told her I'd had enough of what she was feeding me, stood up on my socked feet and lifted Belinda effortlessly into my strong arms. As she smiled lovingly at me and wrapped her arms around my neck as I carried her to the bedroom she kissed my lips, stuck her tongue in my mouth and said that all she had fed me was wine. I didn't need her to tell me that she had somehow tricked me into gulping down some sort of Spanish fly that she had put in the wine. I figured at that moment that I would be the winner in that folly, seeing as I was the one who would be heading over to Stephanie's after I was done there with Belinda. In my young and naïve mind I simply thought how lucky I was that I was a horned up soldier boy with two women at his sexual disposal for that night. In her bedroom I put Belinda down on her bed and was slowly peeling her under panties off her when she reached under the sheet and held up a red silk scarf, very sexy looking. She said she wanted to see me strip her panties and stockings off her while blindfolded. I chuckled stupidly and told her that I was game for anything, nodding downward at my rigidly stiff cock, saying that in this condition I was truly game for anything. As she reached up and tied the silk red blindfold over my eyes I didn't know at that moment what I was letting myself in for. So now, blindfolded I worked slowly and sexily as I peeled her underpants off her. As I was getting her stockings off her she managed to get me lying down on the bed on my back. I felt for her legs and realized she was now straddling me, her legs upward, which meant her pussy was staring me in the blindfolded face. She told me to slow down and I felt her move around on the bed and then she was looping another silky feeling scarf around one of my wrists. I said "Getting kinky on me eh Belinda?" and she replied that she had always been kinky, just that this time she wanted to try bondage with me, although I didn't know just how far she planned on taking me. I pursed my lips, pretended to be mulling it over as she tied my wrist to one of her bedposts and I said, "Okay, sure" as if I had a choice in the matter at that point. By the time I agreed to her little game my arms had been stretched to the sides of her bed and I was tied off to the bedposts at the wrists. My cock, harder than hard, the veins in it pounding pointed straight up at the ceiling as she did her work. Obviously this was a secret fantasy of mine coming true. I giggled a bit and felt my cock twitching as Belinda tongued my jutted up nipples. "Nipples of the gods," she murmured as her tongue worked magic on my nubs and brought them up to the size of two big pencil erasers on my huge soldier-sized chest. As she moved downward along my torso, not once touching my danged hard-on I felt her hands and long fingernails snaking along my hairy muscular legs. I giggled again and said how I still had my danged black dress socks on. Belinda told me not to sweat the small stuff and then I felt my socks being peeled off my feet, one at a time, courtesy of Belinda. I apologized for the sweaty musty scent emanating from my now de-socked feet but Linda said she had something to take care of that. She took the blindfold off me and left the bedroom, momentarily, leaving me tied up at the wrists, my wrinkled socks next to me on the bed. I asked her where she was going and she said it was a surprise. Well, while she was gone her two cats, Nickels and Pickles were their names, wandered into the room where I was now tied like a sexual slave of sorts. I grinned at the two felines, one of them a black and white male, the other a white and brown female. I stupidly said hello to the two cats and then watched as they jumped up onto the bed and sniffed at my socks that Belinda had left there. I laughed heartily and called out to Belinda how her cats were as sleazy as she was. When Belinda came back she was carrying a quart of milk, a jar of honey and some more of those silk scarves that she had used to bind my wrists to the bed with. She closed the bedroom door. Now the cats would not be able to get out I thought fleetingly. My cock was stalked up and huge between my legs by then Vince. I was sporting a hard-on the likes of which I had never before remembered. I asked Belinda what all the stuff was for and she said that I would soon find out, only telling me that she was going to take care of that musty scent emanating from my danged feet. She looked at her cats sniffing my danged socks and without a word went to work tying my feet at the ankles to the legs of her bed. When she was done she looked me over and said, "There, that looks good." I jokingly told her that I was glad she was satisfied with her work and then gestured toward my cock, telling her that my big boy was awaiting her. In response she slithered a silk scarf over my danged manhood. It sent chills through me and yes, it tickled like the dickens Vince. I bucked on the bed and tugged in vain at the scarves that Belinda had used to fasten me to the bed with. Needless to say terrifyingly ticklish thoughts were coming into my mind. I tried to play it off real cool and tell Belinda that that had felt real sexy what she had just done to my cock with the scarf, but when she did it again I laughed loudly and heartily. Her two cats, at the sound of my booming laughter abandoned my smelly socks and bounded off the bed, but they would be back Vince, they would be back for sure..."

While Tim related his tale of soldierly abduction at the hands of Belinda to Vince his wife Stephanie and her friend Valerie were now enjoying the comforts of having their bare feet pedicured at the salon that Stephanie had the gift certificate for.

"Mmmm, this feels great," Stephanie mused as the handsome Asian pedicurist handled her feet.

"Didn't I tell you that it would be worth it to stop here before heading home after the wedding?" Valerie asked in response.

"Yes, when you're right you're right, and if I know that husband of mine he's probably not even home yet either," Stephanie said as Valerie's cell phone rang in her nearby bag.

She quickly reached for the phone and answered it.

"Hello?" Valerie said.

"It's me," Chris replied. "I just spoke to Tim, well, sort of..."

"What do you mean sort of?" Valerie asked, turning her head so that Stephanie could not hear her side of the conversation at all. "Did you speak to him or not?"

"He was too busy laughing his head off to talk," Chris said as he drove slowly up the deserted road back toward the church. "Vince has him Valerie. And he's making the novel of "Timmy's Ticklish Trials" a reality for our friend."

Valerie stifled a laugh as she imagined her best friend's husband totally tied up and being tickled by Tickle Master Vince.

"So where did Vince bring him?" Valerie asked quietly.

"That's what I'm calling you to find out," Chris responded and a look of inquisitiveness came over Valerie's face.

"Me? How would I know where "your" friend took him?" Valerie asked incredulously.

"Come on Valerie, don't play games here," Chris responded. "You helped Kathy with all the wedding plans. You know where the guest brides-maids and ushers stayed while they were in town. You know the addresses of all the caterers, all the guests…everything. And you also know all the men's secret fetishes. Don't tell me that you don't Valerie. You're not exactly Valerie from the stories that Tim and I wrote, but you're not that far from her either. Now tell me, where would Vince have taken a tickle captive? It would have to be someplace that he has easy access to and it has to be a place where Tim's laughing loudly would not disturb anyone…somewhere where someone who resides there would be gone for a while…a long while…"

As Valerie took a breath before speaking Chris reached into his suit jacket pocket and brought out the wedding invitation that Tim had sent him a bit more than a month ago at that point. Curious, Chris thought, how the invite had Leonard the groom's return address on it rather than the mother of the bride or even the bride's herself… Chris listened as Valerie spoke and as he looked at the wedding invitation and as Tim continued relating his past tickle story to his master tickler captor, Vince…

"So, lovely Belinda tricked you into scoffing down an aphrodisiac that she had laced your wine with, she managed to get you stripped of your army uniform, and…and…" Vince chuckled as he squeezed Tim's sheer socked arches as they rested in his lap. "And she even convinced you to let her tie you up to her damned bed. Boy oh boy my laddy, I have to say, you are one gullible guy. I would think that being as ticklish as you are you would be more careful yes?"

"I suppose you're right at that Vince," Tim said agreeably, his cock pounding thick and beefy between his legs as Vince squeezed and teased his feet. "But Belinda was alluring buddy; she had me by the short hairs so to speak. Being tied up to her bed the way she had me was HOT somehow, especially for a soldier boy who entertained fantasies of playing POW games where he's captured by beautiful women. When she teased my cum chock filled cock with that scarf and tickled it I somehow figured I might be in some sort of trouble there. But when she started slopping my tied up bare feet with the milk and honey she had brought into the bedroom was when I knew that I was in trouble…real trouble. I asked her what in dang hell she was doing as she used a basting brush to slather my left foot with the thick sweet scented honey. She simply smiled at me real sinister-like and as she coated my danged foot the basting brush tickled me as well. I giggled like a school girl and told her to stop that now, citing as how I was very ticklish, very ticklish indeed. She said that she knew that. She said that the other women knew that. My heart thundered in my soldier-sized chest when she said that Stephanie knew that. I tried to play it off real clever-like by asking her who Stephanie was. By then my left foot was liberally coated with honey, all over, from my toes, to between my toes, to the fronts and backs of it. As she began next slathering my right foot with the milk she had brought in she smiled at me and asked how I could possibly have forgotten the name of my fiancé. By then I knew I was in deep shit. It was also at that moment that her two cats, Nickels and Pickles did their reappearing act from under the bed. They hopped back up onto the bed, sniffed at my discarded socks a few times but then the scent coming from my honeyed and milked sopped feet reached their curious little noses. I followed their eyes as they started toward my feet and that was when I began struggling in earnest to get myself free of the way Belinda had tied me to her bed. I grunted like a captured soldier, which in essence I really was at that moment. I pleaded with Belinda to untie me, telling her that her danged cats were making a beeline for my sweet smelling bare feet. She simply smiled at me from where she was standing at the foot of the bed and asked me if I recalled yet who Stephanie was. I bantered and swore at her that of course I knew who Stephanie was, I ranted that I was sorry for having deceived her, and I was just a horny soldier boy after all. Belinda smiled evilly and said that she accepted my apology but that I still needed to be taught a lesson where women's feelings were concerned. Did I think it was funny to be engaged to one woman and have sex with another on the side? She asked me how many other women I had deceived. I jibber jabbered stupidly at her as I struggled against the bindings she had tethered me in. My cock was rage hard, mostly from the aphrodisiac she had tricked me into scoffing down with the wine I had drank. My head was spinning in a mixture of an anger and terror combo. Her two cats were now sniffing heartily at my bare feet. And we all know how rough cats tongues are don't we Vince? Belinda then told me how her two cats loved honey and milk, speaking snidely as she said it. I looked down at my feet and tried desperately to get them untied, pleading with Belinda at the same danged time. I realized I would get no help from her. She had me just the way she wanted me. She had planned this. Suddenly, after sniffing at the honey and milk slathered all over my danged feet Belinda's two cats went to work. They started literally licking the tangy stuff off my poor tied up tootsies. Their tongues felt like little pieces of pointy sandpaper as they licked and ate the honey and milk off my tickle sensitive feet. Well, I'm sure you can figure out the rest Vince. I lay there tied to Belinda's damned bed laughing my fool head off...just as I've done most of my life. Seems that just like in the novel that Christopher Trevor and I wrote I do wind up in the most precarious tickle situations."

Tim stopped speaking for a moment and even though he was blindfolded he could feel Vince literally drinking in the sight of him as he sat there blindfolded with his tied up socked feet resting in the tickle master's lap...

"And you mean to tell me that the sound of your insane laughter didn't send those two cats bounding away?" Vince asked, tugging at the toes section of Tim's socks.

"Nah man, they were too enthralled by the taste of milk and honey all over my danged feet," Tim replied. "As those cats licked the tar out of my big ol' feet Belinda participated in tickling me at my upper body. She trailed and railed those long pointy red fingernails of hers all over my torso, my ribs, my nipples; she really knew how to make me laugh and squirm Vince. I screamed my laughter like a banshee, I tugged helplessly at my bindings, I pleaded and begged Belinda to let me go...but it was no use. She planned on tickling me till the cows came home so to speak..."

"How long did she keep you tied to her bed that way?" Vince asked the tied up and blindfolded handsome Southern guy.

"Well, being in the position I was in it's really hard to say man," Tim replied. "But let's put it this way, by the time she untied me, by the time I showered and got redressed in my uniform it was dark outside. I don't recall what all I told Stephanie excuse wise when I got to her place... but I will tell you this buddy..."

Before continuing Tim smiled almost evilly behind his blindfold as Vince went on and on handling his socked feet...

"And what's that pray tell Laddy?" Vince asked.

"Well, while Belinda had me tied up and her tickle captive the bitch gave me no sexual relief," Tim said. "So you can imagine that by the time I got to Stephanie's there was no more room for my army issued underpants to hold my hard cock in. Having been made to scoff down an aphrodisiac, having been tickle tortured and having had a bondage fantasy come true I was really, really worked up to beyond solid in my uniform trousers you can say. That night Stephanie and I fucked like minx, like rabbits, like there would be no danged tomorrow..."

As he spoke Tim's cock twitched long, beefy and hard between his legs... Vince looked at that cock hungrily...

"So there you have it Tickle Master Vince, you managed to force a real-life tickle story from me, in real-time no less, not just in cyber land or in IM fashion..." Tim said, trying to sound miserable, but not succeeding all that much. "You about ready to let me go now?"

"Let you go Laddy?" Vince replied. "Me thinks not..."

That said Vince gripped Tim's feet tight in one of his huge hands and then started trailing his fingertips up and down the bottoms of them in a speedy motion...

"WHOOOOOOOO, OH NO, no, NO VINCE..." Tim squealed helplessly. "HAHAHAHAHAHAHAHAHAHAHAHAHAHAHAHAHAHAHA!!!!!!!!!! AW no, and dang it all man, I'm off to Tickle City yet again!!"

While Tim was again laughing his head off Chris was at that moment parking his car in front of Leonard the groom's house. As Chris turned off the ignition he looked out the passenger side window and saw Leonard standing on the sidewalk in front of the house. The groom was still clad in his tuxedo, his bowtie undone and dangling down around his shirt collar. When he saw

Chris he waved at him in a friendly manner. Chris picked up Tim's shoes and alighted from the car.

"Hey there Chris, what uh, what are you all doing here buddy?" Leonard asked, looking totally dapper in all his six feet tall glory done up in his tuxedo.

"I was about to ask you the same thing, buddy," Chris replied, glancing at Leonard's huge house, the house that would now be the groom's and his new wife's. "Shouldn't you be on your honeymoon...or at least be on your way?"

Leonard shifted around nervously on his patent leather shoed feet, stubbing out a cigarette he'd just dropped to the ground.

"I, uh, had to pack up a few last things," the groom said, gesturing toward his house with a thumb.

As Chris smiled evilly Leonard noticed the shoes he was holding.

"Who, uh, who's shoes are those bud?" Leonard asked.

"As if you don't know," Chris replied.

Leonard shrugged and Chris said, "They're Tim's shoes. You know Tim, your good buddy who was an usher in your wedding today."

"Sure, sure I know Tim," Leonard said, tugging at the end of his bow-tie. "He's a great guy. I told him to invite you along to the wedding. But, uh, what are you doing with his shoes?"

"Again, as if you don't know," Chris said. "They fell off Tim's feet when Vince kidnapped him..."

"KIDNAPPED???" Leonard gasped. "Holy shit, Tim's been kidnapped???"

Chris pursed his lips and looked at the groom in disbelief...

"Leonard, your acting will not win you any awards buddy," Chris said sarcastically. "I know he's here...in your house..."

"WHAT? You, how..." Leonard stammered.

"I figured that the place Vince brought Tim to would have to be pretty big so that he would have plenty of space to tie and tickle torture his favorite Southern laddy," Chris said. "You have a huge basement here. I remember you mentioning that during the reception dinner, saying how all the guys were able to meet at your place and change into their tuxedos in your basement, citing how big it was. Except Tim wasn't on that list to change into his tux in your basement. He changed up at his house before the wedding and you had your other ushers pick him up on the way to the church. You didn't want Tim to see your basement, seeing as you knew Vince would be bringing him there to tickle torture him...once he'd nabbed him out of my car that is...and out of his shoes... If Tim saw your basement he would know where he was once Vince took the blindfold off him."

"T-tickle torture??? Why would someone kidnap a guy just so they could tickle torture him?" Leonard asked, glancing nervously at his house.

"Once more Leonard, as if you didn't know," Chris said. "Everyone knows Tim is very ticklish. He won't admit that he's even more ticklish in his real life than the character he and I created in our book "Timmy's Ticklish Trials.""

"H-his ticklish trials?" Leonard gasped, still looking at the shoes Chris was holding. "And so, what is this, a male Cinderella story? You planning on putting those shoes on Tim's feet for him?"

"Maybe, maybe not, it depends on the condition I find him in when you let me in your house," Chris said.

"Why would Tim be here?" Leonard asked? "Just because I have a huge basement???"

"That, and the fact that Vince needed a place to bring his over-sized tickle equipment, meaning that cabinet with the chair hooked up to it that he more than likely would kneel poor Tim on so he could tickle his bare feet and his spine. Then there's that massage table with the straps on it and the glory hole cut in the center of it..."

"Okay, lets just say you're right and that Tim is here, and lets just say he's here and he's being tickle tortured," Leonard said. "How would I know this Vince?"

Chris smiled wickedly and said, "The internet gives birth to many friendships Leonard. It did for me and Tim, and then it did for Vince and me, and then it did for Tim and Vince. I'm sure you've visited tickle chats and sites. Most guys love tickling a hapless buddy. I'm guessing that's where you met Vince. When Vince told you how he knew Tim and me all you had to do was put two and two together to know that the Tim he was talking about with the author friend named Christopher Trevor was the same Tim you knew with the author friend named Chris. I mean, what were the chances Leonard?"

Leonard tugged at one of the ends of his dangling bowtie and glanced back at his house.

"So, you want to take me inside now?" Chris asked, holding up Tim's shoes. "I think the man needs his shoes..."

"OH heck," Leonard said dejectedly and started walking toward his house, Chris following behind.

As Chris followed Leonard into his house Vince was at that moment just finishing up strapping Tim down to a large oak table. Tim was still clad in his black sheer wedding socks, but now, also his white kangaroo style under shorts, his cock thick and throbbing sticking out of the fly opening of them, pointing up at Heaven, seeping and dribbling his Southern pre seed. The handsome ticklish guy's balls were packed in his under shorts, churning with a life all their own... As Vince strapped his captive down tight Tim couldn't help looking upward at his wedding band as it hung on the gold chain around Vince's neck. The removal of his wedding band and his captor wearing it made him feel doubly captured away from his beautiful wife and somehow tickle/married to this man who had so cleverly nabbed him. Tim wiggled his toes nervously under his black socks when Vince produced the electric toothbrush and held the bristles against the tip of his erection.

"OH my word, Vince, you, you wouldn't..." Tim bantered pleadingly.

"Ah, but my laddy, I would, you know I would," Vince said and caressed Tim's shaft and underside of his cock with the bristles. "All those times I made you cum in cyber-land I had to imagine how a laughing Southern gentleman such as yourself would look as he creamed his guts out...after having been tormented by me as it were. Now I get to do it in real time my ticklish laddy. It's milking time..."

"Vince, no, no, come on man, you've done enough to me, haven't you?" Tim griped. "At least leave my cock alone man...PWAHHHHHHHHH, HAHAHAHAHAHAHAHAHAHAHAHAHA!!!!"

Suddenly, Tim was laughing uncontrollably once more as Vince titillated and tickled his hard cock with the whirring bristles of the electric toothbrush. As soon as Vince clicked it on the sound of buzzing filled the air.

"OH MY WORD, my GAWD!!" Tim shrilled through clenched teeth and bucked and writhed under the straps as he laughed and laughed. "If, if you keep this up you'll get my danged nut Vince!!"

"That is the idea my ticklish laddy," Vince said. "And then we'll find out if what you and Chris said in the story is true..."

"AND WHAT, HAHAHAHAHAHAHAHAHA, what pray tell is that man???" Tim screamed through his laughter.

"That if after a man shoots his load he's even more tickle sensitive," Vince laughed and grinned down evilly at his tickle captive as he tickle tortured his towering erection. "And trust me on this laddy; after you do shoot that load we are going to find out just how very tickle sensitive you are..."

"NO, NO, that was just story fodder, it's not true, VINCE, stop, STOP tickling my danged cock man!!" Tim begged. "I can feel it; I'm getting close already... The way you've tickled me has me so danged worked up and... HAAAAAAAAAA!!!"

Suddenly, from behind him Vince heard someone call out, "Vince, do as the man says and stop!"

Vince turned off the electric toothbrush, turned around at the sound of the voice and saw...

"Christopher, Christopher Trevor, in the flesh," Vince said, smiling and holding up the toothbrush and seeing his favorite tickle author and Tim's buddy Leonard behind him. "Come to join in the tickle festivities?"

"OH sweet balls, help has finally arrived," Tim said in relief at the sight of his author friend, but feeling some embarrassment at his buddy Leonard seeing him in the fashion he presently was.

"As much as I would love to join in the ticklish festivities I really have to get Tim home," Chris said.

Tim smiled happily over at his buddy and saw his shoes in Chris' hand...

"You can take him home, after he laughs just a tad more for me," Vince said and turned his electric toothbrush back on. "And after he's shot his load..."

"NO, NO, Chris, don't let him do this to me!!" Tim hollered.

As Chris was about to step forward to help his friend a chloroform soaked cloth was suddenly slammed over his mouth and nose from behind...

"RRRMMMFFFFF!!!!!!" the author snarled in shock. "WHAT the FUCK???"

When Chris came to a while later he was doubly shocked to find that it was now he who was strapped to Vince's table where Tim had been just a short while ago.

"HOLY FUCK, Vince, what is this?" Chris seethed as he realized that, like Tim, he was wearing just his dress socks and underpants as he lay there.

"Christopher Trevor, my favorite author," Vince said, standing at the end of the table and slowly, so slowly peeling the strapped down guy's socks from his feet an inch at a time smiled evilly at his second captured prize for the day. "Today is a wonderful and very eventful day for me buddy. Today I not only get to tickle the model for your tickle story, Tim Backman himself, but now, NOW, I get to tickle the author himself."

"You wouldn't!!" Chris panted, struggling under the tight and restricting straps. "Vince, don't take my socks off me man! You know what that does to me..."

"Oh I think do Chris, I think I do," Vince said with a smile and glanced at the erection Chris was suddenly sprouting in his underpants. "You and Tim sure can pack a pair of under shorts I'll give you guys that..."

Chris noted that Vince no longer had Tim's wedding band on the chain around his neck. He also noted that Tim's shoes that he had brought with him were nowhere to be seen, as Tim was nowhere to be seen either. And nor was that bastard Leonard who had done the honors of chloroforming him for this tickle master.

"Where's Tim?" Chris asked as Vince finished getting his socks off his feet.

"You know what's funny Chris?" Vince asked. "When we decided to first meet in person, you and I, you were going to de-sock me in a public place. It never happened, although that was not our fault, circumstances were against us. But now I've de-socked you."

Vince laughed and held up Chris' OTC navy blue socks. "And may I say that your feet look very tickle inviting."

"I asked you where Tim was, never mind my damned feet," Chris panted, thinking how he had to find some way out of this mess.

If Tim was ticklish he, the author was triple that, although he had never revealed as such to too many people....

"Not to worry about your and my favorite ticklish laddy," Vince mused as he placed Chris' socks with the rest of his discarded suit. "Leonard took him home..."

"Leonard...you and him planned all this didn't you?" Chris asked as Vince hunkered down at the end of the table, his face perilously close to the author's naked strapped down feet.

Vince simply smiled in response to Chris' question. It was all the reply the author required.

"Now Chris, lets see if you're not as ticklish as you claim you're not," Vince said and began by pressing and nuzzling his prickly goatee against the bottoms of Chris' bare feet.

The sound of the unwitting author suddenly laughing loudly filled the basement turned tickle torture chamber...

"Leonard and Kathy will be on their honeymoon for two weeks Chris," Vince said as he tickled his new captive. "That gives us plenty of time..."

As Chris laughed crazily he told Vince that he could not believe that Tim would have simply left him there in the tickle master's clutches...

Vince grinned and said how Tim really hadn't had much choice in the matter, seeing as before he drove the guy home Leonard had chloroformed Tim for the ride...

Chris realized how Tim had been brought to Leonard's house blindfolded...no way the laddy would figure out where Vince was holding the author.

Chris laughed uncontrollably and nearly sobbed when Vince said he was going to use his electric toothbrush and his feather on the author's armpits...

Timmy tickled by Santa Claus

"WHOOOOOO, HOO, HOO, HOO, HOO, HOO, HOO, HOO!!!!!" I cackled crazily as I lay on the giant caboose of the kiddy train set that the department store Santa had me so cleverly tethered to. "HAHAHAHAHAHA HAHAHAHAHAHAHAHAHAHAHA!!!!! Y-you let me go right now you maniac Santa Claus!!! HOO, HOO, HOO, HOO, HOO, HOO!!!!"

Santa watched with a maniacal look in his eyes as the giant model toy train I was tethered to rolled slowly along the tracks and made its turn. Santa had the toy set at a slow speed. At the front of the caboose that I was on was a forked-like looking device. That device was *not* set on a slow speed. That infernal thing was spinning at what felt like hundreds of miles per hour and it was moving up and down and up and down as well as it spun... I say it felt like it was spinning at hundreds of miles per hour because the two abrasive brush-like attachments at the ends of the fork-like device were pressed steadfastly against the bottoms of my tied down bare feet.

"HAR, HAR, HAR, HAR, HAR, HAR, HAR, HAR, HAR, HAR!!!!!!!" I laughed uncontrollably; my head lifted a tad as I watched that thing snake its way up and down and up and down against my poor bared feet. "OOOOOOO HOO, HOO, HOO, HOO, what a predicament I'm in this time...HAHAHAHAH AHAHAHAHAHAHAHAHA!!! C-captured and tickled by Santa Claus!!! What a fucked up thing to happen to a poor guy!!! And on of all days, on Christmas Eve no less!!! AAAAAHHHHHHH, HAHAHAHAHAHAHAHAHAHA!!! I- I got to get home for Christmas Eve! I got to be there when Tim Junior opens his p-pres-ent-presents!!! PWAHHHHHHHHH!!!! HAHAHAHAHAHAHAHAHAHAHA!!"

Santa quickly stepped next to me, pushed my head down and prompt-ly returned to the control panel for the train-set. He pressed a button on the panel and the train I was on switched the track, taking me along with it, the device at the end tickling my feet as it went... I glanced over at Santa as he sat at his table and saw next to his control panel for the train the comfortable dock shoes I had been wearing when I had come to the department store with my wife Stephanie. Sticking out of my dock shoes were my smelly cotton beige colored socks from The Gap...

"HAR, HAR, HAR, HAR, HAR, HAR, HAR, HAR!!!!!" I guffawed. "Th-that's something I should not, *should not be seein'*, HAHAHAHAHAHAHAHAHAHA!!!! My danged shoes and socks in the hands of a demented department store Santa Claus! OH WOE IS ME, woe is fucking me!! HARHARHARHARHARH ARHAR!!!!!!"

Hanging on a coat rack were my beige khaki trousers, my brown pullover Polo shirt and my white undershirt, all very typical Saturday attire for a business executive who had been so innocently out Christmas shopping with his wife. Santa left me with only my kangaroo pouch style white briefs on, fucking guy had stripped me most efficiently I must say, tricked out of my clothes as it were you might say. Oh yes, good ole gullible and ticklish Timmy Backman had been had yet again buds! I had fallen for it and was being tickled again... As I was moved along on the train caboose my hard cock was tenting my underpants and dribbling pre cum in them... What with all the "Christmas Cheer" that Santa had tricked me into drinking I could not believe that I wasn't shooting huge loads of "Cheer" into my danged underpants... "Christmas Cheer" my damned tickled feet buds!! That stuff was pure and potent aphrodisiac!!! Oh fucking woe is me again, my word, my damned word!!!

"Ho, Ho, Ho..." Santa said meanly from his vantage point as he watched me being ridden along on his evil monstrosity of a creation. "Seems like Santa's not the only jolly guy here today eh?"

"Y-you better let me go Santa, m-my wife is going to wonder where the fucking fuck I've disappeared to!!! HAHAHAHAHAHAHAHAHAHAHAHAH AHAHA!!!!!" I cried out, my eyes filled with laughing tears.

"Your wife knows exactly where you are Mr. Tim Backman," Santa said. "She knows you are with Santa having your picture taken..."

As I laughed and laughed and laughed I was ridden into a tunnel on the model train...

My tied up feet twitched like crazy and my toes flicked around as the device at the front of the train tickled me and tickled me...

As I laughed my fool head off and rode through the dark tunnel my laughter echoed and my mind wandered back to how I had wound up in this most recent ticklish predicament and on Christmas Eve no less...

As I just pointed out it was Christmas Eve and lo and fucking behold my beautiful wife Stephanie had not yet finished up her danged Christmas shopping. And to add to my misery at being shanghaied into going to do that last minute shopping with her my dear brother Bruce had given us a Five hundred dollar gift card to Stephanie's favorite department store. Well, you know how a gift card to her favorite department store would surely burn a hole in my wife's pocket. So, armed with that gift card to get something for her and I armed as well with my credit cards and some cash my darling wife set off (with me) to do her final Christmas shopping's.

"Stephanie, how many more gifts do we have to get?" I asked miserably as I walked along side my wife, clad in casual khakis, dock shoes and a pullover Polo shirt, carrying numerous shopping bags.

The store was well heated; we had left the car in an indoor parking lot so my jacket I had left in the car. Plus being overly dressed in a department store situation makes me feel way too confined... Fucking fucks dudes, talk about an ironic statement huh? Because that's just what the hell happened to me, I wound up confined in a danged department store, my word!

"Well, lets see, I still have to get that new toy that Tim Junior mentioned, I have to get something for your brother Bruce, seeing as he was thoughtful enough to get us that gift card to this store," Stephanie said and I rolled my eyes in my head in disbelief. "Then there's Nancy my CO-worker and Janice my hair stylist and lets not forget Valerie..."

"Oh for Pete's sake Stephanie, I'm sorry I asked..." I drawled in my very Southern sounding accent. "I really wish that I could forget Valerie..."

"Tim, you agreed to come with me and..." Stephanie began to say.

"I agreed? I agreed?" I replied almost angrily. "Last I recall I was sitting in the living room in the recliner at home watching the football game. Who was it that came over to me with my dock shoes and told me that she needed me to go and do the last minute Christmas shopping with her?"

"Oh Tim, lets not argue, it's Christmas Eve after all..." Stephanie said, suddenly trying to work her feminine wiles on me.

"More like Christmas Evil," I responded and we both laughed.

As we walked on through the store Stephanie suddenly blurted, "Timmy look!" and pointed straight ahead.

"What?" I asked her, seeing that she was pointing at a sign that read "Santa's Village" and just behind that sign was an enormous area of the store made up just like what the sign said, "Santa's Village." "Oh my word Stephanie...isn't it a good thing that we left Tim Junior with the babysitter? If we hadn't we would have had to take him to see yet another Santa and to pay for yet another picture of him with Santa and..."

"We could bring him a picture of you with Santa..." Stephanie said, looking straight at a sign that said "Have your picture taken with Santa" as we entered "Santa's Village."

"WHAT???" I asked her, my voice rising a bit as I said it. "A picture of me and Santa??"

"Yes, a picture of his daddy with Santa, Oh Tim, Tim Junior will love it," Stephanie went on.

We stopped walking and I looked at her with an expression of ridiculousness on my square jawed face...

"Stephanie, why would Tim Junior want a picture of his dad with Santa Claus?" I asked her and rolled my fingers against the side of her head. "I think that this time you have really lost some of your marbles..."

"We could say that you and Santa met and that you told him all the things that Tim Junior wanted for Christmas and then Santa wanted for him to see you with him so he had one of his elves take the picture..." Stephanie said enthusiastically.

With a sudden feeling of overwhelming love for my son I realized she was right and that her idea was actually a superb one...

"Okay, I'll do it, a picture of his daddy with Santa," I said dejectedly, not wanting Stephanie to know that I fully agreed with her idea.

We walked further along in "Santa's Village" and it struck me as sort of odd that we were two of very few people there.

"Why do you suppose there's hardly anybody here?" I asked Stephanie. "You would think that a lot of people would have brought their kids to see Santa huh?"

"Well, it's Christmas Eve, so more than likely most people have already brought their kids to see Santa..." Stephanie said by way of explanation. "Lets find Santa, get your picture taken with him and then we can be on our way and finish shopping..."

"Oh lucky me, lucky, lucky me..." I drawled and we followed signs that said "This way to Santa."

When we reached another area of "Santa's Village" we saw a huge throne-like chair set up, prettily decorated in red and green and a camera facing it. Looking around I saw that Stephanie and I were the only two customers in the "throne room" area of "Santa's Village."

"So where do you suppose Santa is?" I asked Stephanie as we walked slowly around the picture taking area of "Santa's Village."

"I don't know, maybe out to lunch with his elves?" Stephanie asked in response and we both laughed.

A few moments passed and from the back of the picture taking area we heard a door close and then the sound of heavy footsteps approaching. Scant moments later we were standing face to face with a very round and encompassing man dressed up as Santa Claus. As he came over to us I had to wonder if he was padded or if he really was that hefty.

"HO, HO, HO, Merry Christmas folks, what can I do you for?" Santa asked us, sounding totally jolly.

Stephanie giggled and explained how she wanted for me, her husband, to have his picture taken with Santa to show our son, Tim Junior and for Santa to write something on the picture saying what a pleasure it was to meet Tim Junior's daddy and what a pleasure it was to make all the new toys for him...

"Ho, ho, ho," Santa laughed, his big belly rocking up and down. "That sounds like a marvelous idea...I'm sure your son Tim Junior would love that!"

Santa hooked a white gloved hand around my upper arm and for a moment I saw him glance down at my dock shoed and beige socked feet...

"So, you want a traditional picture taken on Santa's lap or maybe one with Santa in his workshop or maybe one with Santa on his sleigh..." Santa said to us.

"Well, I wasn't thinking of all that..." I began and felt a tad uneasy as Santa squeezed my arm and slid his thumb up and down very slowly, almost affectionately.

"All of the above..." Stephanie said happily. "That way Tim Junior can see that his dad was at the North Pole with Santa..."

"Now Stephanie, if we do that we'll be here all afternoon with Santa and we'll never get done shopping..." I said.

"I can finish shopping..." Stephanie said and I saw the light go on in her head. "You can stay here and take the pictures and I'll finish the shopping."

"Ho, ho, ho, now that sounds like a good plan little lady..." Santa said and held tighter yet to my arm, his thumb snaking upwards and under my shirt sleeve. "Tell you what Sir, why don't you give your pretty wife all those packages and then come along with me to my workshop and we'll get started on those pictures for your son?"

Stephanie nodded happily, took the packages from me, told me she would put them in the car and then return to the store to finish shopping. She figured that I would be done being photographed with Santa long before she finished shopping.

"Ho, ho, ho, now little lady, just so you're aware, there's a sale going on in the cosmetics and fragrances department that you just *might* want to look into..." Santa said and winked at Stephanie. "So, while I'm being photographed with your handsome husband here you take all the time you need...all the time indeed...ho, ho, ho..."

"Ho, ho, ho," Stephanie said cheerily, thanked Santa for the tip on the sale, kissed me on the cheek and scurried off.

"Okay buddy, that gets her out of your hair for a bit," Santa said to me and winked as he held fast to my arm. "What say we get you a quick drink of some Christmas cheer before I get one of my helper elves to photograph us? You look like a spiced up eggnog sort of guy to me..."

I smiled and let myself be led down a hallway to Santa's workshop...

We entered a room done up totally like a manufacturing toyshop. Atop a huge table was a life-sized model toy train. Actually it was the size of one of those kiddy trains you see in many amusement parks, complete with an old fashioned looking caboose.

"Wow, would you look at this?" I gasped and dashed over to the table where the giant toy train was set up.

"You like trains buddy?" Santa asked me as he opened a small refrigerator and took out a bottle of eggnog.

"Oh my word, yes," I said, sounding like a child myself. "Since the time I was a little kid I've loved toy trains. I'm trying to get my son, Tim Junior, interested in trains as well. When we take him to the amusement park I always make him ride a train almost like this one."

"How do you take your eggnog Sir?" Santa asked me as he poured me a glass of the good stuff. "Straight up or with maybe just a dash or two or three of Christmas cheer?"

"Well, seeing as I was hoodwinked and literally shanghaied into doing all this last minute Christmas shopping and now roped (GAWD) into being photographed with Santa like a little kid I suppose I could use a few dashes of Christmas cheer in my eggnog," I replied gullibly, still taking in the awesome sight of the train atop the huge table. "Does this thing actually work? I mean, does it move along these tracks you got it set up on? Does it really ride through that tunnel at the other side of this giant table? Does it switch tracks? Does it make train whistle sounds and all that such?"

Needless to say I was in awe of the huge model toy train...

"Sure does," Santa said. "It does all that and lots more. We'll use that as one of the props for the pictures for your son."

"Oh my word..." I said in wonderment and ran the palm of my hand over the huge caboose of the train, not knowing of course that all too soon enough I would be tied to the danged thing.

As I looked over the toy train set Santa sprinkled some brown colored powdery looking stuff into my glass of eggnog. I stupidly took it to be cinnamon as he smiled with huge red lips at me through his beard...his eyes glinting as he seemed to be drinking in the sight of me, really devouring me with those steely eyes. I again ran my hand over the caboose of the train, not noticing the forklike looking device at the front of it...not realizing that another implement could be hooked up to that forklike looking device.

"Here you are Sir," Santa said, stepping over to me with the glass of thick white frothy liquid held out to me. "Some Christmas cheer for the patient husband... I made it with a lot of Christmas cheer thrown in, seeing as you seem to be a very cheer-filled sort of guy, HO HO HO!!!"

"HO HO HO and down the hatch," I laughed alongside Santa, took the glass from him and sipped it. "Thank you so much, this really hits the spot... It's delicious actually. Did you make this eggnog yourself?"

"Nah, it's store bought actually," Santa said and watched almost lecherously as I licked the line of white off my upper lip that had strayed there. "I just added what I call the Christmas cheer, HO, HO, HO!!! It's my secret ingredient you might say..."

Santa watched as I sipped the eggnog again. It seemed strange to me that I didn't taste any of the cinnamon that he had sprinkled in it...

"Okay, now, in the next room I have a life-size sleigh set up so we can use that to take some pictures for your kid, Tim Junior you said his name was," Santa mused as I sipped my eggnog and licked my upper lip again. "But for now let's go out to the throne and you can sit on my lap for the first picture."

"That sounds kind of cozy Santa," I said with a stupid looking grin on my face.

"Well, let's face it buddy, everyone who's anyone who ever had their picture taken with Santa Claus has sat on his lap..." Santa said. "HO, HO, HO..."

Santa again hooked a white gloved hand around my upper arm and we walked together back to the room where Stephanie and I had met him just a few minutes ago.

As his hand again tightened on my arm I took a hearty man sized sip of my eggnog. As it slid down my throat, I, for the briefest of moments felt a twitching and a dancing sensation in my kangaroo pouch style underpants under my khakis.

"Say uh Santa, whew, what exactly, uh, what sort of Christmas cheer did you add to this eggnog?" I asked, trying to sound as simple as possible.

"Ah, now Tim Senior," Santa chuckled and gripped my arm tighter. "Like the old saying goes, that's for Santa to know and for you to ponder about...but seriously, just something to take the edge off a poor guy's nerves who's been Christmas shopping way past his limit with the lovely wife..."

"I see," I said and sipped down another mouthful of the eggnog.

"Plenty more where that came from as well Tim," Santa said. "Okay with you if I call you that?"

"Sure thing, my word, it's my name after all..." I said and Santa and I chuckled.

"Ah good, and my faithful elf Sunder is here to help us with our first picture," Santa called out all jolly-like as we approached the Santa throne.

I saw an olive complexioned guy standing behind the camera that was aimed at the throne in Santa's workshop. The guy was wearing a red and green tights outfit with pointy elf style shoes and a silly floppy looking hat on his head. The hat had jingle bells on it and every time he moved the jingle bells jingled, hardy, har, har and ho, ho, ho...

"Sunder, we will need your assistance here," Santa said to the gentleman made up like an elf. "My new best friend Tim here wants to have some pictures taken with Santa to show his son..."

"Yes Sir Santa," Sunder the elf replied and he and Santa looked at each other kind of conspiratorially when he saw the just about empty glass of eggnog in my hand. "I can take that for you if you're done with it Tim, Sir..."

"Oh sure thing," I said and the twitching in my kangaroos had suddenly jettisoned to a very tingly feeling. "My word..."

I quickly gulped down what was left of my eggnog and handed the empty glass to Sunder the elf. Santa and I watched as Sunder turned his back and stepped over to a small table where he placed my empty glass. Sunder was well built buds; his tights elf outfit clearly outlined and really defined his first-rate musculature. His short green coat looked almost like a ballerina's shirt or tutu, or whatever it's called. His tight butt looked like two coconuts that had been positioned next to each other in those danged tights. I suddenly found myself thinking how one could bounce a damned quarter off those tight coconuts of Sunder's. I quickly shoved the thought away, wondering what in the Sam hell had gotten into me...

Once again I felt the twitching and dancing feeling at my danged crotch...

"So Santa, I guess we should get those pictures taken and I'll be on my way and out of your hair, or should I say your beard?" I chuckled stupidly and nearly heaved myself to my tiptoes as the feeling of elation in my crotch mounted to another level. "Oh my word...Stephanie will be back soon enough and..."

"There's time for all that Tim," Santa said jovially, holding tight to my arm as he spoke. "Believe me; the little lady is going to enjoy that cosmetics and fragrance sale immensely. I'm sure she'll lose track of the time so you and I can just take our time."

As Santa spoke and held tight to my arm Sunder approached us, another glass of Santa's eggnog in hand for me.

"Here you are Mr. Tim Sir," the muscular elf said, handing me the second glass of brew. "More Christmas cheer just for you, courtesy of Santa and his elves in the North Pole, ho, ho, ho and down the hatch."

Before I could say that the first glass of the stuff had been plenty Santa held up his glass which was still halfway full and not to be impolite I clinked my glass against his.

"Drink up Tim," Santa said. "Plenty more where that cheer came from... HO, HO, HO..."

As I put the glass to my lips I saw the brown powdery stuff floating at the top of my drink... I held my breath and gulped down a good hearty swallow...

"AHHHH, thanks Santa, thanks Sunder, Mr. Elf," I said with a sheepish looking grin now etched on my face.

At that point I was at full mast in my kangaroo pouch style briefs under my khakis...

I stupidly took another sip of Santa's homemade mixture... Santa and his elf watched in what seemed like wonderment as I slicked the white froth from my upper lip with my tongue.

"So uh Santa, you said that this is a private recipe of some sort?" I asked as I then felt my man nipples tingling on my chest as my cock pounded in my pants.

"My own creation Tim, my own creation, ho, ho, ho..." Santa said and held up his glass.

As he held to my arm with one hand he sipped his drink and I stupidly followed suit... Santa's drink was not mixed with the "cheer" that had been added to mine. I thought about that for a moment but then the feelings in my cock and man tits clouded my thoughts...

A short while later when I was done with my second glass of eggnog mixed with Christmas cheer Sunder politely again took my glass from me and placed it on the small table alongside my other empty glass. Santa had finished his drink as well and Sunder took his glass from him too…

"So, are you just about ready for our "Special Santa" photo shoot Tim?" Santa asked me then as he snaked his other hand around my other arm and squeezed both my biceps tight, almost lovingly somehow.

"Yeah, I would suppose I am at that," I replied grinning as Santa ho, ho, hoed, him holding me in a tight embrace by my upper arms, starting to move me toward the "Santa Throne" for the first pictures for Tim Junior.

Santa let go of my arms, sat down in his "Santa Throne" and I turned to see Sunder step behind his camera set up a few feet away from the throne. Facing me now I could see that directly under Sunder's elf coat his leg muscles were bulging in his tights and so was the plump looking bulge in his crotch. Gawd, my word, and holy tarnation but it sure as all fucks looked like Sunder the elf's muscles and crotch were stretched to the limit in his danged tights, ho, ho, ho!

"Okay Tim Sir, if you would just take your shoes off and then get comfortable on Santa's lap I'll snap the first shot…" Sunder said and at the sound of the words "take your shoes off" my cock leapt to beyond full mast in my kangaroos and my toes scrunched back in my beige colored socks.

"T-take my shoes off?" I asked nervously.

"Sure thing Tim Sir, I'll want you propped on one of Santa's big thighs with your feet resting on his other thigh…" Sunder explained. "Can't have you resting your feet on Santa's thigh when you have your shoes on now can I?"

"M-my feet, my danged feet resting on Santa's thigh?" I asked, reaching up and hooking a finger in my shirt collar and wringing it in there, a nervous tic of mine, just like tugging at my tie when I'm wearing one. "Y-you mean, m-my socked feet???"

As I spoke my toes, all ten of them twitched under my socks and my cock twitched in my pants…

"Well, of course Tim Sir…" Sunder said, sounding somewhat perplexed and exasperated, as if he were speaking to a child.

"Ho, ho, ho…" Santa said. "Come on Timmy, better do as the elf says or you could wind up with coal or some other awful gifts under your tree or in your socks, er, your stocking tomorrow…"

"T-Timmy?" I asked Santa, still wringing my shirt collar. "You said you would call me Tim…"

"Tim, Timmy, what's the difference?" Santa asked. "Now, lets you get those shoes off and get on up here on Santa's lap and make you a Christmas star in your son's eyes…"

"I, ah, I suppose," I said and reached down to untie the laces on my dock shoes.

"Climb aboard Timmy," Santa said, patting his big lap.

I smiled stupidly, the erection in my pants seeming to lead the way for me and thought to myself how this would not be so bad, I was doing it for Tim

Junior after all and the linoleum floor felt cool and soothing under my beige socks...

With that stupid smile still pasted on my handsome puss I stepped up to Santa and climbed onto his right sided huge thigh...

"AH, there you go Timmy," Santa said, grabbing my arms as I got myself situated upon his burly lap, shifting myself onto his right thigh as comfortably as possible.

"Dang, my word, I haven't sat on Santa's lap since I was a little boy..." I commented and then Santa reached under my knees and scooped my legs up with his big arm.

My cock throbbed hard and rigidly in my khakis as Santa then handled my beige socked feet at the ankles, getting them positioned just right on his left leg as I sat on his right one.

"Okay Sunder, I think we're ready over here," Santa called out to the muscular and well-toned elf. "Okay laddy, turn your head and smile real big over at my elf Sunder..."

"L-laddy???" I croaked and with a feeling of sudden dread starting to consume me I did as I had been instructed.

Santa and I smiled at the camera and Sunder snapped off a few good shots... The light from the flash was somewhat blinding to say the least...

"Okay, those will be good I'm sure..." Santa said and looking down I saw that he had his hand wrapped around one of my danged socked feet. "HO, HO, HO..."

Fucking fucks, the way my head was spinning from the feelings of jubilation surging through my manhood and man tits I hadn't even noticed when Santa had gripped my damned foot in hand. But somehow I knew, I just knew at that point that I was in some sort of trouble here...tickle trouble to be exact. My cock was hard as concrete and twitching like crazy by then, my head spun in ecstasy and as I sat there on Santa's thigh with my damned feet resting on his other thigh Sunder snapped more pictures.

"Oh man, Tim Junior is going to get such a kick out of these pictures of his dad sitting on Santa's thigh..." I said, smiling real big now.

I hammed it up a bit by resting my chin on my fisted hands. I smiled coyly over at Sunder. The flash of the camera blinded me for seconds but I smiled and smiled...

Santa trailed two fingers under my feet and pressed hard...and then scribbled them upwards...

"PWWWWWHOOOOOOOO!!! H-hey, careful there Santa Claus!!" I hawed. "I'm real tickle sensitive..."

"Oh my, sorry Tim," Santa said, sounding almost genuinely apologetic. "I just wanted those last few shots to be real good for Tim Junior...wanted to really make you smile..."

Without another word Santa again trailed his fingertips along the bottoms of my feet...

"H-HEY, HAHAHAHAHAHAHAHAHAHAHAHA!!!!" I laughed and squirmed on Santa's knee. "Now you quit that Santa, ha, ha, ha, ha, ha, ha, ha, ha, ha, ha!!!!!"

As I laughed with my head thrown back Sunder snapped the pictures.

"Tim Junior will see how much you enjoyed meeting Santa when he sees how you are laughing and having such a good time in these pictures Timmy my laddy..." Santa laughed. "Now, how about some with my elf in the shots as well? Sunder, put your camera on automatic and please join me and Timmy my laddy for some good smiling laughing pictures... HO, HO, HO...and hardy har and har! MERRY CHRISTMAS!"

Santa continued scribbling his fingertips under my socked feet and before I could decide to bolt off his thigh and away from his tickling torments Sunder was behind me and holding tight to my upper arms, keeping me firmly in place as the camera shot pictures of the three of us on automatic now.

"HA, HA, HA, HA, HA, HA, HA, HA, HA, HA, HA, HA, HA, HA, oh my word!!! What kind of trickery is this Santa???" I gurgled as I laughed and cackled my head off, being held tickle captive on of all places, Santa's lap...

"HAH, HAH, HAH, HAH, HAH, HAH, HAH, HAH, HAH, HAH!!!!!" I crowed crazily as Santa pressed his fingers harder and harder against the bottoms of my danged feet while Sunder held me tight, the muscles in his huge biceps bulging with his effort.

The camera made the pictures look as innocent as could be, just a boy's dad on Santa's lap along with an elf in the picture, the boy's dad delighted and laughing with joy to have met Santa Claus... My word...my fucking word...the things I do for Tim Junior...

Finally, when the camera ran out of film, or it just stopped snapping pictures because it was set for a certain amount Sunder let go of me and Santa helped me off his lap and to my socked feet.

"Good shoot Timmy," Santa Claus said. "Would you agree?"

"I-I, ha, ha, ha, ha, ha, ha, ha, ha, ha, ha," I replied, looking at Santa Claus and standing there semi doubled over and laughing stupidly even though I was not being tickled at present. "I, I guess it was okay, ha, ha, ha, ha, ha, ha, ha, ha, just don't know why you had to tickle my danged feet..."

"Like I said Tim, just wanted you smiling real big...and lets face it buddy, nothing gets a guy smiling bigger than when his feet are being tickled..." Santa replied and as he took me by my arm again we both turned and faced Sunder who was busy at his camera.

"Got all the shots Santa," Sunder said with a leer on his handsome face. "I'm sure Tim's son will be very happy indeed..."

"Good! Ho, ho, ho," Santa replied happily and walked me over to Sunder and his camera. "Now, get Timmy some more eggnog with Christmas cheer in it and then meet me in the sleigh room with your camera in say, twenty minutes."

"Sure thing Santa," Sunder said, looking at me hungrily.

"And make sure Tim is dressed in the overalls for the sleigh pictures…" Santa said, picking up my shoes and leaving the room with them.

"H-hey, where's he goin' with my danged shoes?" I asked, but before I could follow Santa Sunder had me by the arm and was handing me a third glass of Santa's brew.

"Now, now Tim Sir, Santa has to prepare for the next pictures, and so do you," Sunder said as I took the glass from him without thinking about it, it seemed.

"And what overalls is he talking about?" I asked as I held my third glass of eggnog mixed with the Christmas cheer ingredient in it.

"Down the hatch Tim Sir," Sunder said, getting his camera mounted on a dolly with wheels on it. "For the sleigh pictures you'll need to be dressed in "North Pole style" overalls, that way you'll look like a sleigh worker in Santa's workshop…"

I sipped the drink and my head spun…

"Santa has the overalls in the sleigh room," Sunder explained. "You can get changed in there… Say, hop up on my dolly there next to the camera, there's plenty of room. I'll give you a lift to Santa's sleigh room. You're looking a tad peeked there laddy…"

I stepped up onto dolly and sipped my "Christmas Cheer" as Sunder wheeled me and his camera to the "Sleigh Room…"

"OH GAWD, the things I do for Tim Junior," I croaked as my man tits tingled and my cock felt like it was ready to launch in my kangaroo undies.

Sunder wheeled me into the "Sleigh Room" and I stepped off the dolly, my third glass of "Christmas Cheer" half emptied already.

The room was huge and dominated by a life-size sleigh with eight statues of reindeer hooked up in front of it. The lead reindeer had a very shiny red rose. I had to stifle a chuckle as the words for the song "Rudolf the Red Nosed Reindeer" started playing in my head as it spun some more, a feeling of sheer ecstasy seeming to engulf me. In the back of the sleigh were stacked loads and loads of prettily wrapped gift boxes and in the center of it was a seat for Santa, with enough room for a helper elf…or perhaps a ticklish laddy if you would, HO, HO, HO and Merry fucking Christmas buds…

I sipped my "Christmas Cheer" as Sunder got his camera set up, loading it with fresh film… Looking around the large room I didn't see Santa or my dock shoes anywhere. As I sipped my drink again I wriggled my toes nervously under my beige socks. Looking at the sleigh I figured there was no way Santa could tickle my feet in that thing while we took the pictures for Tim Junior. Oh woe is me, how gullible and wrong I was buds…as usual…

"You can step behind that partition over there Tim," Sunder said to me, pointing across the room where a makeshift dressing room had been set up.

Essentially it was one of those three paneled partitions that you would see in a movie where a gorgeous actress stands behind while she changes her clothes. Hanging over this partition was a one-piece pair of what Santa and Sunder the elf had called "North Pole overalls." To me they just looked like old-fashioned blue denim overalls.

"Thanks Sunder," I replied and with my glass now just about drained I walked over to the partition.

I put my glass down on the floor and snagged the overalls from where they hung.

"Say man, I mean Mr. Elf," I laughed. "These overalls look like they're a size or two too big for me, especially the pants legs. They'll be riding over my danged feet for sure...plus I don't see any boots back here to go with the overalls...and..."

I wanted to tell Sunder that I was not all that keen on stripping out of my clothes and getting into those overalls, but before I could finish my thought he said...

"Not a problem if they're a size or two too large for you Timmy," Sunder said. "It's just for the effects of the pictures that Santa wants you wearing them. You can roll the pants legs up to your calves to keep them riding over your feet, that'll make for a good effect I would think. And as for the boots you don't need any, just leave your socks on, you're just helping Santa in his shop, you're not going outdoors. That's the message we want the pictures to convey for your son. Sounds good laddy?"

"I-I suppose it does at that..." I replied and hung the overalls back up as I stepped behind the partition.

LADDY??? Had he called me laddy??? And leave my danged socks on??? Somehow I was getting the feeling that there was evil afoot here, but somehow as well, my mind was clouded and my cock had really STALKED up in my kangaroo undies at that point... Fucking fucks but I was ready for liftoff in my underpants man!!

A few minutes later Sunder called out that he was ready for the pictures. I stepped from behind the partition, feeling totally ridiculous the way I looked decked out in the so called "North Pole style overalls." With no shirt on the straps on the upper part of the overalls hung loosely over my naked broad shoulders. The middle of it hung over my chest area and the underside of the denim was teasing my torched up man tits, DANG! To keep the pants legs from drooping over my feet I had rolled them up a few times till they were aligned with the tops of my calf length beige socks.

"Excellent! You look perfect Timmy!" Sunder said jovially, dashing over to me and hooking a hand around my arm. "Okay, now, let's get you set up in the sleigh. Santa should be here any minute now..."

"With my shoes right?" I asked and Sunder and I looked at each other, me with a look of apprehension in my peepers and the elf with a look of hunger in his.

"Uh yeah, I suppose, with your shoes," Sunder said and his grip on my arm tightened as we stepped over to the life-size sleigh.

The sleigh was actually raised a few inches off the floor and supported on the bottom by what looked like smaller versions of Sunder's dolly with the wheels on it. Looking upward I saw that it was supported from the ceiling rafters by two heavy-duty cables hooked up to it with pulleys at the tops of the cables.

"The sleigh can be moved up and down and side to side via remote control," Sunder explained. "It gives a great impression of flying when Santa is in it and we video tape him for the kids who come to the store to see him. If Santa is delayed in getting to his "Santa Throne" while the kids are waiting we simply show them the video of him in this sleigh as it appears to be flying and we tell the kids that Santa is on his way..."

"Clever...very clever..." I said softly as Sunder and I stood next to the seat of the sleigh, the seat that I would be in soon.

"And with this backdrop behind the sleigh it really does appear that Santa is flying through the heavens to get to the store..." Sunder went on and produced a small remote control from the pocket of his elf jacket or tutu or whatever the hell it was he was wearing.

Sunder pressed a button on his remote control and a screen that had been raised near the ceiling came down beside the sleigh. The screen was actually a huge mural, a painting that depicted outer space with stars on it and planets as well in the distance.

"My word, it seems that this store spares no expense where Santa is concerned," I exclaimed, feeling totally impressed.

"Christmas is our best time of year Timmy," Sunder said.

"What do you do the rest of the year Sunder?" I asked the muscular guy who had the looks of a GQ model turned elf. "I'm guessing you must work in sales or something close to that yes?"

"I'm an elf Timmy, I'm an elf," Sunder replied, looking at me quizzically, as if it was the simplest thing to understand. "I'm here to serve Santa..." I smiled in a silly fashion, Sunder clapped me on the shoulder in a friendly manner and just then the door to the "Sleigh Room" opened and Santa sauntered in.

"HO, HO, HO, everything all set in here for more pictures taking Sunder?" Santa called out jollily as he entered the room, stomping over to Sunder and I in his huge rubber boots.

"Sure thing Santa," Sunder replied.

"And Timmy, HO, HO, HO, don't you look so spiffy all dandied up in those overalls, HO, HO, HO!!!" Santa laughed, his huge belly jostling up and down as he did. "Tim Junior is going to love these pictures."

"I'm uh, I'm glad to hear that Santa, but uh, where are my shoes?" I asked.

"I left them in the room where the kiddies train is Timmy my laddy," Santa said. "Now, as they say in Hollywood, let's get this show on the road, yes?"

"Uh sure, if you say so Santa," I replied, wondering why so many people called me laddy.

"Sunder, lets start with a few of me and Timmy here standing next to the sleigh," Santa said and positioned me on the side of the sleigh.

My cock pounded in my kangaroo pouch and at some point I knew I was going to have to use Santa's private facilities to relieve myself in a manly fashion, ho, ho, ho, Merry Christmas! Whatever the fuck was in that brew I had drank had me balanced precariously on the sexual edge. I wondered if Santa knew of its erotic effect... Watching Sunder walk away from me and Santa I again could not help but take in the sight of his succulent and tight looking ass globes. The way I was so torched up in my underpants and throbbing the thoughts that went through my head where Sunder's delectable looking ass was concerned shocked even me. Once more I tried in earnest to push such thoughts away...

Santa stood next to me, draped an arm around me up near the shoulder and said, "Smile Tim, smile real big for Tim Junior." I did as Santa instructed and then Sunder had Santa and I move to the front of the sleigh so that we stood in front of the reindeers, then to the back of the sleigh so that we stood in front of the prettily wrapped boxes of Christmas presents.

"Okay Santa, that's enough of you and Timmy outside the sleigh, now lets get a few of the two of you in the sleigh," Sunder said, stepping from behind his camera and over to me and Santa. "I'll help Timmy into the sleigh..."

With no hesitation whatsoever Sunder leaned down and scooped me up off the floor and into his huge muscular arms.

"WHOA!!! Holy shit," I laughed as my socked feet left the floor. "You sure are strong for an elf Sunder..."

"As I said Timmy, I'm here to serve Santa..." Sunder said, setting me down in the seat of the sleigh.

"Okay, now, place your hands on the rail in front of you laddy," Sunder said to me and again I did as he said. "And if you don't mind please reach down and get your socks off now and place your feet in that compartment down there..."

I looked down where Sunder had indicated and stupidly did as he asked. I peeled my beige socks off my feet, Santa took them from me and I slid my de-socked feet into two openings at the base of the sleigh.

"What uh, what are my feet in those openings for?" I asked pensively and glanced over at Santa as he folded up my socks and shoved them in one of his deep Santa pants pockets.

"Just to keep you in proper position for the pictures Timmy," Sunder said and again produced his remote control.

He pointed the red light on his remote control at my feet encased in the floor openings on the sleigh and I felt my feet sucked further in and then the edges around the openings seemed to squeeze tight around my toot-sies.

"Hey, I can't move my feet now," I said nervously.

"Good, that way you'll stay just the way Santa wants you, right Santa?" Sunder asked as he stepped back over to his camera.

"HO, HO, HO, righty ho my faithful elf..." Santa laughed and turned to me. "Now Tim, I want you to look over there at Sunder's camera and smile real nice and wide for Tim Junior. And if you don't smile wide enough Sunder has a little magic charm that he can use just for that problem should it arise. Please show him Sunder..."

Sunder smiled from his stance by his camera and again produced his remote control. At the sight of that device I saw Ronald's face in my mind's eye... Ronald and all his danged remote controlled tickle devices...

"Of course Santa," Sunder said and pressed a button on his remote control.

Suddenly, I felt what felt like thousands of spinning brushes against my bare trapped feet within the openings at the bottom of the sleigh...

"WHOOOOOOOOO!!!! HAHAHAHAHAHAHAHAHAHAHA!!!!" I sud-denly blurted as I was being tickled yet again.

I bobbed and thrashed around in the seat of the sleigh as I did my own "ho, ho, ho," version of Santa's classic laugh. I gripped the bar in front of me tighter and tighter and heaved up and down in the sleigh.

"T-Turn it off Sunder, turn it off!! HAHAHAHAHAHAHAHAHAHAHA!!!" I cackled, spittle flying from my mouth, my cock throbbing and beefy hard in my kangaroos. "Santa, make him turn it off, PLEASE!!! HOHOHOHOHOHOH OHOHOHOHO!!!! Oh my word, I'm being tickled tortured by an elf here!!! Of all the blasted things!! HAHAHAHAHAHAHAHAHAHAHAHAHAHAHA!!!!"

But instead, Santa stepped out of the line of where Sunder's camera was aimed at me and the elf snapped off picture after picture of me as I sat trapped in the sleigh laughing my fool head off.

"HAR, HAR, HAR, HAR, HAR, HAR, HAR, HAR, HAR, HAR, HAR," I laughed and whatever the devices at my feet were they were spinning faster and faster it seemed, getting me laughing louder and louder.

"Brilliant pictures Timmy, these will be perfect," Sunder called out and Santa ho, ho, hoed agreeably. "Tim Junior will love these for sure..."

"N-no wonder you wanted my socks off me... PWWWAHHHHHHHH!!!! HA, ha, ha, ha, ha, ha, ha, ha, ha, ha, ha, ha!!!!" I laughed and clenched my teeth... "I-I can't believe I fell for that, HA, HA, HA, HA, HA, HA, HA, HA, HA,

HA, HA!!!!!"

Sunder then pushed another button on his remote control device and the sleigh started swinging back and forth, making it appear as if it was flying.

"HAH, HAH, HAH, HAH, HAH, HAH, HAH, HAH, HAH, HAH!!!!" I laughed as I was tilted backward, looking up in a diagonal position as I laughed and laughed.

"WH-what the fucking fucks is this???" I chortled crazily.

"Like I showed you earlier Tim, the way the sleigh is situated makes it look like you're flying through the air on it," Sunder said to me and Santa nodded agreeably. "Your son is going to be so impressed with these pictures!"

Sunder snapped shots of me as I was propelled back and forth in the sleigh. Somehow the movements made my dancing cock sway more-so in my kangaroo pouch underpants. Woe is me buds... The underside of the denim overalls I had on pressed against my man tits and rubbed them hard. Fucking fucks, fucking double fucks buds, it felt as if sandpaper was being rub-a-dub-dubbed against my danged sensitive nipples... And all I could do was ho, ho, ho and ho, ho, ho some more...

After what seemed like a long while Sunder turned off the tickle devices at my feet and as I slowly stopped laughing he instructed Santa on how to pose behind me in the giant sleigh... Sunder used his remote control device to set the sleigh facing forward and straight and then Santa was seated behind me in the sleigh. We both smiled at the camera and made it appear as if I was helping Santa transport his sleigh of toys and goodies for the children of the world.

"My, my, I'm sure your son will love these shots for sure Tim," Santa said as he sat with me in the sleigh. "Imagine you flying in Santa's sleigh..."

"Yeah, imagine that huh?" I asked and pursed my lips between pictures as I tried unsuccessfully to pull my feet free of the compartments they were trapped in. "Just wish that elf of yours hadn't locked up my danged feet the way they are..."

"But Tim, if he hadn't done that how else would we get you to laugh and smile so much for the pictures?" Santa asked and then pointed a white gloved finger at Sunder. "Now Sunder..."

Suddenly, the brushes that my feet were pressed against in the compartments at the bottom of the sleigh came to spinning life yet again...

"OH NO OH NO!!! HAHAHAHAHAHAHAHAHAHAHAHAHAHA!!!!!" I chortled anew as I was again tickled.

Santa sat behind me with his hands on my shoulders as I laughed and laughed like a hyena. To anyone looking at the pictures that Sunder was snapping it would most certainly have appeared that I was simply having a grand old time flying in Santa's sleigh...not being awfully tickled tortured...

"HARHARHARHARHARHARHARHARHAR!!!!!" I roared and then

Santa was laughing as well, but not from being tickled as I was being, he was laughing at my awful plight, although to anyone watching it would simply have appeared that Santa was ho, ho, hoing…

"Laugh my laddy, laugh," Santa said into my ear, his lips almost nuzzling my lobe as he spoke. "And when we're done here we'll get you another glass of Christmas cheer…"

"OHHHHHHHHHH NOOOOO NOOOO, that's a danged sex pot drink!!" I cried laughingly. "HARHARHARHARAHARHARHARHARHAR!!!!!"

"Have yourself a merry little Christmas Timmy…" Santa laughed as I laughed and laughed.

Santa put an arm around me in the sleigh and with my head pressed against his enormous chest I haw, haw, hawed. As I heaved myself upwards in the sleigh the denim overalls rubbed my man tits and I hee, hee, heed against Santa's enormity. My cock throbbed like a thing alive in my kangaroos and I was helplessly guffawing my head off as Santa climbed out of the sleigh.

"You're on your own for now Timmy my laddy," Santa chuckled as he stepped next to Sunder as the elf went on and on taking pictures of me as I laughed and laughed.

"YAAAAAHHHHHHHHHH, Ha, ha, ha, ha, ha, ha, ha, ha, ha, ha, ha, ha, ha, ha!!!!" I screamed my laughter with my head down now, gripping the bar in front of me.

I heard Sunder's camera clicking away as my tickle torments were captured on film…

"Very good Tim, very good indeed…" Santa called out. "When your lovely wife sees these pictures I'm sure she'll want to purchase enough of them to fill a large photo album, ho, ho, ho!"

"M-MY wife, my danged wife!!" I chortled. "HAHAHAHAHAHAHAHAHA!!! Stephanie, she got me into all this!!!! HARHARHARHARHARHARHARHARH AR!!!! She should see her poor handsome laddy husband now!!!!"

I gripped the bar tighter and for some danged reason it felt as if my feet were being sucked deeper into the compartments and somehow it felt as if the whirly devices down there were spinning faster and faster…

"HAHAHAHAHAHAHAHAHAHAHAHAHAHAHAHAHAHA!!!!" I laughed uncontrollably, sweating like crazy now as well.

When I looked over at Santa and Sunder I saw that Sunder was no longer taking pictures. They were simply watching me laugh my head off as I was tickled and tickled… My heart broke when I saw that Santa was holding another full glass of the "Christmas Cheer" in hand…

"NNNNNOOOOOOO, HOO, HOO, HOO, HOO, HOO, HOO, n-no more tickling, no more Christmas cheer, oh please no more!!! HAHAHAHAHAHAHAHAHA!!!!" I pleaded.

Finally, Sunder stepped over to the giant sleigh with his remote control and pointed it at my feet. The spinning brushes came to a slow halt and I gradually stopped laughing.

"There you go Tim, we're all done with the sleigh pictures," Sunder said as he pressed another button on his remote control. "Hasn't this just been a great day?"

I felt the holes that my feet had been trapped in expand and I quickly and without thinking about it pulled my poor tickled feet upwards and out of the compartments.

"Yeah, just about the best danged day I could have imagined," I heaved as Santa handed me the glass of "Christmas Cheer."

"There you go Tim, that'll cool you down a bit and then we'll go and take pictures with your favorite toy kiddy train..." Santa said and because the thought of being photographed with that danged train excited me so I didn't think twice as I sipped the "Christmas Cheer." "I added some ice to that one to help you cool off a bit laddy."

"OH MY WORD..." I gasped and my head spun away into orbit.

Santa quickly took the glass from me and I slumped into a stupor in the sleigh...

"Looks like my Christmas laddy needs a rest..." I heard Santa say laughingly as I then felt strong hands hoisting me out of the sleigh. "Okay, no problem at all. While he rests up I'll get him ready for the train, ho, ho, ho...ho, ho, ho..."

It was that evil sounding ho, ho, ho that I kept hearing as I was carried from the sleigh room...eventually the world went dark and I must have slept a while...

It was when I came to that I found myself tethered to the kiddy train that I had been so fascinated with when I first met Santa, which seemed like eons ago at that point... Actually Santa was just finishing tying up my danged bare feet to the front of the caboose as I came to. The rest of my body was already quite well and efficiently tied the fuck down. As I opened my eyes the first thing I did was look around the room I was now in with Santa. I recalled being in the room when I first saw the kiddy train set. Glancing over at the table where the control panel for the train was I saw my dock shoes with my beige socks sticking out of them. My other clothes hung on a coat rack that Santa had set up in the room.

"OOOOOOHHH my word, wh-what happened?" I croaked.

"You fell asleep Timmy my laddy," Santa said as he wound the rope around and around my feet, lashing them tightly to the train's caboose I was stretched out on my back. "I guess all that picture taking tired you out eh?" "More like all that tickle torture that you and that sadistic elf dished out on me, ho, fucking ho Santa Claus!" I replied angrily and it was when I tried to sit up that I realized I was tightly tied down...and wearing just my danged kangaroo pouch style briefs. "OH HOLY CRAP and fucking TARNATION!!! I-I've been stripped down and tied up!!"

"Very well stated laddy," Santa said and finished tying my feet.

Smiling evilly he hunkered his head down a tad and gave each of my big toes a hearty slurp each. The sound of my toes being sucked on seemed to fill the room and my stalked up cock in my briefs churned like nobody's business... HO, HO, HO!!! Santa sucked my big toes so powerfully that it felt as if it was a motorized device hooked up to them, rather than a human mouth doing a job on them... Seeing that long tongue of Santa's snaking out between his lips and from out of his beard was erotically driving me crazy somehow. He sucked my toes with gusto and chills coursed through my being.

"Wh-what the fucks man? I'm tied up to this danged train of yours! And you're sucking my stinking toes no less!!" I gurgled angrily, my fists clenched at my sides. "S-Stephanie my wife, she'll get you for this Santa, this was *not* what she had in mind when she left me with you to take pictures for Tim Junior!!"

"Ah Timmy my laddy, the real question here is, will your wife get you?" Santa asked me and squeezed my bare feet almost lovingly.

"What is that supposed to mean???" I asked in angered reply.

"I'm sure that by now she's very entranced over at that special sale I told her about," Santa laughed and squatted down to kiss the bottoms of my feet a few times each. "I'm positive that she will not be looking for her handsome husband any time soon..."

"Oh dang, oh woe is me," I swooned as Santa sent chills through me as he gingerly kissed my feet. "If Stephanie could see her handsome hubby now I doubt she would believe it..."

"I don't doubt that laddy..." Santa snickered.

Santa kissed the bottoms of my feet over and over and my cock strummed up more-so in my kangaroos...

"AWWWWW man, what a Christmas this turned out to be, dang, y-you're sending chills through me the way you're kissin' the bottoms of my feet Santa Claus!!" I groaned as my head spun, my nipples sizzled and my cock pounded. "Wh-where's Sunder?"

"I gave Sunder some time off Mr. Tim Backman," Santa said, reaching into his pocket and bringing out a forklike looking device of some sort. "He had been so cooperative in photographing you that I felt he deserved it...plus it affords us some Christmas time together...wouldn't you agree?"

"I-I'm sorry I agreed to all of this Santa! I didn't plan on being tickle tortured..." I grunted. "And what pray tell may I ask was in that so called "Christmas Cheer" you gave me to drink?"

"Just a little sprinkle of potency Mr. Tim Backman..." Santa snickered and I watched then as he clipped the forklike looking device up to the front of the caboose of the train, directly in front of my danged tied up feet.

"WHAT the devil is that?" I asked the deranged Santa.

"Ah, my latest trickery Timmy, all the kids will want one this year..."

Santa replied jovially and then clipped the small brush-like attachments to the fork shaped device.

As Santa tested the device by moving it manually up and down slowly against the bottoms of my feet I gulped hard and gurgled the words, "Ah no, no, oh dang it all, you're plannin' on ticklin' my damned feet again..."

"And this time you'll be riding your favorite toy train as they are tickled my laddy," Santa said and stepped next to my crotch area, placing the palm of his hand over my erection and outlined juicy balls in my kangaroos, patting them gently too. "Nice impression you're making here in these kangaroo pouch underpants of yours Timmy..."

That said, I groaned as Santa took his hand off my crotch, no chance of him giving me a man's relief it seemed. He had tricked me into being all worked up in my kangaroos via tickling my danged feet and feeding me an aphrodisiac, but like so many others in my ticklish past history he was not about to give me release...

I watched then with my head raised as Santa stepped over to the control panel for the toy train set...

"All set for your train ride my laddy?" Santa asked as he sat down at his control panel. "HO, HO, HO!!!"

"The way you got me all tethered and tied here I don't think you've left me with much choice Santa," I replied miserably. "Dang it all and my word but this Christmas photo shoot has turned into a horrendous ticklish situation for me here..."

"Very well stated my laddy, if I do say so myself that is," Santa chuckled.

Santa pushed a lever on his control panel and the sounds of whistles rang out from the train and the train itself starting moving slowly along the tracks...taking me with it...

"And off you go on Santa's private train line Timmy my laddy." Santa ho, ho, hoed at me, his white gloved fingers pushing a lever upwards on the control panel.

The train moved slightly faster along the tracks. I felt the rumbling against my naked back and the strumming of my cock in my underpants was otherworldly by then. My nipples were jutted up to the size of pencil erasers. I lifted my head for a second to take in the sight of my plumped up man tits. GAWDS, it looked like someone had done the honors of really sucking them up past erect. I wondered just what Sunder the elf and Santa had done with my tits in between the time I had slept and then Santa had gotten me tied to his kiddy train. The train made whistle sounds and I heard bells clanging as I was rolled along the tracks.

"I got to say, I'm glad you're not taking pictures of me tied up like this," I said, looking over at Santa as he controlled the train from where he was seated. "I doubt Tim Junior would understand..."

"Ho, ho, ho, so right you are my laddy," Santa said agreeably. "No pictures after all of you on the train, ho, ho, ho! This will be just our little private session so to speak...and so to laugh..."

That said Santa pressed a button on the control panel and suddenly the brushes attached to the forked-like looking device at the front of my tied up bare feet came to rotating and up and down life at a high speed...right against my poor tied up feet...

"HARRRRRR!!!!!!!!!!!!!!!!!! HA, HA, HA, HA, HA, HA, HA, HA, HA, HA, HA!!!!" I cackled loudly and crazily. "OHHHHH NO NO NO!!!!!"

"Don't you mean oh Ho, Ho, Ho, my ticklish laddy?" Santa asked me... "Off you go my laddy, to the North Pole on the Santa Claus Express train..."

And so now you know how I came to wind up as a tied down decoration on Santa's kiddy train's caboose...and how I came to wind up clad in just my danged kangaroo pouch style underpants while in the deranged Santa's clutches... Oh Stephanie, why hadn't she come looking for her poor imperiled husband??? Could that sale over in the cosmetics area be that enticing that she had completely forgotten about me???

"HAH, HAH, HAH, HAH, HAH, HAH, HAH, HAH, HAH, HAH!!!!" I laughed as I was moved through the dark tunnel, my laughter echoing as I went. "SANTA, you release me, you let me loose now!!!!"

As I saw the light at the end of the tunnel the train slowed down and switched the track again atop the table, making the sounds of a real train as it rode along...

"HAR, HAR, HAR, HAR, HAR, HAR, HAR, HAR, HAR!!!!!" I laughed loudly as my tickled feet emerged first into the light as the train exited the tunnel.

When the train exited the tunnel I quickly cocked my head and looked over at Santa at the control panel. His hands were moving quickly over the board, pressing buttons.

"Timmy, it sounds to old Santa like you're having a good time riding that train eh?" Santa called out to me. "HO, HO, HO, Merry Christmas my laddy!"

"Oh, oh, ha, ha, ha, ha, ha, ha, ha, ha, ha, ha, ha!!!!" I replied. "Oh yeah, can't think of anything else I would rather be doing right about now you maniac Santa Claus, ha, ha, ha, ha, ha, ha, ha, ha, ha, ha, ha, ha, ha, ha, ha!!!!!"

"Choo, choo and Merry Christmas Mr. Backman..." Santa laughed and pushed a button on his control panel.

The train switched back to his original track and the device at my feet snaked meanly upwards, spinning fast as it tickled and tickled and tickled my bound bare feet...

"HAHAHAHAHAHAHAHAHAHAHAHAHAHAHAHAHAHAHA!!!!" was all I

could say at that point.

Finally, after a long while more and a few more times sending me through the echoing tunnel Santa brought the kiddy train to a stop in its original position...

"OHHHHHH, ho, ho, ho," I bantered, feeling totally exhausted. "I-I have to get out of here Santa. It's Christmas Eve and I have to be there when Tim Junior opens his Christmas presents... OH PLEASE..."

"And so you shall be my laddy," Santa said and standing next to me he untied me as I sat up atop the caboose, sweating and gasping for breath, my cock stalked up and mighty hard in my kangaroo pouch undies.

I sat up on the caboose and straddled the thing, draping my muscular legs over the sides, my hands still tied behind me. As Santa was putting the rope away somewhere under the table that the train was set up on it was at that moment that Sunder the elf returned.

"Ah good, and right on time as always Sunder, my faithful elf," Santa said. "HO, HO, HO, I'm happy to say that Timmy our ticklish laddy here just enjoyed a wonderful trip on the Santa express train."

"I bet he did," Sunder said meanly, flicking his fingers over the brushes on the fork-like device attached to the front of the caboose.

"Now, Sunder, I have to go and see if Mr. Backman's pictures are all developed and ready for him and his lovely wife to choose from," Santa said to Sunder, gesturing over at me as I sat atop the train in just my danged underpants. "Would you be so kind to finish untying our laddy and then meet me and his lovely wife in my workshop where we'll work out the details of prices and such for the pictures?"

I could not believe it, tickle tortured as I had been yet again I was going to be charged full price for the pictures. To Timmy Junior it would look like his dear dad was having a grand time with Santa and his elf, while the reality for me, every time I looked at those pictures it would be a memory of yet another tickle torture episode in my ever-ticklish life, GAWD!

"Of course Santa, always happy to oblige," Sunder said and reached up to take the string of jingle bells off his floppy hat.

As Santa left the room where the train was set up Sunder approached me, waving his string of bells, smiling evilly...

"So Timmy, tell me, did you enjoy your time with Santa?" Sunder asked and I could not help noticing that he was looking lecherously and hungrily at the huge stalk in my kangaroo pouch under shorts.

"I, uh, suppose "enjoyed" really isn't the word that would apply here at the moment Sunder," I said breathlessly, knowing all too well what he was about to do.

My cum filled nuts churned in the white under shorts I was wearing...

"I'm just glad that Timmy Junior will have some good shots of his dad with Santa and…" I suddenly found myself gasping as Sunder brazenly reached into the fly opening of my kangaroo pouch underpants, forcing his fingers in and expertly tying his jingle bells from his hat to the base of my balls…real tight I might add. "AHHHH my word, what, what in tarnation are you up to now you crazy elf???"

Moments later Sunder had me lying on my back on the caboose of the train, my hands still tied behind me. (The fucking elf had taken advantage of that fact, that Santa hadn't yet untied my hands.) The perverted elf had blindfolded me and he was singing "Jingle bells, Jingle bells, jingle ALL THE (damned) way" as he stroked my jingle belled cock and balls through my kangaroo pouch undies. Oh woe is me buds, much as I wanted to cum I did not feel like filling my pouch under shorts with my own blend of Christmas cheer.

"Jingle bells, jingle bells, jingle all the way," Sunder sang and stroked my Yule log faster and faster as he held it tight in hand. "Oh what fun it is to ride in a stalked up open sleigh, HEY!!!"

"Sunder, you crazy elf, you, you untie me now man," I gurgled through clenched teeth, sweating profusely as the Christmas cheer I had been tricked into drinking did it's devilish work all too well. "And, and take this danged blindfold off me, my word!! Oh my, what a Christmas present I'm getting here!! I'm going to slop my mess in my danged kangaroos!"

"Dashing through the snow, in a one horse open sleigh," Sunder sang, and rather badly I might add as he pumped my stalk faster. "What fun it is to ride and stroke and choke a ticklish laddy in a plight…"

"S-sunder, I'm sure Santa didn't want you decking my balls with your jingle bells," I cawed, listening in blindfolded darkness to the sounds my shaking maracas in my underpants were making as I was pumped and pumped.

"OH!!! Jingle bells, jingled balls, jingling every which way…" Sunder sang. "Oh what fun it is to stroke Timmy the laddy today…HO, HO, HO, and away we go…"

He laughed raucously and then I was spewing my Christmas eggnog, right into my damned under shorts.

"AAAAAAHHHHHHH…oh Merry Christmas," I sang out, my muscular body arched upwards on the caboose as Sunder sang and my cock sprang and sprang its Christmas donation. "OOOHHHHH and happy New Year too…" My man tits were jutted up, as usual as I sprayed my spray into the pouch of my kangaroos. When I was done I lay there gasping for breath. The orgasm seemed to go on and on, non-stop. My under shorts were filled to just about overflowing with my sticky cheer. I shuddered and there were goose bumps all over me as I felt Sunder reaching into my now cum sopped undies to retrieve his danged jingle bells. The feel of his fingers handling my balls sent chills through me…I lay there grunting, gasping and sweating…

"And jingle all the way…" Sunder finished and whipped the blindfold off me.

He stood there leering at me as I panted and heaved...

"Merry Christmas you handsome laddy," Sunder said softly and held up his jingle bells.

They were dripping remnants of my slop... I grimaced miserably as the elf claimed his prize...he slid my danged kangaroo pouch style underpants off me and a feeling of loss and humiliation filled me as he deposited them in an over-sized plastic zip-lock bag. I looked in awe as my sticky mess coated the sides of the bag...

When Sunder untied my hands I made a beeline for my clothing...not caring at that moment that I would have to free ball in my khakis for the ride home...

Later...

"Stephanie, I cannot for the life of me believe that you purchased every single one of those pictures of me with Santa for Tim Junior," I said in disbelief. "Thank God my brother Bruce gave you that danged gift certificate for this store. The price was unbelievable."

"Oh come on Tim, cheer up, it's for Tim Junior after all," Stephanie said as we walked toward the exit of the store, me carrying still more packages, filled with still more stuff she had purchased at the danged cosmetics sale.

The only good thing about having to carry the packages was that I was carrying them in front of me, covering up the new erection I was sporting in my damned khakis. My word, and without my kangaroo pouch undies to hold my equipment in I was really showing off my Christmas log. My balls bounced around in my pants like no one's business.

"I suppose, but you have no idea what I went through to smile and laugh just right for those pictures Stephanie," I said, wondering if she got my meaning at all.

As we walked on I heard a booming voice call out, "Timmy? Timmy Backman? Merry Christmas buddy!" My jaw dropped and as Stephanie and I looked to our right where the voice was coming from I was astonished to see "Bull" the bartender from the infamous leather bar where I had been duped into being tickle tortured not all that long ago.

"Oh uh, hello there Bull, good to see you, Merry Christmas," I said, shaking hands with him as I held the packages quickly in one hand.

I quickly introduced Bull to Stephanie, they shook hands, we all wished each other a Merry Christmas and as Bull walked off he howled out a "HO, HO, HO" and suddenly I realized who I had been tickle tortured by yet again...

When we got home I quickly dashed to our bedroom to get a pair of underpants on...

Stephanie caught me standing there with my erect tool sprouted up in my fresh underpants. She was under the impression that I was changing into more comfortable clothes. When she cuddled up against me I would finally know some real relief…GAWD!

Timmy confronts his Brother Bruce
(and the tables turn and turn…)

Author's Comments: When I first introduced the character of "Ticklish" Timmy in the novel length tickle story "Timmy's Ticklish Trials" to the story of "Timmy at the Leather Bar" and the most recent installment of "Timmy and the Hong Kong Tailor" we learned that Timmy's conniving brother Bruce is the one who usually sets Timmy up for playful capture and tickle torture. Throughout those stories we never saw Bruce or any confrontation between the two brothers. Needless to say, after all Timmy the ticklish laddy has suffered tickle-wise I (and my buddy Bill) figured it was time for the brothers to have that confrontation. But, as usual, things will not go exactly the way Timmy would like them to, as you will find out in this latest installment where "Timmy confronts his brother Bruce…"

I left work early that Wednesday afternoon. I figured for one afternoon the bank could do without good ol' reliable and always dependable Timothy Backman. After what had happened with Steve the tailor, oh, excuse me, Steve the *Master* tailor and after what had happened at the leather bar with Bull the barrel chested and muscle bound bartender and his buddies I decided it was time for my older brother Bruce and I to have a little talk. I knew full well that it was Bruce who had set me up both times for tickle torment! And both times I was naïve and gullible enough to fall for his trickery. Well, for Bruce the day of reckoning had come. As I rode the train to his house I thought about how after each of the times I just mentioned Ronald was there to pick me up, literally, he picked me up. Fucker that he can be, he picked me up and carried me off, hardy, har and har! But truthfully, as much as Ronald makes me laugh it's no laughing matter. (Ronald, owner of the tickle palace that's set in a very remote area of somewhere I can only guess is upstate New York. Ronald, who had the audacity and cunning to kidnap me, *fucking guy kidnapped me,* right out of my own house during the wee hours of the night when I had woken up to use the bathroom; Ronald, who brought me to his tickle palace on that fateful night and for the better part of three days tormented me continually with his devilish inventions of tickle torture devices. I said that I could only guess that the tickle palace is located in a very remote area of upstate New York. The reason that I can only guess at it's location is because each time Ronald has had the cunning to bring me there I was either sleeping off a dose of chloroform he had given me or I was blindfolded or both. What I have seen of the outside of Ronald's tickle palace is a huge house surrounded by mostly woods, which leads me to guess it's location as being somewhere in upstate New York.) And woe of fucking woes, as if I hadn't been worked over enough in tickle fashion at the leather bar and at the tailors, Ronald held onto me *again* for a few hours each time, really putting the tickle screws to me some more. Gawd, you're probably thinking what a ticklish life I have, and you're right, sadly you're right! My brother Bruce works nights for some privately owned company that creates and constructs novelty items. We never really talk about our work so I really don't know what kind of novelty items the company my brother works for constructs. But on the day I took off work to have a little meeting with my dear brother I figured I would find out just what it is the company he works for constructs. I had told my vice president at the bank that I had something personal to take care of that day and that I needed the afternoon off. Seeing as I rarely take any time off whatsoever he quickly granted me the time I needed. I didn't even call my wife Stephanie to let her know that I would be leaving early. No, I didn't want her to know about this little folly I was embarking upon. This would be between *only* me and my ever conniving brother Bruce…

    I got off the train an hour later and clad in a charcoal colored Brooks Brother's suit I walked the short distance from the station to Bruce's house. Bruce is gay, (which was never a problem for me) single and lives alone so he and I would have his place all to ourselves while we had a nice brother to brother chat. I hadn't even called Bruce to let him know I was coming over, oh no, this was to be a total surprise buds, just as he had worked his trickery in surprising me all those times in my ticklish past! Well, now we would see just how much my brother appreciated being surprised. I had to chuckle at the thought that he would jump out of his socks when he saw me… As I walked up the short path in front of Bruce's house I had fleeting thoughts of perhaps interrupting him while he was in the middle of some sexual trite with a new buddy or potential life partner. I also thought very fleetingly that he might not be home at all and I would have wasted an afternoon off. These thoughts came to a halt as I rang the doorbell and a few moments later I heard the sound of heavy footfalls approaching the door. As I stood there the door opened and there stood my very handsome, very muscular brother Bruce. He was all sweaty, very pumped up and breathing heavily while clad in a pair of black cotton gym shorts, a gray tank top, white ankle length sweat socks and sneakers. I had obviously caught my older brother in the middle of his after-noon workout. Bruce is a real fanatic about his daily workouts, so fanatical that he transformed his basement into a makeshift gym, complete with weight benches, dumbbells of varying weights and even Nautilus brand machines. When Bruce saw me standing there his mouth widened into a huge smile. He was obviously happy at seeing me and surprised at the same time that I was there at his house.

"Hey little bro, what are you doing here?" Bruce asked me. "Is everything okay at work? Shouldn't you be home with Stephanie if you're not at work?"

As he spoke he reached out and tugged on my tie, a habit he had gotten into ever since I started working in the corporate world and was required to wear a suit and tie...

"The hell with Stephanie for the moment Bruce," I said, standing there with my hands balled into fists. "Stephanie has no goddamned idea that I'm even here! This is a brotherly meeting just between you and me!"

"The hell with Stephanie?" Bruce asked me. "Say, what's gotten into you Tim?"

"I'm mad at you Bruce, or can't you see that?" I asked him.

"Mad at me, what for?" Bruce asked. "What the hell are you talking about?"

"I'm talking about all those things you've had done to me, all the tricks you set me up for..." I ranted at him, my teeth clenched.

God, if he wasn't my older brother I would have decked him right there...

"What things? Oh man, I think you had a really bad day or something Tim," Bruce said, letting go of my tie. "Come on in little brother, take your shoes off, relax and we'll talk..."

"Oh yeah, we'll talk *big* brother, that is for sure," I said sternly as I walked into Bruce's house, him closing and locking the door behind me. "And after we're done talking you are going to pay for what you've done..."

"Pay for what?" Bruce asked me in a high pitched tone of voice. "Tim, I swear that I do not know what the hell you're talking about. If I've done something that offended you, you need to be more specific here."

I sat down on the couch in Bruce's living room, unlaced my wingtips, slipped them off my tired feet and propped my black nylon socked feet on the coffee table. Bruce hates for anyone to prop their feet on his coffee table but when he saw the smug look on my face he didn't say a word. He was still looking at me as if he didn't know what the hell I was talking about.

"What the hell I'm talking about is the set up at the leather bar when I wanted your help in playing a trick on Jim, what the hell I'm talking about is what your good friend the tailor did to me when he fit me for the tux for Jim's upcoming wedding..." I seethed. "Come on Bruce, don't try to play all cocky and innocent with me here..."

"What about those things Tim?" Bruce asked, looking at me as I sat there on his couch, my dress socked feet still propped on his coffee table.

"You went to the leather bar on your own, I told a couple of the guys there to expect you and after you got there you were, as I just said, on your own little bro. And what the hell happened with the wedding tux? I sent you to the best tailor possible. Steve said he fitted you real well…"

"You know fine what happened at the leather bar," I went on, sounding sarcastic as hell now. "And yeah Steve fitted me? It was more like he fitted me *up* big bro!"

"Okay, look man you come here accusing me of things I really don't know about," Bruce said and from the way he sounded I almost believed him. "If, and I mean if, if anything did happen I really do not know anything about it. Now, if you don't mind I would like to get back to my workout. Hey, come on downstairs and let me show you the new equipment that I added to my home gym."

As Bruce left the living room and walked toward the stairs I stood up and padded on my socked feet behind him.

"Hell no, I couldn't give a shit what you've done with your gym Bruce," I ranted behind him. "We are going to clear this all up here and now…"

"Okay, okay, whatever you say Tim," Bruce said as we walked down the stairs into his gym/basement.

Once we were downstairs Bruce stood in the center of his nearly state of the art gym and looked at me staring at him from a few feet away.

"Just tell me exactly what Steve did to you and I'll try to take it up with him little bro," Bruce said, sounding almost sincere. "But as for the leather bar and Bull…"

"Bull, how the fucking fuck would you know Bull's name?" I asked Bruce and from the look on his face he knew that he had just stepped in it.

"Whoops, you uh, you got me there little bro," Bruce said with a stupid looking grin on his face as he picked up a large sized medicine ball.

"Come on Bruce, just admit it man, you know what happened to me at the leather bar and with Steve the so called "Master" tailor."

Suddenly, my never loving brother hefted the medicine ball and tossed it in a very fast speed at me.

"Think fast Timmy, and catch!!" Bruce hollered.

I stupidly caught the ball by wrapping my arms around it but it landed hard against my stomach, which sent me spiraling and propelling backward on my socked feet.

"HOOFFFFFF!!!" I huffed stupidly.

With no control over my bearings for the moment I spun around a few times and then landed on a weight bench behind me, first hard on my ass and then stupidly still holding onto that medicine ball I wound up slap dang right on my back…

"Wh-why'd you do that???" I whined and dropped the weighty ball, somewhat in a daze.

My suit jacket was splayed at my sides, my shirt a tad wrinkled and my tie askew and laying over the side of my shoulder. Before I could get my bearings to get up Bruce dashed over to me, yanked my hands together under the weight bench I was lying on and tied them at the wrists with a workout jump rope that had been under the bench.

"Damn you Bruce, stop it, *stop this now*," I grumbled. "What the fuck do you think you're doing here??? No more of this nonsense…untie me!!"

"So tell me little bro, exactly what did happen at the leather bar and at the tailor shop?" Bruce asked me mockingly.

"You damn well know man," I griped up at him. "I'm sure your two sadistic buddies, Bull and Steve gave you a full report."

Once my hands were tied good and secure Bruce stepped to the end of the bench, set up a chair for himself and then, horror of all horrors he hoisted my dress socked feet into his lap. Oh woe is me, woe is fucking me and I had taken my shoes off upon my older brother's suggestion! Although, being with the way he had me tied up to that weight bench I was sure that if I hadn't taken my shoes off Bruce would have happily done it for me right about then.

"Oh Gawd Bruce, no, no, no!!!" I bellowed, struggling like a madman to get my hands untied. "You know what I'm like when it comes to, to…PWAAHHHHHHHHH HAHA, HAHAHAHAHAHAHAHAAHAHAAHA!!!" I suddenly guffawed as my older brother trailed his fingertips in a fast motion up and down and up and down the bottom of one of my feet. "OOOOOOOOOO GAWD, d-don't tickle me Bruce!!! HAHAHAHAHAHA!"

"Did Bull and Steve do something like this to you little bro?" Bruce asked me and tickled the bottom of my other foot next, scribbling and scrabbling his fingertips up and down it at what felt like hundreds of miles per hour. "Or was it something like this?"

"HAHAHAHAHAHAHAHAHAAHHAAAHAHA!!!" I screamed. "Oh Gawd, y-you're my brother, ha,ha,ha,ha,ha,ha,ha,ha,ha,ha,ha,ha, y-you shouldn't be doin' shit like this to me man!! HAHAHAHAAHAHAHAHAHAHA AHA!!!!"

"Why not?" Bruce asked. "I tickled the hell outa you when we were growing up. Why not now too?"

"PWWWAHHHAHAHAHAHAAHAHAAHHAAHAHA!!!!" I laughed. "OHHHHRRR FUCKING FUCKS HAHAHAHAHAHAHAHAHAHAHAHAHAH A!!!!!!!!"

I writhed and squirmed miserably on that bench, trying to pull my feet free of my brother's grasp, trying to get my hands untied, trying not to laugh so heartily at the tickling misery he was now heaping on me.

"HARHARHARHARHARHARHARHARHARHAR!!!!!" I cackled real deep throatily as my brother's fingertips worked their evil over the bottoms of my black socked feet. "L-let me up Bruce, ha, ha, ha, ha, ha, ha, ha, ha, ha, ha, ha, f-fucking untie me man!"

Bruce's fingers then found their way to my ultra tickle sensitive arches and he dug in on them real deep, sending chilling ticklish sensations through my feet...

"AAAAYYYYYYYHAHAHAHAHAHHAAAHAHAHAHA!!!!" I screamed. "Bruce, please stop!!!!! HAHAHAHAHAHAHAHAHAHAHAAHHAAHAHAHAA A!!!"

"So tell me, did Bull and Steve do something like that to you little bro?" Bruce asked me after he had stopped tickling me, still holding my socked feet in his lap. "Or maybe they firstly did something like this..."

That said Bruce slid his hand up and under my pants leg, his fingers searching diligently for the top of my dress sock.

"Heh, heh, fuckin' OTC office socks you wear little bro," Bruce chided me as his fingers found the top of my sock. "I always thought that it was my gay office buddies who wear OTC socks for their office jobs Bro. All you straight guys seem to favor calf lengths, heh, heh! So tell me, did Bull and Steve take your socks off you Tim?"

"Y-you bastard," I seethed as Bruce started pulling my socks off me one at a goddamned time. "Yesssssss, th-they took my socks off me man. You know that damn well, now stop this and untie me Bruce."

Once Bruce had my socks off me he held them up, let them dangle all wrinkly, smelly and long, snickered again at the fact that I favor OTC socks and then tossed them aside on the floor.

"So, after Bull and Steve got your socks off you was it then that they did this to you little bro?" Bruce asked and pressed his fingertips once again against my arches (my ultra tickle sensitive arches) and began tickling them.

"EEEEEEEHHHHHHHH HAHAHAHAAHAHAHAHAHA!!!" I laughed, writhing on the bench.

"NO, no, no, th-they did not," I lied as I wiggled like a fish out of water. "HAHAHAHAHAHAHAAHHAHAHA, I-let me free Bruce!!!"

As I sang my song of laughter my scheming brother held tight to my bare feet and tickled them harder and harder.

"OOOOOOOOOOOOHHHHHH nooooooooooo HAHAHAHAHAHAH, B-Brucie noooooooooooopleeeeeee no more oh man, plleeeeeeeeeeee!!!!"

Fucking fucks, I was being tickled by my own brother here...

"B-Bruce, w-will I never win??? Ha, ha, ha, ha, ha, ha, ha, ha, ha, ha, ha, ha, ha, ha, ha, ha!!!!!!" I laughed. "NO MORE!!!"

"No more Tim?" Bruce asked me, sounding totally fiendish by then. "But I'm just getting started here little bro. And you yourself told me that Stephanie doesn't know that you're here, so I can hold onto you for the remainder of the afternoon and tickle torture the fuck out of you..."

"You, you're what??? You've got to be kidding me man!!" I roared through bouts of laughter upon hearing my dear brother's ticklish plans for me.

"No, no, *no way!! No fucking way!! Oh fucking fucks!!!* I want out of here!!"

"Captured again Tim, you are tickle captured again little bro..." Bruce laughed and he tickled my feet some more. "Remember all the times when we were kids when me and my buddies captured you and tickled you?"

"Damn, damn you," I reeled. "HAHAHAHAHAHAHAAHHAHAHA, h-how the fucking fuck can I forget? You're always there to remind me big bro!! M-my life hasn't ch-changed, ha, ha, ha, ha, ha, ha, ha, ha, ha, ha, ha, ha, ha, ha, all that much!! HAHAHAHAHAHAHAHAHAHA!!! Oh fucking fuck, fuck me and my bright idea to have come here!! HAHAHAHAHAHAHAHAHAHAHA I-I've walked right into tickle Hell!!!"

Bruce then squatted in front of the bench I was on, grabbed my feet by the ankles, held them straight out, toes pointing upward and to my shock began to slather his tongue over and over the meaty bottoms of my feet. Fucking totally fucks, he, my brother, my own brother, he was lick tickling my danged stinky feet!"

"Br-Bruce, wh-what are you doing??? HAHAHAHAHAHAHAHAHAHA HA!!!" I screamed as I tried to wriggle away.

"Why, I'm tickling you bro, what the fucking fuck does it look like I'm doing?" Bruce asked me snidely, mocking the way I swear and also sounding eerily like Ronald when he tickled me.

"Y-you don't know what this is doing to me man!" I bellowed as my hard cock tented the crotch area of my suit pants.

"Oh but I do know bro, I know *exactly* what it's doing to you..." Bruce laughed. "It's tickling you."

That said he resumed slathering and slithering his tongue over and over the bottoms of my feet, really licking and slurping at my arches, my heels and when he licked my toes I nearly went crazy.

"AAAAAAYYYYYYY HAHAHAHAHAHAHAHAHAHAHAHAHAHAHA!!!" I laughed crazily.

"Damn little bro, for a regal looking and snappy dressed corporate exec you sure do have stanky feet," Bruce chuckled and slathered the tip of his tongue over the tops of my toes as he dug his thumbs and fingers into the bottoms and sides of my captive feet.

"N-never you mind about how my feet, s-smell,hahahahahahahahaha !!!!" I cried out, sounding nearly insane already. "You just untie me and let me the fuck outa here, NOW!!! HARHARHARHARHARHARHARHARHARHARH ARHARHAR!!!!"

Finally, Bruce stopped licking my bare feet and stood up, towering over me as I lay on the weight bench.

"I-I'm glad you finally came to your senses Bruce," I said, still breathing a tad heavily from all the laughing I had done. "Now, untie me..."

But instead of doing as I asked my older brother began unbuckling my belt...

"B-Bruce, *Bruce, what the fucking fucks are you doing now man???*" I screeched, disbelief filling me even more at that point.

"Well, you're in my home gym little bro, and now I want you to see the massage room I had installed down here," Bruce said and in a fast sweeping motion de-panted me. "So with that in mind I think you should be clad in the proper manner befitting a massage room..."

"OH FUCK!!" I growled through clenched teeth as my brother tossed my suit pants aside and then got busy undoing the knot in my tie.

Unbelievably my cock was plumped up and hard as steel in my silk scarlet colored executive briefs.

"Wow, you really are a true blue executive boy aren't you little bro?" Bruce chided me as he tied my tie over my eyes, turning it into a makeshift blindfold. "Not only do you wear OTC silk socks but you wear silk briefs too... I would just bet that Stephanie loves seeing you in those..."

"Bruce, stop this now, let me out of here..." I pleaded as I was plunged into darkness.

Once my eyes were covered Bruce reached under the bench I was splayed on, untied my hands, but being blindfolded there wasn't all that much I could do as he quickly grabbed my wrists and hauled me roughly to my feet, me clad now in just my danged briefs, my suit jacket and button down shirt.

"Okay little bro, lets get you stripped the rest of the way down and then I'll set you up good and proper the way you should be in a gym..." Bruce chuckled as he hauled me forward in his iron-like grip.

"NO, NO!!!" I grunted as Bruce roughly yanked me forward, holding tight to my damned wrists as he did so.

Bruce slipped my watch off my left wrist and the next thing I knew my feet left the floor...

"ULP!!!" I bantered as my never loving brother hauled me upwards and above his head with his huge bear-like hands, gripping me at the chest with a handful of my shirt and at the thighs.

He held me so that my blindfolded face was facing the floor...

Suddenly, I was being spun and spun...

"H-HEY!!! B-BRUCE, stop this!! I'm getting dizzy here bro!!" I screeched as Bruce's hands did their work, spinning me and spinning me above his head.

I felt like I was trapped in an out of control washing machine of sorts...

Bruce chuckled and said how all his hard workouts had really paid off for him...

My arms flailed at my sides and I was so disoriented that I couldn't even reach to try to get the blindfold off...

When Bruce finally stopped spinning me he set me down on wobbly feet and as I tried to balance myself on my bare feet I felt my suit jacket being taken off me followed by my button down shirt being undone…GAWD!!

A short while later, wearing only my scarlet colored executive style briefs I was tied up again and in position to be tickled once more by my goddamned conniving brother…

In most gyms, whether they be home or professional gyms there is usually a standing lat-pull machine. It is basically an almost straight handlebar with a cable attached at the center. My arms had been yanked up above my head and my hands were secured with Bruce's workout jump rope to that almost straight bar at the wrists. My goddamned brother had taken advantage of my dizzied and blindfolded state and hooked me up to the lat-pull machine real sweet and secure I got to tell you. The cable went through two pulley wheels at the top of the workout device. The two pulleys can change the direction of the force where the cable is lifting weights that are in a track and are added onto by a moving pin. (Oh let me tell you a tad early here, that those pins used in Bruce's workout machines became part of my own brand of tickle hell, as you'll soon find out buds…) Bruce had set the pin so that enough weight had been added to the mechanism so that it exceeded my weight, thereby I was unable to pull down on the bar, and thus, I was just left hanging there by my wrists like a side of beef in a butcher's freezer, my bare feet in such a position so that I was just about standing on my tiptoes. The lat-pull machine is a lot like the danged "Spinning Chinaman" that Stephanie and I have at home and I guess you could say that I somehow felt right at home the way my dear brother had secured me. Like the "Spinning Chinaman" the lat-pull machine is set up inside a strong metal frame that accommodates the full of the apparatus. It was also apt for having spread my legs real wide apart and it had made it simple for Bruce to secure my ankles to the vertical bars of said frame, thus being secured that way and up on my toes gave my dear brother the access he would want to the bottoms of my ticklish feet…

"Timmy my laddy, as Ronald would call you, hardy fucking har," Bruce said as he took the blindfold off me. "It would appear to me that just like at the leather bar you've went and gotten your ass in another heap of trouble! Man oh man little brother but you just keep looking for boiling water don't you?"

"Bruce, let me free man!!" I rattled loudly, struggling to get my hands untied as his fingers began trailing over my stretched triceps. "How would you know of Ronald's sadistic pet name for me? Fuck, how would you even know of Ronald??? You son of a bitch! Don't do this to me! You don't know what this is doing to me!!"

"Oh I think I can take a guess or two of what this is doing to you little bro," Bruce said, a chilling smile on his face as he trailed his fingers some more over my triceps.

"Okay, now look Bruce, this has all gone far enough," I said through trembling lips, knowing he was getting ready for a real ticklish onslaught. "I came here only to have a talk with you! Getting captured again and tickle tortured *was not* part of the plan!! Untie me man, let me get dressed and I'll get on my way and…PWWWWWWAAHHHHHHHHHHHHHHH!!!!!! HAHAHAHA HAHAHAHAHAHAHAHAHAHAHAHAHA!!!!!!"

As I was speaking Bruce chose that moment to dig his fingertips real deep into my very exposed armpits.

"AAAAAAAYYYYYYYYHAHAHAHAHAHAHAHAHAHAHAHAHA Y-you fucking tickle fiend!!" I cackled and visions of our past when Bruce and I were kids filled my head, visions of him tickling me even back then.

"Well little bro, getting captured may not have been part of the plan when you decided to come here and confront me, but it sure as fuck looks like that's what you've gotten for your trouble," Bruce said meanly. "What's happened here today is called cruel irony little bro."

As Bruce spoke he dug his fingertips into my armpits and whirled them around in there, getting more hoots and screams out of me as he did so. In between tickling my bushy and sweaty armpits he trailed his fingertips down my sides and over my ribs, getting more loud laughter out of me, getting me squirming in the bondage at the same time. My hard cock jutted up even more in my silk briefs and stained and spotted them with my pre cum. I prayed that Bruce wouldn't notice that…

"HARHARHARHARHARHARHARHARHARHAR!!!!!" I screamed louder and louder.

Bruce even trailed his fingertips over my silk covered ass cheeks, making me jut myself forward involuntarily as far as the bondage I was tied in would allow.

"ST-stop, oh good Gawd, p-please stoooooopppp!!!" I screeched. "HAHAHAHAHAHAHAHAHAHAHA!!!! D-didn't you say you were working out when I got here??? Fucking fuck Bruce, you should be working out, not, not tickling your younger brother!! HAHAHAHAHAHAHAHAHAHAHA!!!"

"Oh I really don't think it'll hurt me to miss one workout Tim," Bruce laughed and drove the tip of his index finger deep, deep, and deeper into my sweaty armpit, twirling it as he did so. "And lets face it, how often do I get to tickle you now that we're adults? I have to admit, I've really missed this."

"HAHAHAHAHAHAHAHAHAHAAHHAHA!!!!" I laughed crazily as Bruce then trailed his fingertips over my stretched torso, aiming meanly for my ribs and stomach regions.

Finally, after a good fifteen minutes of straight and non-stop tickling he stopped…

"Okay laddy, I mean Tim, come up for some air and then I'll get started back on you again," Bruce said, giving my nipples a squeeze as he stood in front of me. "Boy oh fuckin' boy laddy, I mean Tim, but your tits really do get erect as a building when you're tickled…"

"Laddy, laddy, just how well do you know Ronald???" I seethed as my brother twisted my nipples. "OHHHRRRR GAWD Bruce…"

"Tits all plumped up and nowhere to go huh little bro?" Bruce teased me, but made no mention of just how plumped up I was in my silk briefs as well.

My eyes rolled in my head and I was already sweating when Bruce pulled a pin from one of his other workout machines, held it up for me to see and said, "I'll try one of these on you next little brother..."

"H-hey man, d-don't," I squabbled. "What the fucking fuck are you planning on doing with that?"

Smiling fiendishly Bruce said, "Oh come on Tim, you really don't need for me to answer that question now do you?" and he stuck the tip of the blunt bottomed pin into my belly button.

"GWWWWAAAAAHHHHHHHHA!!!" I screamed at the sudden and maddening invasion. "HAHAHAHAHAHAHAHAHAHAHAHAHAHAHAHAHA!!!"

I was breathless yet laughing my head off anew...
"PWWWWWWWWWAAAAHAHAHAHAHAHAHAHAHAHAHAHA!!!!!"

"Aww, poor Tim, now even I have to say that this is a shitty way to tickle a poor sap of a guy in his unnerwear," Bruce teased me and twirled the pin harder in my belly button. "Why, I can just imagine just how ticklish the inside of your belly button must be. I've heard it said that that area is really ultra tickle sensitive... But I sure as hell am finding out wouldn't you say?"

Laughing meanly at my ticklish plight my brother tickled my inner belly button with one pin and suddenly, as if by magic, he produced another and used that one to tickle my nipple tips at the same time.

"HARHARHARHARHARHARHARHARHARHARHARHAR!!!! N-not my man tits too Bruce!!!" I screamed.

I cackled and guffawed insanely as Bruce worked those pins on me...

Then, my brother stepped behind me, squatted down at one of my legs and began trailing his two pins up and down the back of my calf and up and over the back of my upper thigh...

"HAHAHAHAHAHAHAHAHAHAHAHAHAHA!!!" I screamed my operatic sound of laughter filling my brother's gym as he tickled me with the pins from the workout machines. "P-PLEASE STOOOOOOP Bruce, please stop!!! HAHAHAHAHAHAHAHAHAHAHAHAHAHA!!!!"

As tears of laughter filled my eyes my vision blurred and I and the tickle sensations became one with each other it seemed... The way Bruce was once again on his feet and tickling the inside of my belly button was beyond enough to make a poor guy crazy...

Bruce alternated between tickling the inside of my belly button and the backs of my calves and thighs...

"HEEEEEEEEEEEEEEEEEEEEEEEEEEEEEEEEEEEEE!!!" I screeched when Bruce again squatted behind me.

He grabbed one of my calves, forced my bound foot upward to expose the bottom of it and trailed the pin over and over the meaty bottom of my foot.

"HEEEEEEEEEEEEEEEEEEEEEEEEEEEEEEEEE!!!!" I screeched even louder as he tickled the bottoms of my feet alternately now.

I bumped and grinded against that danged lat-pull machine, swearing and laughing as my brother worked and wreaked his ticklish havoc on me... As I laughed and laughed I then heard my brother's voice telling me that that was enough for the moment. Everything suddenly went black, as it usually does when I'm tickled to just over the edge...

"Th-thanks Bruce thanks for st-stopping..." was the last thing I heard myself saying as the world went black.

A Short While Later...

"Okay, that's perfect, that looks good," I heard Bruce's voice musing, sounding more as if he were talking to himself as he worked at a task that he was deeply engrossed in. "This is a perfect position..."

"Ohhhhhhhh sh-shit, what happened?" I gasped as I tried to open my eyes, but found that I couldn't.

Obviously Bruce had blindfolded me again...

"H-hey, Br-Bruce, what the fucking fuck is going on here?" I called out as I felt rope being wound around and around my bare ankles.

Blindfolded I definitely was but I was still able to feel that I was tied up stretched out on my back and laying on a cushioned table of some sort. I tried to sit up but my upper body was roped tight to the table, my arms at my sides, my wrists tied off to the sides of said table.

"Bruce, what's going on here?" I repeated miserably.

I was able to smell scented lotions and perhaps oils of some kind, incense seemed to fill the air as well. The scents were a mixture of aloe, lavender, chrysanthemum and hibiscus. Hadn't Bruce mentioned something about having had a massage room installed in his basement/gym? My heart suddenly thudded in my chest as I felt him working at tying up my feet and the scent of the lotions and oils filled my nostrils. My cock also thudded in my executive briefs...

"Relax little bro, you're in good hands here with your big brother," I then heard Bruce say. "I'm going to take good care of you."

"Oh lucky me, I'll just bet a week's salary you're going to take good care of me," I prattled sarcastically. "And I'm sure that your idea of taking care of me entails tickling me some more huh?"

"Bingo little bro," Bruce said and whipped my necktie/blindfold off me. "You win the tickle prize...take a look around..."

As my eyes adjusted back to the light I saw that I had been right. I was now tied to a massage table in my brother's newly installed massage room in his basement/gym. Shelves were adorned with all kinds of bottles of scented lotions and skin oils. Incense was burning in a potpourri burner nearby on a small table. New age music was piped in. The room was dimly lit...

"Do you tie up all your massage clients like this?" I bantered miserably as I lay there in just my danged underpants, raising my head and taking in the sight of myself. "Holy fucking fucks, what a position to tie a poor guy in..."

"I figured you would approve, coming from someone who spends a lot of time tied up I would say that's a real compliment little bro," Bruce chuckled.

"Hardy fucking har and har," I replied miserably.

With my head still raised I looked down at my bound feet and saw that Bruce had them dangling off the end of the massage table. Fucking fucks buds, but my poor bare feet were hanging there and totally on display and accessible for some real tickling. My calves however were bound good and tight to the table, it was just my bound feet that dangled perilously off the end. Fucking totally fucks, but when the tickling of my feet began they would be thrashing helplessly... As I lay my head back down I softly breathed the words, "oh shit..."

"Now you know Tim, a lot of people pay a lot of money for what I'm about to do to you here," Bruce said and took a bottle of aloe scented massage oil from a shelf.

"You fucking prankster Bruce," I seethed. "Let me out of this! What the fucking fuck are you up to now?"

"Well, the way I see it little bro, its time to massage and of course tickle your feet..." Bruce replied and as if on cue he poured a goodly amount of that massage oil into one of his hands.

He set the bottle down on the small nearby table and rubbed his hands together vigorously...

"Oh Gawd Bruce, no, please man, please bro, don't do this..." I whimpered.

Bruce smiled real fiendishly and grabbed my left foot with both his hands, his oily fingers entwined around the top of it, his thumbs pressing hard into the meaty bottom of it. As he began massaging the aloe scented oil into my foot he also began pressing his thumbs meanly against the bottom of my poor foot, twirling and swirling his thumbs all over the bottom of my foot.

"FWWWWWWWWAAAAHHHHHHHAHAHAHAHAHAHAHAHA!!!" I burst out laughing yet again.

"God almighty little bro, but I have to admit, I sure as all heck do love that first sound that erupts from you when the tickling starts up..." Bruce commented and worked the massage oil well into my foot at the same time tickling me.

He moved his fingers upward on the front of my foot and strummed them up and down as if he were playing a piano.

"HAHAHAHAHAHAHAHAHAHAHAHAHAHAHAHAHA!!!!!" I guffawed,

sounding like a goddamned hyena in the throes of some twisted passion.

"Fuck man, and then the way you follow up that first laugh filled erup-tion with your hawing and heeing sounds, man, it's just music to my ears," Bruce said. "It reminds me of when we were kids and me and my friends used to get the drop on you and tickle you…"

"HAHAHAHAHAHAHAHAHAHAHAHAHAHA!!!!!" was all I could say because Bruce was now massaging that oil into both my feet at the same time and tickling them as well as he did so.

Fucking fucks, but when my feet are tickled all I can do is laugh…

"Oh what a twisted turn of events eh little bro?" Bruce asked me, pressed my feet together, grabbed my big toes with one hand and snaked a finger of his other hand up and down the bottoms of my oil slicked feet alternately. "You came here to pay me back for your past tickle torments and you only wind up getting more of the same… Oh how the tables do turn eh laddy?"

I arched my chest upward under the tight and binding ropes and my head arched back a bit as well as I laughed and laughed…

"HAHAHAHAHAHAHAHAHAHAHAHAHAHA!!!!" I screamed as Bruce next went for my arches, darting his fingers deep into the sexy curves of them.

"Got to say it again little bro, nothing sounds as insanely rhythmic as a guy in the heat of laughter…" Bruce said, verbally tormenting me as well as tickle tormenting me.

Bruce then picked up a second bottle of massage oil, lavender scent-ed this time and went to work slathering that onto my toes and in between them as well. He hunkered down a bit and really got me screaming as his strong fingers trailed between my toes, tickling the fuck outa them. He again slithered his fingers over and into my arches and moved down to my strong heels to tickle them as well.

"HARHARHARHARHARHARHARHARHARHAR!!!!!!" I cackled like a banshee.

When Bruce produced two of the pins from his workout machines and began sliding them between my oiled toes I sort of thanked God that I was bound to that table. If I hadn't been the way I was laughing I would've flown clear off it and smashed into the ceiling. Fucking fucks buds, all throughout the tickle tortures that my dear brother was heaping on my feet I bucked and writhed under the tight ropes, sweating my guts out and laughing and laughing till I thought I couldn't laugh anymore…till the only sounds emanating from me were breathy sounding gasps…

Hunkered down right in front of my aloe and lavender scented feet Bruce trailed the two pins up and down and up and down the bottoms of my soles, over the balls of my feet, against my heels and up again.

"OOOOOOOOOOOOOOOHAHAHAHAHAHAHAHAHAHAHAHA!!!!" I

screamed my laughter anew.

It looked like I still had some real gut curdling rasps in me huh? Hardy har and har buds...

My upper body arched upward some more against the binding ropes as my brother trailed those pins from my heels up to the balls of my oily slicked feet. My brother was quite wise in having oiled up my feet and made them all slick and slimy. It served to make them even more tickle sensitive.

"HARHARHARHARHARHARHARHARHARHARAHAR!!!!!" I laughed like a loon.

The ticklish sensations emanated from my tortured feet, up my spine and the tingling sensations found their way to my hard cock in my silk briefs...

"HAWHAWHAWHAWHAWHAWHAWHAWHAWHAWHAWHAW!!!" I cried out, sounding real husky by then. "B-Bruce, PL-PLEASE stop!!! HAHAHAHAHAHAHA!!"

I balled my hands into tight fists at my sides, lifted my head up and watched as my erect cock twitched and danced in my silk briefs, oozing pre cum. My brother hadn't seemed to notice that, or if he did he wasn't making mention it, thank God for small favors. No, my never loving brother was more interested in tickling my tied up oil slicked feet and hearing me laugh my head off...

Bruce then trailed the pins from his workout machines along the inner parts of my arches, really getting me laughing some more...

"HAHAHAHAHAHAHAHAHAHAHAHAHA OH GOD STOP!!!" I ranted crazily.

My head spun into orbit and then I heard someone screaming insanely in the throes of helpless and forced laughter. Fuck, fucking fucks, I was so far gone that I stupidly realized that it was me who was making those sounds...

Then, to really get me laughing and hawing like a madman Bruce spun the pins around and around the centers of the bottoms of my meaty feet. My feet twitched in the bondage, I clenched my teeth and screamed, "RRRRRRHHHHHHEEEEEEEEEE!!!!!!"

Hee, hee, hee, hee, hee, hee, hee, hee, hee, hee, hee, hee, hee!!!!!!" I then cackled in a high pitched tone of voice, directly from deep in my sore throat.

Gawd, but I had the stupidest of grins on my face as I writhed and squirmed in the bondage on my brother's massage table...

Finally, Bruce stopped tickling my feet with the weight pins... He looked me over and took in the sight of me as I lay there sweating from my head to my oily feet... Amazingly I didn't pass out after all the tickling that Bruce had just done to my feet...

"Fuck man, tickling you after all this time sure is fun little bro," Bruce said and stepped over to a mini refrigerator. "It's bringing back such *great* memories from when we were kids..."

"So glad you're having such a grand trip down memory lane..." I replied sarcastically.

Bruce took a bottle of cold mineral water from the refrigerator and came over to me with it...

"But we're far from done bro," Bruce said, snaking a hand behind my head and lifting it up a bit so he could feed me the water. "The afternoon is still young and as you said Stephanie doesn't know you're here so she won't worry..."

I chugged down the water and cursed my bad luck at having come to my brother's house...

When I was done drinking Bruce put the bottle back in the mini refrigerator and stepped over to his shelf of oils and lotions. This time he selected one bottle of vanilla scented lotion and one bottle of cocoa scented lotion.

"These will make your feet really smell and feel great bro," Bruce said and next stepped over to a supply closet of some kind. "These lotions are real invigorating when massaged into the skin..."

"Don't you mean *tickled* into the skin?" I rasped angrily and strained against the unforgiving ropes. "GAWD!!"

"Tickled, massaged, in your case it's all the same at the moment Tim," Bruce laughed and took a hand-held hairdryer from his supply closet.

"What the fucking fuck?" I asked. "You planning on doing my hair too Bruce?"

"Not only is this lotion that I'm going to massage into your feet invigorating it also tingles the skin when it's heated up a bit and then dried..." Bruce said, stepping over to me with his cache of new tickle torture supplies. "And once the skin is tingled and heated you of all people should know what that means dear brother..."

"Oh Gawd Bruce, it, it means," I began miserably.

"Go ahead little bro, say it, say it and you'll be laughing in a short time..." Bruce verbally tormented me.

"It means that my feet will be even more tickle sensitized," I said woefully. "Oh fuck Bruce, I won't be laughing in a short time, fucking fucks man, I'll be laughing in no time..."

"Well said my banker bro..." Bruce said.

"Oh but holy fucks man, I somehow get the feeling that those invigorating lotions really aren't meant for a guy's bare feet..." I said. "The skin on the feet would be too sensitive for lotions of that caliber..."

"So true, but in your ticklish situation it's well meant for *your* feet bro..." Bruce chided me.

He put the cocoa scented lotion and the hairdryer down on the small table next to me. He then stepped to my bare oiled tied up feet with the tube of vanilla scented lotion.

"We'll start with this one," Bruce said and squeezed a good dollop of the lotion onto each of my feet.

It dripped from the tips of my toes down the fronts and backs of my bare feet. The cool feeling of the lotion as it mixed with the oil already on my feet felt real soothing somehow, but sadly that soothing feeling would not last long...

Bruce set the tube of vanilla lotion down on the small table, rubbed his hands together and then gripped both my feet in his hands...

"And here we go again little bro..." my brother said and began tickle/massaging the vanilla lotion into my soles and tops of my feet with his thumbs and fingers.

"GGGAAAAAHHHHHHHHHAHAHAHAHAHAHAHAHAHAHAHA!!!!"   I screamed and then I was off and laughing again. "OOOOOHHHHH GAWD STOPPPPP!!!!! Stop tickling me Bruce!!!"

Bruce swirled his thumbs around and around against the bottoms of my feet, really working the vanilla lotion in vigorously. His fingertips played the piano at the top of my feet, tickling me there as well.

"OOOOOOOOOO HAHAHAHAHAHAHAHAHAHAHAHAHAHAHAHA!!!!" I laughed loudly as my brother did his dirty work.

As he massaged the lotion into my feet I started to feel the tingling sensation he had mentioned. It felt like tiny crystals were being rubbed against my feet and they were literally coming alive...Actually it felt like my feet were being exfoliated but at one hundred miles per hour...

"AAAAAAWWWHHHHHH, ha, ha, ha, ha, ha, ha, ha, ha, ha, ha, ha, ha, ha, ha, if- if you weren't tickling the bejesus out of me that lotion would feel great..." I stammered.

"Just enjoy it bro, just enjoy it..." Bruce said and gripped my danged feet tighter.

I pursed my lips together, trying to stifle my laughter as Bruce swirled his thumbs real hard against my heels...

"PPPPPPWWWWWWWAHHHHHHHHHAHAHAHAHAHAHAHAHA!!!!"   I laughed.

I had not succeeded in not laughing... GAWD!!!

A few minutes later Bruce was squeezing a goodly amount of the cocoa scented lotion onto my bare tied up feet.

"Man, this much I can say, your feet are going to smell great when you get home tonight..." Bruce laughed and quickly went to work tickle/massaging the cocoa lotion into my soles.

"HARHARHARHARHARHARHARHARHARHARHARHAR!!!!" was all I could say in reply to the fact that my feet smelled so damned good...

Bruce again played the piano atop my feet with his fingertips while at the same time swirled his thumbs in a circular motion against the bottoms of my feet, really digging his thumbs into the meat of them...

"HAHAHAHAHAHAHAHAHAHAHAHAHAHAHAHAHAHAHAHAHAHAH A!!!!!" I screeched helplessly, my laughter filling my dear brother's massage room.

As I lay there having my feet tickle/massaged my cock oozed more pre cum in my silk executive briefs...

Smiling fiendishly Bruce slid his lotion slicked fingers between my toes, tickling the tender sections of them...

"HAWHAWHAWHAWHAWHAWHAWHAWHAWHAWHAWHAW!!!!!" I ranted as my toes flicked and twitched.

Then, to my horror of horrors Bruce grabbed the toes of my left foot and glided one fingertip up and down the bottom of it, using his fingernail as well as he did so...

"OH NO, NO, HOHOHOHOHOHOHOHOHOHOHOHOHOHOHOHO! !!!" I laughed like Santa Claus.

He squeezed my toes tight and slid that danged finger slowly up and down the bottom of my left foot. He soon did the same thing with my right foot, really gripping my danged toes...

When I thought that I could laugh no more Bruce let go of my toes and as I stopped laughing I heard him say, "Okay, time to dry up those feet of yours..."

Bruce wiped his hands clean on a small towel and as my feet tingled he picked up the hairdryer...

Moments later the sound of the turned on portable hairdryer filled the room as Bruce aimed it at my vanilla and cocoa creamed feet. The feeling of tingling/exfoliation was seared up nearly about one hundred notches as my dear brother blew-dried my tootsies.

"Oh man, check it out little bro, the skin on your feet is glistening, almost baked enough and ready for more tickle torments..." Bruce said laugh-ingly and sadistically.

He cupped my dangling feet in one big hand and then aimed the hot blow-dryer directly at them, really cooking my lotioned up feet. My toes flicked around as Bruce blew-dry my feet some more. When he turned off the dryer he set my feet down to dangle again and from a pocket of his gym shorts he produced a stiff looking goose feather.

"OH NO, NO, of all things, a blasted feather!!" I screeched and was almost laughing already, even though I was not yet being tickled.

"Like Superman has kryptonite as his vulnerability so it is with you where feathers are concerned dear brother," Bruce said to me, looking down at me with a maniacal grin on his face.

"PWWWAHHHHHHHHH!!!! HAHAHAHAHAHAHAHAHAHAHA!!!" I laughed anew as my never loving brother began strumming the bottoms of my oily and lotion blow-dried feet alternately with the feather. "B-BRUCE, st-stop, oh for the love of GAWD, but that tickles bro!!! That tickles!!! It fucking tiiiiiicccckkklleeesss!!!!"

HEEEEE, HEEE, HEEEE, HEEE, HEEEE, HEEEE!!!!!"

Bruce, being a tickle expert was right. Having my feet slathered in lotion and then blow-dried really had made them hundreds of times more tickle sensitive. As I lay there laughing crazily the room again spun in front of me... I nearly sobbed when Bruce began slathering my feet with the vanilla and cocoa lotions a second time... By then I was so laughed out that I couldn't even beg him not to blow-dry my feet a second time. The feather was on the table next to me, mocking me, taunting me...

All totaled Bruce slathered my poor feet three times with the lotions and blew them dry. Three times he tickled me with that damned feather and for better than a half hour each time, continuously, non-stop...

By the time he untied me from the massage table I was a sweaty, heaving mess...

I sat up on the table and whimpered "thank you" as my dear brother handed me a bottle of mineral water. I gulped the water slowly and my hard cock churned and danced like Fred Astaire in my silk style executive briefs...

"Well bro, now I suppose you can honestly say you're pissed with me," Bruce said, standing near the table, him also sipping a bottle of water.

"J-just admit it man, after what you just did to me it's the least you can do, just admit it," I bantered, sitting atop that table in just my danged briefs. "Just fucking admit that you set me up for tickle capture at the leather bar and with your friend Steve the tailor..."

Bruce smiled at me, spread his muscular arms, shrugged, and said, "Okay bro, guilty as charged, but I assure you, it was all just in good fun."

"I'm sure glad you think it was good fun, for me it was torments upon torments," I replied and gulped down the rest of the water. "What about Ronald?"

"What about him?" Bruce asked.

"Was it you who set me up for his so called playful kidnap stunt that night when he snagged me right out of my own house when I had gone to take a leak during the night?" I asked and hopped down off the table.

Bruce seemed to mull a bit before he responded this time...

"Well, when he came to me to construct the tickle devices that he has at that place of his I didn't realize that you would become his patsy so to speak," Bruce said.

"So because of the company you work for that constructs novelty items Ronald approached you..." I said and Bruce held up a hand, halting me in mid sentence.

"No, more like because of you he came to me," Bruce said and I looked at him quizzically. "You told Ronald at one of your dinner gatherings with him and a girlfriend of his that I worked for a company that builds novelty devices. He came to me after that. Again, when he contracted me I didn't realize that he would choose you as his guinea pig."

"Well, choose me he did big bro," I said, sounding somewhat miserable.

Bruce simply looked at me as if trying to make an inaudible apology...

"I better get dressed and get out of here," I said. "Coming here was totally tomfoolery. All I got for my trouble was more tickle tormented."

I stomped past my brother and up the stairs...

As I dressed in Bruce's living room my dear brother came up the stairs...

"Tim, I arranged a ride for you buddy," Bruce said, sounding like he really felt sorry for me, looking at me almost woefully as I tied the laces on my shoes. "It uh, it's the least I could do..."

"It's okay, I have my car here," I said, gesturing toward the window.

"I'll drive your car to your house bro," Bruce said. "A good buddy of mine will be here soon to give you a lift."

As I finished knotting my tie and climbing into my suit jacket whoever it was that Bruce had arranged to drive me home still hadn't arrived. Fuck it, I figured, I would simply drive myself home and forget all about this latest twisted turn of events.

Just as I was saying good-bye to Bruce and was about to head out the door the doorbell rang.

"Ah good, there's your ride now, I feel better already," Bruce said and dashed past me to the door. "This way I can make it up to you Tim."

Bruce opened the door and my jaw dropped when I saw who was standing there in the archway...

"R-Ronald..." I whispered, wondering why in the fucks I kept falling for these things.

As I backed away from the door I saw that Bruce was smiling devilishly. My dear brother told me how he had created a brand new tickle device for Ronald and that Ronald could not wait to give it its first run...

Before I could dash out of there past the two men a chloroform soaked cloth was pressed hard over my nose and mouth. As I slipped into dreamland I heard my conniving brother and Ronald laughing meanly...

Piss Fried (Literally)

What a night it was last night, that's all I can say. No, fuck that, *that's not all I can say*. Fuck it all I can say a lot more, a hell of a lot more! Okay, again, what a night it was! There, I said it again! And there's going to be a lot more to be said! What a fucking night, all the beer I could drink but boy howdy did I have to go some to really keep those two prissy yuppie executives entertained. And I do mean it when I say, "Go some..." I really did fucking "Go some" and fuck but I went! And to think that it all started in a men's room because that dude named Alex liked my damned hairy chest and my goddamned fat and stout nipples. Let me backtrack for you... It really didn't start in a men's room, not exactly anyway; it started when I decided to have a few cold ones before heading home from my job. It was a weeknight. I had just worked an entire fucking nine hours and then some outdoors in the raging hot sun at my job as a construction worker. I work for the reputable construction company of "Green and Sons." Actually, Green is dead, may he rest in peaces hardy fucking har. His sons run the business but they still call it Green and Sons. Go figure, what the fuck! My name is Craig and because of my job where I lug cinderblocks, sling two by fours and swing sledge hammers all goddamned day I'm built like a fucking bull, a thirty-three year old bull at that. Couple my job as a construction worker with the fact that I also workout lifting weights at the gym three to four times a week and you got a fucking guy who's been referred to as a goddamned mountain of muscles! I also have the big husky balls of a bull if you wanna know, hardy fucking har, har! Actually, for the purposes of what I'm telling you here it's good that you know that my balls are of the jumbo sized. I mean, okay, I don't usually talk about my goddamned privates, especially my jumbo-sized balls, but for what I'm writing here you need to know all the facts, and my big balls relate to the facts...

Any fucking way I was being served my third twelve ounce bottle of cold brew when those two prissy suit boys sauntered into the bar called "The Local." "The Local", in case any of you out there aren't familiar with it is a real sleazy fag bar. I heard it told once how some fucking shmo of a hunky sailor boy managed to get his stupid ass tied up to a stall door in the men's room, the *infamous* stall door with the glory hole wedged in the front of it. Fucking glory hole is cut in the shape of a goddamned pussy, if you can imagine that in a fag bar, again, go fucking figure! The way it was told to me was that the sailor had wandered into "The Local" while he was in town on a pass from his ship which just happened to be docked in the harbor. The uniformed handsome and hunky, *straight*, twenty-two year old sailor boy wasn't wise to the fact that "The Local" was a sleazy fag bar and that the fags there devoured military types like him. And man oh fucking man, the way I heard it told he was more than devoured that night, like I said the stupid schmuck managed to get himself tied to the stall door with the glory hole wedged in it, and his cock and balls were tied off nice and tight and hanging out of that glory hole for all the cock hungry fags to suck loads out of. That made a real pretty porn picture bud, that sailor boy's big meat stick and his juicy balls dangling help-lessly out of a hole cut in the shape of a pussy! Hardy fucking hardy har, har! (Can you believe that shit though? A straight horned up sailor boy in the US navy sucked off all night long by cock hungry faggots? Hardy fucking double har! I have to wonder if he told his shipmates about it when he finally returned to the ship.) To tell it real quickly, to make a long story short the way it was told to me was that the sailor had wandered into "The Local" looking for some female action. He stupidly asked the bartender where all the women were and the bartender quickly told the horned up sailor boy that this was a gay estab-lishment, hardy fucking har, har! Well, needless to say the kid nearly bolted from the place but the bartender slyly told him how he could still *possibly* get his rocks off. The sailor, instead of bolting from the place listened in awe to the bartender as he told him about the glory hole that's wedged in one of the stall doors in the men's room. He told the sailor boy how he could stand in the stall, stick his cock and balls out of the glory hole and let whoever comes in the men's room suck him off. He also told the sailor how in most other sleazy bars the glory holes are cut in the sides of the stall walls, but not here at "The Local", oh no, here we go all out for you when you want to get your cock sucked and your balls licked! The bartender told the sailor how lucky the men were here that the goddamned glory hole was cut in the front door of a stall in the men's room. And to hammer his point home to the straight horned up sailor boy the bartender winked when he told him that it was cut in the shape of a pussy. The sailor stupidly gave it some thought, figured he could pretend it was a woman sucking him off, seeing as he would be behind the door as his tube steak was serviced and he wouldn't see who was doing the nasty on him. The sailor set himself up in the stall, lowered his uniform pants and stuck his pride and joy through the glory hole. To keep the story real short, just so I can get to mine here's what the fuck happened. The owners of "The Local" walked into the men's room and took turns sucking Sailor boy's cock; while one of them sucked him the other one licked his balls, and man, they milked him real good of his pent-up sticky juices. It was said that he shot a whopper of a god-damned load. The owners took turns scoffing it down as best they could as the sailor seemed to cum and cum. What they couldn't catch in their mouths and get down their throats wound up splattering on the floor and even on the front of the stall door as that kid's cock twitched and danced with a life all its own. They say that he grunted and ranted in pure ecstasy in that stall as he came and came. Legend has it that he was in a class by himself when it comes to shooting a hefty sized load, that it was a record cum to tell it plainly. I suppose being cooped up on his ship with no women around for months on end really got to the handsome and hunky sailor boy. While the kid was breathless in the stall after having just shot a load big enough to choke a horse and just as he was about to pull his cock and balls back into the stall so he could hike up his uniform trousers and be on his way was when he felt it. What he felt actually was a length of rope looped around the base of his cock and balls and yanked tight, preventing him from pulling his pride and joy back into the stall. The way I heard it told his cock was horse-sized and like me, he had the balls of a bull. He yelped as his cock and balls were tied up outside the stall door and yanked forward, and then he started swearing at the two guys to let him go, stating how with his nuts tied up the way they now had him there was no way that he could pull himself back into the stall. Well, to finish this up I heard that those bar owners stripped the sailor boy down to his black socks, tied him to the stall door, blindfolded him with his own goddamned neckerchief and left him in there to be sucked off *all goddamned night*. Fucking sailor swore just like what he was, a sailor! Har, har, har! I heard that someone saw the sailor boy leaving "The Local" around five AM and they said he could barely walk. I suppose you wouldn't be able to walk too well either if you had been sucked off so many times that by the time the night was over you were spewing out dry loads. But that's what "The Local" is all about buds, sleaze, and total fucking sleaze at that! And the night I'm telling you about now I got *my* share of just that, *sleaze*...

It was just about five PM so the place wasn't overly crowded as yet, plenty of seating still available at the bar. As the bartender (I had to wonder if he was the same bartender who had coaxed the sailor boy into the men's room that night) placed my third beer in front of me I pushed the two empty bottles aside. As I did that the two prissy looking suits sat down directly across from me, brazenly drinking in the sight of me in all my sweaty, smelly and muscular glory. I was clad in a pair of worn blue Levis, a really scuffed up pair of mustard colored work-boots that climbed up to just above my iron-like calves and a dark blue cotton button down shirt with the sleeves chopped off a bit, (by Dickies) wide open at my bull-sized neck and down to my barrel-like huge hairy chest.

"What'll it be boys?" the bartender asked the two suits as they got comfy on their barstools.

I meanly imagined huge dildos wedged in the center of those barstools and ramming the cute suits real hard right up their tight-wad asses as they sat down. That would really get them screaming in their silky socks and designer outfits. I had to stifle a laugh as I chugged at my beer as they sat down.

"Two cold Buds," the blond haired blue eyed suit said in reply, straightening his necktie as he said it, but at the same time his eyes suddenly riveted on me as he placed his drink order.

"Same for me," the brown haired, brown eyed stockier suit said to the bartender.

Like his blond buddy the brown haired suit was suddenly staring at me in awe. They also seemed to be noticing the empty bottles by my side on the bar as I chug-a-lugged at my third beer. The bartender set two cold Budweiser's in front of the suits, they picked up their bottles, clinked them together and took a dainty sip each. As they sipped their beers I took another hearty chug of mine and belched loud enough for both of them to hear me. They put their beers down and as they began discussing their work day they kept stealing glances over at me. To really fuck with their heads I showed them some tit, accidentally on purpose pulling my shirt aside a bit so one of my really fat, really fleshy brownish pink eraser sized nipples was on display, hardy fucking har, har. Fuck, I got tits bigger and squishier than a woman's let me tell you buds and they're just as fucking sensitive too! Once squeezed and teased just the right way they're no longer squishy however, then they become as hard as steel. You've all heard of the man of steel I'm sure, well I'm a man with tits of steel! I chugged my beer again till there was just a drop or so left, belched again real loud and the bartender was at my service almost instantly.

"Ready for another?" he asked me, placing a fourth cold bottle of Bud in front of me.

"Yeah, sure thing, thanks," I said. "But keep it cold for me will ya? I need to go and take a monster sized leak!"

As I was about to hand the bartender some money before heading to the men's room he held up a hand.

"This one is on the two gentlemen sitting across from you," the bartender said as he refused my money.

"Say what?" I asked him, sounding dumbfounded and belched real heartily again.

I glanced across at the two prissy suits and they both smiled at me, real pearly whites let me tell you, held up their beer bottles and took a sip each. I called out a "Thank you", held up my fourth beer, the one they had just bought for me and took a good long chug of it. My Adam's apple bobbed up and down and I swear I could feel those two suits really drinking in the sight of me now. I suppose that my little X-rated performance of showing off a tit ala Janet Jackson had really gotten to the two prissy boys. Or maybe it was my musculature, or maybe it was my overly hairy chest, or fuck it, maybe it was all of the above! When my fourth beer was just about gone I slammed the bottle down on the bar. The need to piss had REALLY set in hot and heavy at that point. As I would call it I was at the boiling point. I felt as if my cock was going to overflow in my under shorts buds!

"Now I really gotta go and take that monster sized leak," I announced proudly to the bartender as I stood up and stretched my muscular legs, looking across the bar at the two suits, they really were quite the handsome boys I'll say that for them. "Thanks for the beer you guys!"

Smiling, they again held up their beers and said that I was most welcome...

I walked quickly from the bar and to the men's room. My over-sized cock was piss hard in my pants buds and putting on a show called "Erection" in my Levis. I made sure to saunter past where those suits were sitting on my way to the bathroom. I have to say that they both looked real regal in their finely pressed suits, their lace-up shined shoes and even their goddamned silky socks I mentioned earlier. They smelled real nice too, of some kind of designer cologne I would imagine, and there I smelled all sweaty and randy like a goddamned locker room...

I dashed into the men's room and walked past the stall I had told you about earlier, the one with the glory hole wedged in it. I trailed a finger around it and imagined that hunky sailor boy tied up in there. I chuckled meanly and then stepped over to one of the three urinals lined up against the wall. I chose the middle one to make my piss deposit in. I yanked down my zipper, reached into the fly opening of my sweaty and piss stained white briefs and brought out my whopper sized cock. I had to wait a few seconds for the big guy to deflate a bit before I started pissing. If you're like me you know what the fuck I'm talking about here. It ain't all that easy for a guy to piss with a raging hard-on. Seems like any time I see some cute suits I get a real hard-on in my jeans. A lot of times while I'm working outdoors I'll purposely take my shirt off to give passerby a real show. What those Wall Street bulls don't know is that while they're checking me out in all my bare chest glory I'm checking them out too in their suits and ties. There's something real exotic and sexy about a studly guy in a suit, silk underpants and silk socks, Gawd! Come on, you know that all those prissy hard-nosed Wall Street bulls wear silky underpants and knee high silk socks, hardy fucking har, har! I knew a guy a year or so back who even wore garters with his goddamned silk socks, he favored the ones that climbed only up to his calves. Fucking fuck man, I snapped the elastic in his garters so many times while I sucked him off that just handling those prissy items kept my cock real hard till he blasted his load down my throat. My cock went down a bit and I began a slow trickle into the cold water of the urinal. A feeling of relief started filling me as I slowly emptied my bladder. As I pissed I heard the men's room door open behind me and someone come in. I thought of the sailor boy trussed up in the stall and how every time he heard the men's room door open he cringed miserably in his tiny prison, or so it was told to me. He knew that every time some cock hungry shmo came into the men's room it was nursing time again, hardy fucking har, har. And woe was him that he was the fount that all those cock hungry guys were nursing on that night. I mean, okay, lets face it, there ain't a guy out there who doesn't LOVE shooting his load! It's his pride and joy; it's a rite of his manhood! But that poor swabby was forced to shoot his load so many times that he nearly went crazy in that stall. I continued pissing as whoever had just come into the men's room approached the row of urinals. The blond haired suit sidled up to one of the urinals next to the one I was pissing in. He grinned at me real fiendishly and set a fresh cold beer down on top of my urinal.

"Hey man, thanks again," I said, looking at what would be my fifth cold brew for the night.

"Down the hatch big fella," the handsome blond suit said to me, picked up the beer and held it out for me to take.

"Yeah, thanks again man, but as you can see my hands are a bit occupied at the moment," I said, grinning also and glancing down at my huge cock as I held it balanced over the cold water of the urinal.

My yellow stream had yellowed the water real nice and a sour piss odor was wafting up at me and my bathroom companion.

"Stop pissing and take a chug," the blond guy said, sounding almost authoritative and looking down at my frothy yellow stream at the same time.

We looked intently into each other's eyes and I decided to see just what the fuck this cute suit boy was up to here. I clenched my cock muscles and halted my stream. Leaving my meat stick hanging out of my Levis and over the urinal I dutifully took the cold brew from my benefactor and put it to my lips. I threw my head back and chug-a-lugged my fifth beer.

"AHHHH!!!" I grunted after I had downed a good mouthful. "Thanks man, that was real sweet of you and your buddy out there to buy me the beers…"

I took another chug and as I did I saw the blond suit looking down at my cock as beads of piss emanated from the sexy tip of it. I felt real sexy and totally on display buds as I stood there chugging a beer with my cock dangling out of my Levis and hanging in a urinal.

"Drinking a lot of beer really makes you have to piss big and strong huh big fella?" the blond asked me, moving stealthily and taking up a position behind me.

I liked the way he had pet named me "big fella" and I was starting to see where this was going… Not only was the prissy blond suit checking out my huge pissy cock but he was also taking in the sight of my gloriously hairy chest and the two huge nips that were nestled in all my fur. Fuck yeah buds, I knew where this was going, what I didn't know was the kind of night it would turn out to be for yours truly here…

The blond suit positioned himself behind me as I chugged down another swallow of beer and then placed the bottle on the urinal. What a feeling is all I can say. I had to piss to start with. I had already begun my stream and stopped in midway, but each time I chugged down some beer my cock inflated some more, like I said, what a feeling! As I reached for my cock to begin pissing again the blond brazenly reached around my musculature and helped himself to my big fat man-sized nipples. (A guy I dated a while back, a real queen he was, called my nipples nipply nips, hardy fucking har!) He took my nipples in his thumbs and first two fingers of each hand and squeezed down good and fucking tight.

"OHHHHHHRRR FUCK..." I groaned and the second he squeezed down on my tits (nipply nips?) my stream halted involuntarily.

It was a weird feeling let me tell you buds, to have my piss suddenly stopped up in my baby maker because this blond handsome suit had just grabbed my big nubs. And God of gods he had them by the meat of them, holding them real tight at their sides as he squeezed and teased the bejesus out of them. The way he squeezed at the beefy sides of my tits really made the tips of them bubble up nice and sexily let me tell you! Instead of telling the brazen and prissy suit boy to get his mangy manicured mitts off my tits I grunted again; the sound of a real man's passion emanating real huskily from deep inside me.

"Fucker, *fucking guy*, I knew that you and your buddy out there at the bar were up to hi-jinx and mischief when you bought me that damned beer," I muttered in a real guttural tone.

In response to all my swearing and muttering the blond suit squeezed my huge nips even harder, giving them a good twist for good luck in the equation... I chuckled a bit as my nips were toyed with, thinking of how someone had once told me how its good luck to have your tits squeezed and teased. I could never figure out though who had the more luck. Was it the guy having his nubs squeezed and worked over or was the lucky guy the one doing the squeezing of the other guy's tits? In my opinion, it brought luck to both parties.

"Drink your beer before it gets warm big fella," the blond suit whispered in my ear, sounding like he was in love with me, squeezing my tits harder yet.

I glanced at the bottle on the sill of the urinal and surprisingly found myself doing what he had just instructed me to do... I'm actually more used to *giving* the orders in these kinds of situations, but fuck, he was the one kneading my tits and making them feel real good, so I figured what the fucking fuck, I'll play his game for now. As I chugged down a good swallow of the cold brew the blond suit kept toying with my damned tits in pure earnest. At one point he let go of them, ran the palms of his smooth hands over my rock hard furry chest and quickly re-grabbed my nubs. That got another good breathless sounding grunt out of me let me tell you...

"There's thousands of ways to make a guy's nipples feel real happy," the blond suit whispered in my ear as he leaned in real close to me, grabbing my tits harder yet in his finger and thumb grip.

Fuck, I could feel his erection in his suit trousers as it pressed against my chunky and hard ass cheeks. There was something erotic about that too, his erection at full mast in his prissy trousers pressed against my rough Levis... Chills and thrills shot through my very being...

"If you don't drink that beer now it'll be warm before you know it and it'll taste like piss big fella," the suit whispered in my ear, reiterating about the beer getting warm.

When he was done whispering for the moment he meanly nipped at my earlobe with his front-most teeth. I let out another deep guttural roar, the sound of my voice bouncing off the bathroom's tile walls.

"Speaking of *piss* Fucker," I said, nearly breathless as he whirled and twirled the very pudgy tips of my nips in his fingers and thumbs. "HUUUHHHHH GAWD, I can't *piss* while you're working your magical hi-jinx on my damned nips!"

I looked down at my cock as it hung over the urinal. It had jutted up to a steel-like erection and I saw that now my big guy was oozing beads of piss *and* beads of cum as well... The blond suit giggled like a real fag, let go of my tits and I took a deep breath. I managed a few trickles of piss into the urinal but when the blond grabbed my tits again my stream halted. Amazing huh? I grunted miserably, the need to piss overwhelming by then and the need to shoot a load gaining on me too. Fucking fucks! Was I actually going to let loose with a mess of construction worker sticky juice right here in the men's room of "The Local?" Ah, what the fuck right? That sailor boy I mentioned to you earlier had shot off countless loads in the men's room of "The Local." So what would be the big fucking deal if I shot one? The blond suit again let go of my tits. Again I heaved a deep breath, trickled some piss into the urinal and then he re-grabbed my tits. My yellow stream was again halted midway.

"Looks to me like you've got a real problem there big fella," the prissy and pert suit said to me, sounding somewhat fiendish as he said it. "Every time I squeeze your tits it stops your stream. And fuck Mister, I can do this all night with tits the size of yours!"

Then, he took one hand off one of my nubile nipples, placed it palm-up under the beer bottle in my hand and pushed upwards gently, coaxing me along to drink.

"Down the hatch big fella, don't want that brew to go to waste now do we?" he asked me tauntingly.

As I chugged another good and hefty swallow of the beer the suit reached over and took my now much jutted up nipple back in hand, or back in fingers and thumbs if you would.

"Gawd, I can't piss normally when I'm sporting a goddamned hard-on and especially when some prissy suit has got me by the tits!" I murmured and again looked down at my steely erection as it dribbled beads of piss into the urinal.

It's been said that my nipples (nipply nips?) are the control knobs for my big cock... And boy howdy was that theory ever being proved right at that fucking moment. I felt like I was being held prisoner in front of that fucking urinal. I mean, okay, I could've swatted that blond haired suit away from myself like he was a bug, but Gawd, what he was up to doing to me felt so fucking *good* buds. Then, the fucking prissy guy increased the tempo in his fingers and thumbs as he played my goddamned tits like they were musical instruments. I grunted real loud and a thick dollop of pre seed dripped from my wide sexy piss slit.

"GAWD, if you keep this up you're goin' to get my goddamned nut man!" I said throatily.

"Then I suppose I should just keep at my work wouldn't you agree big fella?" the blond suit asked me and mashed my tits at the sides.

"AAAAWWWWWW GAWD man, my tits are alive with the sound of music!" I said ala Julie Fucking Andrews.

"Finish up that beer big fella, there's another one on the way for you," the blond said to me, gyrating his crotch against my ass, his erection in his suit pants feeling like steel by then.

"A-another beer?" I asked. "Fucking fucks you handsome suit, that'll make six for me tonight, a whole goddamned six pack!" I said breathlessly and then did as he said and chugged down what was left of the beer in the bottle he had brought me.

I put the bottle down on the sill of the urinal and leaned my head back further as the blond suit made real sport of teasing and pleasing my nipples. By then he had them real tight by the tips and was stretching them forward as far as they would go...

"OOOHHHRRRRR MAN, I don't believe this shit, I'm not even touching my goddamned meat stick and just from you playing my tits like they were a squeeze toy I'm gonna erupt like a volcano in this goddamned pisser I'm standin' in front of!!" I seethed in forced ecstasy.

"Go for it big fella," the blond suit said, squeezed the tips of my tits real hard, leaned in real close to me and kissed me softly on the cheek.

"AAAARRHHHHH GAWD, but I gotta piss too," I said somewhere between ecstasy and agony and then I felt my juices churning in my bull-sized nuts. "And I always have to piss after I shoot a load man!!"

"So what's the problem big fella?" my blond tit player and beer benefactor asked me teasingly. "You're rooted in the right place to do both after all..."

"If, if you keep on kneadin' my tits the way you are I'll never piss my whole stream," I seethed. "OOOHHHHHHH OHHHHH man, OHHHHHH FUCKING FUCK, I'm gonna shoot a load like you can't believe you prissy yuppie boy!!"

"Actually I think I can believe it big fella," the blond laughed and rolled my tits in his fingers and thumbs.

It was a fucking unbelievable feeling buds, my entire cock felt like it was tingling and jingling. I shot a load the size of which would have choked a horse into that urinal, and my hands were pressed against the wall. I was not touching my goddamned baby maker! Fucking fucks, it was true what had been said, that my tits were the control knobs for my cock! This prissy suit boy was proving that totally at the moment. He squeezed my tits hard, twisted them left and right and I spewed yet another good thick dollop of my good stuff into the urinal. I heard it land with a plopping sound into the yellow water... I involuntarily heaved myself up to my tiptoes and did a stupid and sexy dance against the prissy suit's erection as I spewed jets of man juice into that urinal...

"OHHHHRRRRR fucking A!!" I grunted as the last of my loads were deposited into the cold water of the urinal.

The blond suit meanly jiggled my tits now, up and down and side to side...

"OHHHHHRRR hey man, easy with my tits now," I said, sounding real authoritative myself at that point. "After I've shot a load like that every part of me becomes real sensitive and sexy feeling you know?"

"Especially your tits big fella?" the blond asked me.

"OH yeah, especially my goddamned tits you prissy suit boy," I seethed and lowered myself back to flat on my booted feet. "OHHHHRRR fuck, after all those beers now I really have to piss like a racehorse!"

But he didn't let go of my tits. If anything he held them even tighter and only tiny trickles of piss emanated from my cock.

"OH man, come on, lemme piss and then I'll let you back at my tits fucker," I said almost pleadingly.

As sensitive as my poor tits were feeling by then there was a part of me that wasn't ready for this to end just yet; what I didn't know at that moment was that it really was just beginning buds...

But then, the door to the men's room opened and the blond guy's brown haired suit buddy walked in, and yep, you guessed it, he was carrying a cold bottle of beer.

"Hey, just like you said man," the brown haired suit said and put the beer down next to the empty one on the urinal sill.

"Sure as shit man," the blond said to his buddy. "I told you I would have this big fella by the tits in no time. The way he was teasing us out at the bar attests to what he's letting me do here...he loves to have his tits worked over...and get this, he can't piss while I've got his tits in my clutches..."

"Storing it up for us huh big fella?" the brown haired suit asked me and reached into the urinal to give my shaft a feel and a squeeze or two.

"OOOOHHHHRRR, d-don't know what the fucking fuck you mean by that Mister," I said to the brown haired guy, glancing in his direction.

Naïve little me huh? I still hadn't deduced that they were planning on having a piss party with yours truly here! The need to piss my guts out had become almost painful by then but for some reason I found myself guzzling at my seventh beer, nursing the tip of the bottle like a baby at its mother's tit...

"Down the hatch big fella, down the fucking hatch," the brown haired guy said to me, grinning at his blond buddy as he said it.

Again my Adam's apple bobbed up and down real sexily as I guzzled the beer...

"Can I get at those tits of his for a bit?" the brown haired guy asked his buddy.

"Sure thing man, squeeze em' enough and maybe you'll get another load of goop from him as well," the blond chuckled. "I already made him cum..."

The two suits laughed meanly...

Then, the blond let go of my nipples, stepped away from me and his brown haired buddy quickly stepped up behind me next. Before he reached around me to grab my manly tits though I trickled a few droplets of piss into the urinal, giving myself a quick moment of relief.

"OHHHHHRRRR fucking fuck," I grunted breathlessly all over again though because then it was the brown haired suit's turn to play with my tits.

He gave my furry chest a rub and then grabbed my nubs real tight. He was stronger than his blond buddy that was for sure...

"OHHHHH you fucking guys," I panted in between chugging my beer, feeling my piss retreating back into my tube steak. "What's the point of all this?"

"Well big fella, lets just say this, if you're willing to cooperate you'll get all the beer you can drink tonight, after a few more here you hold onto your piss as long as you can," the blond guy said to me as his buddy kneaded the fucking fuck out of my now getting sore nipples. "After a few more beers here we'll all pile in my van and drive back to our place, Ronald here and I live together."

"G-go on," I said, taking in what he was saying while being taken to the heights of ecstasy by his buddy.

"When we get back to our place we'll feed you more beer and then, and only then will we let you piss till your heart's content!" the blond guy said and leaned in close to me to kiss me on the cheek. "We got a deal?"

"I-I suppose so fucker," I said sternly. "But you'll have to allow me one piss at least before we leave here..."

The two men smiled at each other meanly...

"Go get him another beer Alex," the brown haired guy said. "I'll keep him busy here till you get back..."

"Sure thing," Alex chuckled and left the bathroom.

As Alex walked out of the men's room I took a swig of my seventh beer and as Ronald toyed with my tits like crazy other guys came into the men's room to piss. Unlike me when they stepped up to the urinals they had no problem whatsoever in relieving themselves.

"Looks like you're having an interesting evening here tonight Sir," a guy said from next to me as he stood and pissed into a urinal.

I glanced to my side and saw that he was a young, handsome and hunky sailor...

I nearly let out a laugh that would have bounced off the tile walls. Instead I went on enjoying the chills and goose bumps that had broken out all over me while Ronald now played with my tits and I chugged down a seventh beer... The sound of the sailor's piss as it streamed into the urinal he was standing in front of sent waves of jealousy through me...

"Fucking fucks Sailor boy, but I really got to take a leak that would put that tiny trickle of yours just now to total shame," I huffed as Ronald squeezed my tits harder yet. "OOHHHHRRRRRR FUUUCCK!!! But you see the way this prissy suit behind me has me by the tits seems to have made that nearly impossible..."

"Yeah, I'm the same way Mister," the handsome sailor chuckled. "Whenever my tits are squeezed I can't piss either, no matter how strong the urge for it is..."

The sailor got himself packed back into his uniform pants and he and Ronald smiled at each other...

"Hope you enjoy your evening Sir," the sailor said to me, flushed his urinal and exited the men's room, leaving me and my tits in Ronald's clutches.

"OOOHHHRRR man, you fucking yuppie boy, I really got to piss!!" I heaved loudly at that point.

Ronald let go of my tits, grabbed my upper arms and slowly turned me around facing him...

"What do you have in mind Fucker?" I asked, knowing all too well just what this sleazy suit had in mind.

A few seconds later I was huffing and puffing real sexily and loudly as Ronald the brown haired suit knelt in front of me with the very tip of my cock wedged between his bulbous lips. My muscular legs were spread real wide and I was sort of straddling the urinal behind me. It was an awesome feeling, my cock tip wedged between that suit's lips. Reaching down I held him by the back of his neck, running my fingers through his sexy hair as I trickled my piss drip by drip into his warm and velvety mouth. His lips worked like he was drinking a beer, his Adam's apple bobbing up and down as he scoffed down my sour yellow stream.

"OHHHHHHH yeah, nice, good feelin' of relief," I garbled with a sly looking grin on my face. "No wonder you and your blond prissy buddy filled me up with beer! You two are into goddamned piss sports! I shoulda known that was what your buddy was talkin' about when he talked about takin' me back to your place after I had chugged down more beers and then lettin' me relieve myself when you two get me there. You two are gonna be my urinals huh???"

Ronald ran his soft hands up and down my sweaty and scuffed Levis, over my clonky work boots and dutifully drank down my stream as I deposited it a bit at a time into his mouth. His eyes were open in ecstasy and he was looking up at me in awe.

"Fucking fuck, I get the feeling that when you and your buddy out there get me back to your place the two of you are gonna be chug-a-luggin' my piss all goddamned night," I said meanly.

He nodded his head in an affirmative and I grinned wickedly as I pissed the rest of what I had into his mouth. The fucking suit didn't lose a drop of my yellow liquid. He swallowed it all, not wanting to get it on his fancy suit I suppose...

When I was done my cock felt relieved somewhat but lo and fucking behold there was still some piss in there buds... I got the feeling that my two beer benefactors were going to make sure I stayed good and needy in that area buds.

Ronald got to his feet, quickly took me by my arms as I was catching my breath and turned me back to the urinal so that my semi hard erection was again dangling over it...

"O-okay Fucker, I'll keep playin' your game here..." I murmured as he grabbed my big tits again from behind me. "Fucking prissy suit boys up to shenanigans with me..."

I heard him smacking his lips together in ecstasy and a few moments later Alex returned, carrying what would be my eighth beer for the night...

"Here you go big fella," Alex said to me and placed the beer on the sill of the urinal for me.

"Fucking guys man, you two are gonna have me pissin' all the live long night," I grunted as Ronald squeezed my tits from the sides and twisted the fuck outa them.

My cock had gone back to an erect state as it dangled frustrated, hard and still chock filled with piss over the urinal...

Looking down into the urinal I was treated to the sight of my earlier yellow stream which was erotically mixed with my spews of cum that I had also deposited in there while Alex had been working my tits over...

I picked up my eighth beer, scoffed down a good mouthful and the need to piss again increased...

"His piss tastes like magic," I heard Ronald saying softly to Alex as I was getting ready to spew another load of construction worker jazz into the urinal.

"Good deal," Alex said sounding real corporate, watching to make sure I drank down the beer he had just brought me. "Before we leave here we'll get him a couple more beers, a few tall glasses of cold seltzer and then be on our way…"

I glanced at Alex with a look of disbelief in my big now wide opened eyes… These two pranksters were really planning on filling me to the goddamned brim and I was going to allow it all. I was going to be beyond what I call the boiling point buds! I didn't say a word however because it was at that moment that I was grunting and groaning as I shot a second load into the urinal, it making plopping sounds in the water as Ronald used my tits as control knobs for my huge cock…

"OHHHHHRRR GAWD, fucking tricksters, got me shooting another load of my goddamned sticky juices!" I crowed loudly as my cum landed in the urinal.

I threw my head back and leaned it a bit on Ronald's shoulder as he held tighter and tighter to my manly nipples…

"AAAAARRRHHH FUCKING A, what a night this turned out to be for me!" I said throatily.

"And you're not to piss another drop until we get you to our place big fella," Alex taunted me meanly…

"Yeah, sure as shit man, the way you two are squeezing my goddamned tits I won't piss for days it seems," I replied loudly.

When I was done spewing my load Ronald let go of my nipples, ran his hands over my furry chest and pulled me away from the urinal by my upper arms.

"Don-don't you think we should flush that?" I asked stupidly as I packed my sexy and sensitive feeling cock into my pants and zipped up.

As we walked out of the men's room I spied the sailor from earlier make his way over to the urinal I had just pissed and cum in. The mangy sailor knelt in front of the urinal and started lapping my good stuff from it like it was a fountain.

"OH GEEZ," I said softly and with a wicked looking grin on my face.

A short time later me and two new buddies, my beer benefactors I suppose you would call them were back at the bar, having a few cold ones for the road I suppose you would say. I was seated between the two prissy suits. Actually it was me having a few cold ones for the road. Being that Ronald would be driving he didn't have any more beers, except for the one he had downed when he and Alex had first sauntered into "The Local." By then the place was pretty crowded with the after work crowd but no one was the wiser to what was transpiring between myself, Alex and Ronald.

"Down the hatch big fella," Ronald said to me, squeezing my iron-like thigh as he sat next to me while I chug-a-lugged yet another beer.

As soon as I put the beer bottle down Alex moved a cold glass of seltzer in front of me.

"You boys picked the right one for your tricky tricks and goddamned hi-jinx," I said as I picked up the glass of seltzer, the need to piss almost pain-ful at that point.

I was sure that I was spotting my grimy under drawers with beads of piss by then.

"When we get back to your goddamned place you boys will be drink-ing piss all night long," I laughed meanly.

As I scoffed down the seltzer I heard Alex call out real mockingly, "Barkeep, two more beers for our buddy here and then he'll pay the tab!" I nearly blanched and nearly spewed seltzer when I heard that. Fucking totally fucks, these two jokers had filled me to the eyeballs with beer and seltzer and I was being handed the goddamned bill... Hardy fucking har, har, what a joke played on yours truly here huh buds?

Well, after I managed to down the last two beers and a total of nearly three glasses of ice cold seltzer I found myself being led, nearly floating actu-ally out of "The Local", through the parking lot and toward a large van that obviously belonged to Alex and Ronald. The two suits held me tightly by the upper arms, kneading my bowling ball sized biceps as we walked along. I swayed a bit between them, mostly from the fact that I had to piss like never before in my life and from the fact that I had lost count of how many beers the two prissy suits had fed me.

"G-Gawd, can't believe you two didn't have to carry me out here to your goddamned van," I slurred slightly. "I can't feel the fucking ground under my boots you guys...The way you two jokesters filled me up with so much beer and then that seltzer makes me feel like I'm fuckin' walkin' on air!"

"Well, you'll enjoy the relaxing ride then big fella," Ronald said, him taking me now by both my upper arms and keeping me balanced by the van as Alex opened the back doors of the vehicle.

"You'll have to ride in the back big fella, seeing as there are only two seats up front for me and Ronald," Alex said to me and then, holding my arms tight Ronald moved me and positioned me so I was looking directly into the back of the van.

"HOLY FUCKING SHIT, what in the hell...?" I blurted when I saw the kinky and monstrous looking contraption that was hooked up in the back of their van. "What is that goddamned thing you guys??" By then Alex had again taken my other huge arm back in his hands... He and Ronald held me real tight and I was rooted to the spot, my cock churning in my Levis with what felt like gallons upon gallons of piss in it...

"Well, like I just told you big fella, you'll have to ride in the back, see-ing as there are only two seats up front for me and Ronald," Alex chuckled as I took in the sight of the gizmo in the back of the van.

"B-but what is that thing??" I asked as my two new buddies each held tightly to one of my arms each, reached down with their other hands, gripped me by the backs of my knees areas, clenched their teeth and lifted me up off the concrete.

"H-hey, put me down fuckers, and answer my goddamned question, what is that gizmo you got hooked up in your van here?" I asked them and belched real loudly as they started swinging me back and forth like a god-damned pendulum, the bottoms of my booted feet aimed perilously at what now looked like the wide open mouth of the van that was ready to devour me. "UULLPPPPPPPP!!! H-HEY, take it easy you two huh???"

"Man, he sure is one heavy big fella huh?" Alex quipped as he and Ronald hoisted me higher and swung me faster and faster between them.

The device in the van looked like an oversized harness that was dan-gling from the ceiling of the vehicle from what looked like heavy duty cables. It looked large enough to slip a guy of my musculature into and somehow I got the feeling that that was just what my two beer benefactors had in mind as they swung me faster and faster between them...

"AAAAAAHRRRRRRR, p-put me the fuck down you pranksters!" I seethed.

"Sure thing big fella," Alex chuckled and just as they swung me for-ward they each let go of me and I was propelled through the air.

"AAAAYYYRRRRR SSSHIIITTTT!!!" I ranted as I landed in the van in a heap of muscle, my head spinning...

I looked up and saw Alex and Ronald stepping up into the van. Fuck, but they were beyond handsome in their suits, ties and sexy lace-up shoes and silky socks...

"Wh-what do you two have in mind?" I asked as they reached down and helped me off with my sleeveless shirt.

A short time later, with my head spinning I found myself in a most embarrassing and yet erotic of positions... I had been slid into the leather har-ness up to my mid section, like I said the harness was big enough to house a guy the size of me. I was dangling in an upside down letter "U" position, my arms dangling down in front of me, my wrists tied up and lashed to a handle in the floor of the van, my legs dangling behind me and roped at my booted ankles and lashed to another handle in the floor of the van.

"You fuckers, what a position to put a poor beer filled dude in," I grunted throatily, looking at their legs from my upside down perspective and feeling my Levis being pulled down in the back along with my mangy white briefs. "Wh-what the fucking fucks are you two up to now huh???"

You would have thought that being in the position I now found myself in that I would have been screaming my head off for help, I mean, lets face it buds, I was bein' kidnapped here...

It was Alex who was doing the honors of lowering my Levis and put-ting my hairy ass on display as it faced the goddamned ceiling of the van while Ronald squatted behind me all handsome and macho in his suit and holding a pair of tit clamps. He reached under me and snapped the sharp-teethed tit clamps onto my erect and overworked (nipply nips?) nipples, the connecting chain on them dangling against my hairy, furry chest.

"YAAARHHHHHH GAWD OF GAWDS!" I blubbered and squirmed in the harness as my tits felt seared.

"That'll keep him from losing his piss during the ride," Ronald said as he stood up next to Ronald. "Those clamps will keep the big fella good and stopped up, ha, ha!"

I felt the palms of their hands being run over my hairy ass and they probed in my scruffy crack with their fingertips, really digging for gold in there...

"HUUHHHHHHHHHHH!!!!" I panted as they probed me anally.

A few times they took turns spreading my cheeks real wide; spit into my most private crevice a few times each and they sniffed, snuffed, licked and ate around in it as well. What a feelin' I got to tell you boys! It's not all the time that I get my cruddy hole sniffed at and eaten up while I have to take a monster sized piss! My piss hard cock throbbed real beefy and thickset between my legs, my bull-sized balls feeling like they were still chock filled with my manly juices, even though I had shot two whopper sized loads back in "The Local."

"H-how long is the ride to your place fuckers?" I asked them.

"About a half hour, depending on traffic," Alex replied and gave one my chunky hairy ass cheeks a good whack.

"OUCH!!! A half hour??" I blurted. "A half fucking hour??? You two are gonna make me wait a half hour so I can piss my goddamned guts out???"

"Keep prattling like that and we'll take the scenic route, that'll take forty five minutes at best," Alex laughed meanly.

Ronald again squatted behind me, hooked a cock ring up to my cock and balls and Alex inserted a long tube-like hose into my wedged open shit chute. I farted a couple of times real embarrassingly as the hose was inserted in me good and fucking deep.

"HHHHHHUUUHHHH wh-what the fuck have I gotten myself into here???" I garbled, my eyes crossing in my head as Alex inserted that goddamned tube in me. "EEEERRHHHHH!!!!! More shenanigans huh fuckers?"

I glanced to my side and saw that the hose was actually hooked up to a large plastic tank. The tank was filled with water...

"OH FUCKING FUCKS!" I cried out and as Alex and Ronald stepped out of the back of the van I felt my bladder being filled with warm water.

As I hung there like a side of beef in a butcher's freezer I could actually feel the lips of my goddamned shit chute sucking that tube-like hose further down into my raunchy anal canal.

"Man, by the time we get home he's *really* going to have to piss," I heard Ronald laugh and then the van doors were slammed shut.

I clenched my teeth and rolled my tied hands into fists as I was filled up rectally…

A few seconds later the van was pulling out of the parking lot of "The Local." I stupidly wondered if I would be able to go to work the next day. I chuckled real loud from deep in my belly and farted around the hose in my hole as it continued its trickle into my shit chute… When the van moved down a small hump I knew that we were now leaving the parking lot of "The Local." Like I told you buds, "The Local" is a real sleazy dump, a real seedy and slimy place, and I, like the sailor I told you about earlier had fallen victim to its wiles it would seem… I clenched my teeth and the need to piss increased with each harrowing and passing second…

The ride seemed like it was more than a half-hour, it could actually have been less for all I know but in the position I was in and the way I was feeling, all filled and stopped up at both ends I couldn't make head nor tails of time…

The van picked up speed a short while later and I supposed that we were on a highway at that point. I glanced to my side and the water tank mocked me. The water sloshed around in it and my stomach made gurgling sounds as said water was siphoned from the tank and into my shit chute, filling my bladder to what would surely be overflowing. I crossed my eyes in my head and farted loud and smelly around the hose in my hole…

Before the van came to a complete halt we stopped for a few seconds and I heard the sound of a garage door being opened via a remote control from within the van. We moved slowly into the garage and then the ignition was shut off.

"Let's see how our big fella is doing back there," I heard Alex say in between laughing as he and Ronald stepped out of the van.

The back doors of the vehicle were thrown open and looking between my legs I saw my two (captors?) new buddies step up into the van. I noticed that Ronald had undone the knot in his brown silk tie and it was now dangling around his neck along with the topmost button of his white shirt undone.

"How are you doin' in here big fella?" Alex quipped. "Whew, smells like a goddamned men's room…"

In response I farted again…

"Fuckers," I whispered as the water trickled into me, as I sweated like a stuck pig and as my cock was rage hard and in need of relief like never before in all my goddamned life.

The two men stepped to my sides and got busy real quick. Alex did the honors and slowly slid the hose from my shit chute. It felt awesome I gotta tell you as that hose was taken from my hole boys. As soon as the hose was out I could feel water bubbling and trickling out of my well sopped, well filled asshole. Ronald reached up onto a shelf on the other side of the back of the van and produced a medium-sized butt-plug. He inserted it fully into my asshole.

"AAAAAAAWWWWWWHHHHH...fuckers, stoppin' me up real good huh?" I blubbered as the pink latex device was inserted inside me.

My cock twitched and dribbled a good dollop of pre seed which landed on my upturned chin...

"You two sure know how to play real sleazy and kinky I gotta fucking say," I said gaspingly as the two men then squatted down one in back of me and one in front to untie my hands and feet.

Once I was untied they left me dangling a few moments more so that they could unlace my boots, get them off my feet and then de-pants me as well along with my mangy piss and sweat stained briefs...

"GAWD almighty, I gotta fucking piss you guys, hurry up and do your dirty work and get me outa this goddamned infernal contraption," I garbled, massaging my wrists as the two men worked at stripping me.

A few moments later, wearing nothing but my goddamned smelly white sweat socks and Ronald's tie now tied over my eyes as a makeshift blindfold Alex and Ronald helped me from the van, again holding one of my arms each. They squeezed and kneaded my iron-like bowling ball sized biceps almost lovingly. My cock was beyond rock hard, still erect, and still cock ringed, sticking out in front of me like a goddamned flagpole. My balls hung real low and chock filled with my sexy ball juice, swinging from side to side as I trudged along in the blindfolded darkness. GAWD, even though I had shot two hefty sized loads of cum back at "The Local" my balls felt like they were still filled to the max with my sexy juices. I supposed that that was because of the need to piss like never before in my life! My tits were still clamped mighty tight and the butt-plug in my juicy and soaked shit chute kept me stopped up real well let me tell you bud. My stomach made embarrassing churning sounds as I was heralded out of the back of the van. I jutted my furry chest forward, almost military like because of the pressure in my anal canal. One of the guys meanly reached behind me and gave the butt-plug a few twists and turns followed by thrusting it out and then back in as well...

"OHHHHHRRRR GAWD, what's the point of blindfolding me fellas?" I asked as I was guided along by them, the smell of Ronald's designer cologne on his tie intoxicating me a bit. "Looks like I'm in for more surprises huh?"

"You'll see soon enough big fella," Ronald said and kissed my cheek.

I smiled through pursed lips...

"For some fucking fucked up reason I get the feeling that I'm in for a long night of hi-jinx and mischief with you two eh?" I asked them.

"That would be an accurate assessment big fella," Alex said. "Okay, one step up into this room now and then we'll take that tie away from your eyes..."

I did as he said and we entered the room where I would be made to piss my guts out like never before in all my life...

The two men positioned me where they wanted me standing and then Ronald did the honors of taking the necktie/blindfold off me...

My chin dropped when I saw the set-up they had for what would obviously be an all night pissing-fest for yours truly...

We were standing in a spacious room that was dominated in the dead-center by a good-sized concrete post. At the bottom of the post was what looked like a platform of some kind for a dude to stand on, me being the said dude I supposed. The room was hardly furnished except for a few stray chairs strewn here and there.

"Welcome to your private latrine big fella," Alex quipped as the two men walked me over to the post.

"What the fucking fuck do you two prissy suits got in mind for me now?" I asked as I was ushered up onto the platform at the bottom of the post and positioned real sexily with my back against the structure, my furry and muscular chest jutted out real soldierly-like, my clamped nipples (nipply nips?) making a real nice erotic picture.

From out of nowhere it seemed (at least it seemed to me) the two prissy suits produced a few good lengths of rope and before I knew what the fucking fuck was happening they had my muscular arms pulled back around the post. They roped my stretched out arms together at the wrists, securing me to the over-sized post.

"OHHHHRRRR GAWD of gods, bosses of bosses, trying me the fuck up again," I garbled and squirmed miserably against that post on my socked feet as those two faggots did their dirty work behind me.

I felt like one of those Greek god statues... I could actually feel the veins in my huge biceps being stretched and plumped up as my two new buddies roped me real tight to the post at the wrists...

A short while later my wrists were tied good and fucking tight around the back of the post, a rope had been secured under my huge pecs, pinning me to the structure and my socked feet were spread wide and also tied off to the structure. I was positioned and balanced real well let me tell you bud...

"Fucking fuck, what a position you two got me in," I ranted, squirming in the tight bondage. "You have to tie up a man so he can piss?"

The butt-plug in my shit chute drove me crazy and I wriggled like a fish out of water against that post. No wonder my two beer benefactors had tied me up the way they had. Just for the record here I want to clear up any misinterpretations you might be having. Yeah, those two prissy suits had in fact kidnapped me, they had in fact stripped me, they had in fact filled me to the point of overflowing with beer and seltzer and they had in fact tied me the fuck up, twice at that! But despite all that I wasn't afraid and I was actually inwardly enjoying every second of this ride that I had been taken on...

"When the fuck do I piss fellas?" I asked, looking down at the tit clamps on my nipples and the cock ring still snapped around my cock and balls.

"Hold your water a tad more big fella," Alex mused. "Enjoy the show…"

"Enjoy the show?" I asked. "What the fuck show is that?"

In response to my question the two suits faced each other. Alex shucked off his suit jacket followed by Ronald. Ronald slowly undid Alex's necktie as Alex started unbuttoning Ronald's white shirt.

"Ah shit, a goddamned strip tease," I chuckled and my hard cock oozed beads of piss and pre seed.

They each helped the other off with their button down office shirts and then their white tee shirts. Alex was lankily built with a smooth chest and two of the pinkest most nubile nipples I had ever seen on a guy. Ronald was more the hairy type, not as hairy as me mind you, but his chest was of the robust and muscular sort, adorned by two silver dollar sized nipples nestled in his fur. I could see anyone with a man tit fetish wanting to chow down on Ronald's big tits. However, at the moment it was my nipples (my nipply nips?) that were two of the star attractions for the upcoming pissing event. Next, the two men got their shoes off and they each unbuttoned the other's suit trousers, teasing each other by running their hands over each other's crotches as they did so, teasing me mercilessly at the same goddamned time. I watched with an erection of steel as their suit trousers fell to the floor and bunched around their ankles. It was a comical yet erotic sight at the same time. With their suit pants down around their ankles they both looked real sexy somehow in their boxer briefs with their dark colored silky socks up to their knees sticking upwards out of their suit pants around their ankles… They stepped out of their suit pants, took off their boxer briefs and then looked at me hungrily. Like me they were both sporting erections of steel. Alex had a long wiry looking cock between his lanky sexy legs, nestled real sexily in a blond thick pubic bush. The crown of his manhood was a delightful looking mushroom cap and just the thought of sucking on that cock-tip caused a good dollop of pre seed to ooze from my own piss slit. Ronald on the other hand had a fat cock, not as long as Alex's and his was surrounded by dark curly pubic hair, not to mention that his ball sac looked real sweaty from being so hairy.

"Fucking prissy sexy guys," I muttered as they sauntered slowly over to the post I was securely bound up to.

My steely erection saluted them as it twitched in front of me like it was alive, filled to overflowing with piss and my balls aching to be relieved of yet another load of my manly juices.

"You ready to be piss fried big fella?" Alex asked me, looking at me as if he were in love with me.

Somehow I got the feeling that the beautiful blond prankster was in love with me… The memory of when he and Ronald had settled down across from me at "The Local" filled my mind and I recalled just how very lustfully the blond suit had looked at me. He had his designs on me the moment he saw me it seemed…although I had to wonder if those designs of me included getting me so stopped up with piss that I would be sweating it out of my pores…

"I was ready to piss before we left "The Local" you hoax player," I garbled and squirmed in the bondage, my eyes rolling in my head. "So let's get this show on the road huh? Let's get me pissin' here…Fucking fucks man, I'm feelin' like I can piss a waterfall for you two water sports junkies…"

"Not so fast big fella," Ronald chuckled. "We're going to piss fry you a little at a time and then some and then some more…"

"I don't think I understand you buds," I said as Ronald stepped next to me and Alex hunkered down in front of my crotch.

My cock twitched as he sniffed under it and lapped at my husky balls a few times…

"OHHHHRRRR, yeah, fucking beautiful blond prissy guy is lickin' my gonads," I sputtered.

Then, Ronald reached across my tied up chest and unclipped the tit clamps from my nipples…

"AAAAAAYYYYRRRRR!!! GODDAMNIT all!!" I roared, my loud voice echoing throughout the room my two new buddies had me in.

"Yeah, it tends to feel worse when the clamps are taken off after having been on you for so long," Ronald said meanly, giving one of my bloated up looking nipples a good squeeze, sending thrilling sensations through my entire musculature. "But at least you can piss now right?"

"Fucking A faggot!" I garbled and looked down at my swollen cock.

Alex quickly took the cap of my cock into his greedy mouth and Ronald said, "Go for it big fella, a trickle at a time. My buddy there wants to savor every mouthful you give him…then it'll be my turn, then we'll fill you up with some more beer…"

A feeling of disbelief filled me. More beer??? But at that moment I couldn't really mull on it for all that long. I had more pressing matters in front of me, namely a beautiful blond on his knees in front of me with my cock head securely planted between his lips. I took a deep breath, actually felt the blood rushing back through my nipples and started a slow trickle into Alex's mouth.

"AAAHHHHHHHH, nice, feels real nice," I gasped and grunted as I did as Ronald had instructed me, pissed small trickles of my yellowish stream into Alex's mouth.

On his knees with my erect cock in his mouth Alex looked like he was in ecstasy as my warm flow filled his craw and he swallowed it. Each time he gulped down my mess I quickly trickled some more into his mouth. He rubbed my muscular legs and toyed with my white smelly sweat socks as I fed him my frothy piss.

"AAAARRRRHHH, fucking hot man, never knew how good it could feel to piss," I said throatily.

I trickled a few more good pisses into Alex's mouth and then Ronald said, "Okay big fella, that's enough for the moment," and then he clipped the tit clamps back onto my goddamned nubs, stopping my piss flow...

"AAAAARRRRHHHH fucker, *fucking fuck*!" I gasped somewhat miserably. "Fucker stopped me up again!"

My cock ringed cock and balls still felt all bloated. What I had just fed Alex was barely the tip of the iceberg with how much more piss I had stored up in me...

Alex let my cock head slip from between his lips and he stood up at my side as Ronald hunkered down at my erection.

"You ready big fella?" Alex asked me, his lips grazing my ear as he spoke directly into it.

"I'm really not in much of a position to be debating with you buddy," I snickered as Alex kissed my cheek and then took the tit clamps off my nipples again.

"AAAAARRRRHHHHHH!!!!" I screamed. "GAWD you guys, I don't know whether to hate or to love that feeling when you unclamp my goddamned nipples!"

I hunched my broad shoulders up a bit, took a deep breath and as Ronald gobbled my cock head into his mouth I started again a slow trickle piss, into the guy's eager craw...

"HHHHHHOOOOOO, n-now I know what you two prissy and sadistic suits meant when you said I was going to be piss fried..." I grunted.

"Yeah, you're going to piss like never before in your life big fella," Alex laughed, holding up the tit clamps. "After Ronald gets his fill of your mess I'll drink from you one more time and then we'll give you a few beers to guzzle."

"FUCKING fucks..." I snarled.

I happened to look up at the ceiling and when I looked back down it was Alex again scoffing down my trickles of piss and Ronald was standing next to me, the tit clamps at the ready to stop me up again. Fucking fucks man, I didn't even see those two tricksters switch places on me. There would be no rest for the weary that night let me tell you buds.

After they had both scoffed down a few mouthfuls of my piss they clamped my nipples again to keep me from pissing anymore until they were ready for me to.

"OHHHRRRRR fucking guys man, you two sure know how to make a man piss crazy," I blubbered, sweating in my socks as I stood tied up on that platform, giving those two prissy faggots a real show let me tell you.

"Time for a drink I would think big fella," Alex mused, gave the chain on my tit clamps a tug and chuckled as he and Alex left the room.

"Hey, where are you two pranksters off to huh?" I shouted at their backs as they sauntered off, looking real sexy and hot in just their knee length silk dark colored socks. "Fucking shitty thing to do to a guy you mugs, to tie him up like this when he's all piss sloshed and waterlogged..."

Well, they weren't gone all that long, just long enough to get some kinky equipment...

I *was* going to drink more beer, but definitely not in the traditional sense let me tell you buds...

"OHHHHRRR fuckers, fucking guys man, what are you two up to now?" I growled as they carried in a few lengths of flexible rubber tubing, a couple of bottles of cold mineral water and a six pack of ice cold long-necked bottles of beer.

"Time to fill you back up again big fella," Alex chuckled meanly.

The answer that I was seeking to the question I had asked myself earlier had just been answered. I was definitely not going to be showing up for work the next day, hardy fucking har, har...

Standing there tied up the way I was there wasn't much I could do to stop the two prissy faggots from hooking me up for a real beer tasting let me tell you man. Alex squatted in front of my spread legs, reached up between them and grabbed the butt-plug that was wedged in my shit chute. He got it out with one good yank and quickly replaced it with a length of rubber tubing. I clenched my teeth and goose bumps broke out all over my muscular body as Alex inserted that tube good and deep up inside me.

"EEEEEEHHHRRRRRR wh-what's the point of this fuckers?" I screeched through my clenched teeth.

Standing next to me Ronald held a bottle of cold beer to my lips and I chugged it down a bit at a time as he fed it to me.

"Fucking totally fucks, I'm gonna be piss fried and not to mention piss drunk you guys," I blubbered and was fed more beer orally.

As I swallowed the beer the need to piss increased tenfold it seemed. My eyes rolled in my head. Alex, still squatting between my spread legs gave the rubber tube in my shit chute a few tugs. He deemed that it was in there good and secure and got to his feet, holding the slack of the flaccid tube in his hand.

"OH God man, I really hope you're not thinking about doing what I think you're thinking about doing," I garbled at him as the guy opened a cold bottle of beer.

I watched as he slid the end of the tube he was holding over the opened bottle of beer.

"Ronald, while I start filling him why don't you hook up that other tube to his cock and mouth?" Alex asked his buddy.

"WH-WHAT???" I shouted.

Smiling almost evilly Ronald picked up a very thin length of the rubber tubing. I watched in horror as he attached a clear and very thin catheter-like tube to the end of the rubber tubing. Fucking fucks bud, I didn't need three guesses to know where that was going. Suddenly, I felt it in my shit chute. The beer that Alex had poured into the rubber tubing that was wedged in my hole started filling my bladder.

"OHHHHRRR you fucking fucked up dudes," I grunted as my head spun. "GAWD, I'm drinking beer through my goddamned asshole!!"

Holy crap buds, but I could actually feel my shit chute sucking on that tube wedged up in my ass. It was as if my hole was thirsty for the beer and was involuntarily scoffing it in. Suddenly, the sound of a big construction dude screaming in erotic agony filled the room. When I saw that Ronald was wedging that catheter-tube like thing into my piss hole I realized that it was me who was screaming. Sweat poured off me in rivers...

"AAAAYYYRRRRRRRRRRR!!!!!" I reeled.

The other end of the rubber tubing that was inserted into my piss hole had a mouthpiece on it I saw as Ronald held it up, a mouthpiece along with a length of rubber tubing that would feed me the piss that I pissed when it was hooked up in my mouth.

"NO, no, you wouldn't," I stammered as Alex's beer bottle emptied into my asshole.

My cock was rigidly hard; beyond hard, beyond belief I got to tell you...that tube inserted in my piss hole was a monster. When the beer that Alex had siphoned into my asshole was gone he quickly hooked up a second bottle to the end of the tube.

"GAWD, I gotta piss," I said desperately.

"All in time big fella," Ronald said and held up the mouthpiece attachment at the end of the tube that was inserted in my piss hole.

"GRRRRFFFFFFF!!!!" I grunted as Ronald slid the attachment into my mouth, forcing my jaws slightly wide.

"When the trickle starts in your mouth swallow fast," Ronald laughed.

I simply looked at him in disbelief then faced forward. I could not believe the way the night had turned out for me...

Then, another loud grunt of erotic agony escaped me when Ronald took the tit clamps off my nipples again... And this time I would be drinking down my piss rather than my two beer benefactors.

The second bottle of beer was gone, straight into my shit chute and Alex wasted no time bud. This time he hooked a bottle of cold mineral water to the end of the tube in my ass. He turned the bottle on its side and seconds later I felt it seeping into me.

"Piss fried big fella," Ronald laughed at my side as I suddenly felt the trickles of my own piss dripping into my gaping open mouth. "You are going to be better than piss fucking fried..."

My head spun wildly from having had the beer fed to me through my raunchy asshole and I swallowed, gulped and scoffed down my piss as fast as possible as it trickled into my mouth through the attachment hooked up there from my piss hole. Fuck, I didn't even feel myself pissing buds. It seemed that it was happening involuntarily. Fucking fucks, like I said already, what a night it had turned out to be for yours truly here!

"RRRRFFFFFF…r-rastards…" I garbled over the mouthpiece wedged in my mouth.

I stood there being filled with mineral water while I scoffed down my own piss, what a sight I was huh buds???

"I would think you didn't expect to be drinking your own piss huh big fella?" Alex asked me meanly as he and Ronald sidled up next to me at my sides.

I simply glanced at them from side to side, my eyes shifting back and forth as they ran their hands over my furry chest. I was at a point where I was beyond speaking, seeing as my mouth was filled with the device they had wedged in it and not to mention that I was scoffing down my piss as fast as possible. It tasted sour and vile buds…

I swooned as Alex and Ronald leaned down and slurped my jutted up nipples into their mouths. They lovingly licked my man-sized tits as I sweated my guts out and drank down mouthful after mouthful after mouthful of my piss… The combination of them sucking at my tits like nursing babies, my cock at full mast and rock hard and drinking down my piss was intense I got to say here.

After what felt like a long while my head was spinning and when my two beer benefactors felt that I had drank enough of my frothy yellow nectar my tits were again clamped, stopping me up real good once more…

"RRRRRHHHHHHH!!!" I reeled into my mouthpiece.

The feeling of bloating in my cock was over the top. I opened my eyes real wide…

"RET nee riss!!!!" I ranted, trying to scream "Let me piss!!"

"All in time again big fella," Alex quipped and checked on the bottle of mineral water that was still seeping into my asshole. "Wow, halfway emptied already. His bladder is going to be real sloshed by the time we're done with him…"

"RRRRRRRRRRR!!!!" I screamed as the two men laughed meanly.

When the bottle of mineral water was just about empty Alex disconnected it from the rubber tubing in my hole. Now the need to piss was astronomical man! I heaved my chest upwards in the tight bondage after Ronald had taken the mouthpiece out of my craw and slowly slid the catheter-like device from my piss hole.

"OHHHHRRRRR you fuckers with your goddamned shenanigans," I pouted breathlessly. "I gotta piss now like you cannot fucking believe!! Get these goddamned tit clamps off me once and for all huh?"

They were smiling evilly those two beer benefactors of mine, smiling evilly and wickedly as they looked me over in my goddamned bound up bondage state. What I saw in their eyes was total and complete satisfaction. What they had in my guts, kidneys and innards felt like gallons upon gallons of beer and cold mineral water. I felt as if I could piss enough to fill a few quart-sized containers.

"I told you he would take to this like a fish to water," Alex chuckled.

"P-please man, don't be mentioning water, just thinking about it has got my cock churning and burning," I ranted crazily. "Come on you kinky yuppies, un-clamp my tits so I can fucking piss here…"

"Isn't it just too much Ronald, how when his big plump nipples are clamped or squeezed and mashed he can't piss?" Alex asked his buddy. "Even if he's filled to overflowing…"

"RHHHHHH!!!! You fucking guys, you goddamned prankster bastards, I need to fucking piss NOW!!!" I growled crazily.

Then, to my much needed relief a few moments later the tit clamps were off my nipples and Alex was standing next to me sucking one of my bubbled up nips. As Alex made like a nursing calf Ronald had my cock head between his lips. He also was making like a nursing calf as he drank down my trickles of piss…

"OH YEAH, fucking A, great to be in control of my piss again," I gurgled, clenching my tied hands into big fists as I fed the guy kneeling before me trickles upon trickles of my yellow pulpy nectar.

After a few moments my two new buddies (captors) switched places. Ronald did the honors of licking and sucking one of my man-sized tits while Alex helped himself to my brew, via my cock font…

It took nearly a half hour to really drain my vein buds. Those two guys really knew how to make it last so that I had enough of my mess to feed them while they alternated at my cock head. When I was finally empty they untied me from the post and we all bear hugged each other…

Like I said earlier what a night it had turned out to be for me…

I had found out what it meant to be piss fried…totally piss fried buds…

The Abusive Wager

"OOOOHHHHHHHHH!!!" my new buddy Daniel moaned, deeply and throatily as I again squeezed his very jutted up nipples, followed by giving them yet another good twist each just for good measure (and for good luck as well.) "OHHHHHHHHHH FUCK MAN!!!!!!"

"Feeling good buddy?" I whispered in his ear, my lips grazing his earlobe as I spoke, sounding as sadistic and menacing as hell as I leaned up against him from behind, my arms wrapped lovingly and crossed around his upper, fairly muscular torso, my thumbs and first two fingers of my hands gripping his gorgeous, bulbous and plumped pink nipples.

The way I was working Daniel's nipples was causing the sexy nubs to jut up more and more with each passing second, getting them harder and harder as I twisted and squeezed the life out of them…or perhaps I had that in reverse, perhaps I was squeezing life *into* those oversized nipples of his… It was amazing really, how receptive the handsome guy's nipples really were! When we had gotten started on this little voyage his nubs had been fleshy and all squishy, but the moment I had begun squeezing and teasing them they came to erect and rigid life. And not only was it his nipples that were jutted up. He had a real plumped up chub tenting his sexy (tighty whiteys) white boxer briefs. It looked to me like I had chosen well for my game where Daniel was concerned. Just as I had hoped the handsome stud had very sensitive and *very* responsive nipples.

"Fuck, fuck, *double fuck,*" Daniel said breathlessly in his half Asian half New York sounding accent. "When you invited me here for a game I didn't think for a second that it would be *my tits* that would become the main event man…"

"Welcome to my world," I laughed meanly and twisted Daniel's nipples hard.

"AAAAAWWWHHHH GOD!!! Double fucks again!!" Daniel blurted and for a moment arched his upper body real sexily, jutting his bulging cock forward, fucking the air, and then settling back as I again twisted and tweaked his nipples. "AAWWWWWHHHHH!!!"

"I find that a pair of nipples like these makes for a great game buddy boy!" I chuckled meanly. "And like I said earlier, squeezing a good pair of tits and working them over this way is really good luck."

"Yeah, good luck, *sure, good fucking fucked up fucking luck,* but for whom?" Daniel squeaked. "God man, my poor tits…"

"For both of us," I laughed. "Firstly, for you, because you're getting all horned up for free and secondly, for me, 'cause I just love playing with and torturing a meaty pair of nubby nipples!"

"OOOHHHHHHHHH fucking fucks Fucker, nubby nipples, what a hell of a fucking way to refer to my goddamned tits!" Daniel chirped throatily as he stood in front of me, totally helpless (yet inwardly loving the trip I had taken him on) with his hands roped tight behind him. "God almighty and all the angels in heaven, you're sending chills through me buddy... I got friggin' goose bumps all the fuck over me!"

"Yeah, I can sure as hell see that, I never saw a guy with such bubbled up goose flesh before," I guffawed and squeezed his nipples tighter, getting a few good loud moans and groans out of him. "And those friggin' goose bumps just seem to be multiplying with each passing second bud..."

"I'm feeling crazy here Chris," Daniel panted.

Dressed in just his white (tighty whiteys) boxer briefs style underpants and calf length nylon navy blue dress socks the handsome Asian guy made a real exotic and pretty picture let me tell you... Getting his hands roped behind him had been a bit of a chore but when I reminded him of the rules of the game that he had agreed to he gave in. (I'll tell you more about that very soon I promise.) Breathing heavily now I tweaked the very tips of Daniel's meaty nipples a few times (that really got him dancing in his socks for me), then tugged at them, then grabbed the beef of them again, and continued tugging on them, enjoying the nubby hardness of them between the rough skin of my fingertips. Daniel's nipples were like magic. I would squeeze the hard nubs down, squishing them between my fingers and then instantly they were hard again, ready for more tweaking and squeezing. I could actually do this all night if I wanted to I thought.

"AAAAARRRRHHHH man, th-this is too much now buddy, I'm all worked up and steaming in my damned boxer briefs!! Fuck, a little more and you'll see my crotch smoking!" Daniel grunted, leaning his head back a bit. "FUCKING *totally fuck!!!* Never knew that my damned tits were so fucking sensitive!! *And I'm a guy!!* Fucking fuck, I thought that just women had sensitive tits!! RRRRRRRHHHHHHHHHH!!!!"

"Looks like we learn something new everyday huh?" I teased him and rubbed savagely at the sides of his nipples in a very fast and very circular motion. "And if your crotch were to start smoking I'm sure that would be a sight and a half to see..."

"AAAYYYYYY, yeah, and what an education I'm getting where my tits are concerned," Daniel reeled.

He pulled himself to his socked toes and danced real stupidly and sexily for me as I pointed his nipple tips upwards at the ceiling, stretching them far for him, squeezing the tips of them real hard as I did so, him looking down and seeing the fleshy and juicy skin of his nubs being elongated with each squeeze and tug I gave them.

"L-looks like you're planning on tearing my tits from my chest buddy," Daniel panted.

"Nah, I wouldn't do anything that extreme," I laughed. "You'd be surprised though just how much these nubs of yours can handle."

"I-I guess I'm finding that out now huh bud?" he asked me, gasping as he spoke. "L-like you just said you learn something new everyday... GODS!!!"

"You should have your girlfriend do this for you once in a while buddy," I laughed and whirled his nipples with my fingers. "You really do seem to be enjoying it. I mean, like you just said, you're steaming in your boxer briefs!"

"OOOOOOOOOOO man, fucking totally fucking totally fuck!!!" Daniel cried out, swearing in that unique style of his, sounding like he was in a state of total disbelief as I whirled and twirled his nipples like they were a windmill. "Like that old song says, "What a feeling!!!"

"Yeah, what a feeling is right," I chuckled and squeezed his nipples harder yet, causing my new friend to clench his teeth. "Man, I would bet money that if I keep this up long enough these leathery feeling man tits of yours would spurt milk!"

"*What a twisted fucking thought,*" Daniel grunted and lowered himself to his feet as I twisted his nipples like they were two old fashioned television knobs. "Fuck man, if my tits squirted milk we could both make good money, me because they're *my* goddamned tits and you for discovering that my goddamned tits had milk in 'em! D-did you just call them man tits buddy?"

"Yeah, a guys nipples are his man tits, to call them just tits would imply woman's tits," I said right into his ear, the hardness in my pants caressing the back of Daniel's white boxer briefs as I teased and tormented him in a totally erotic fashion. "But I will say that there are some guys out there who would indeed call these jutted up nubbies of yours womanly, very womanly man tits indeed! Does it bother you that it's a guy doing this to you buddy boy?"

"I-I highly doubt that a woman would want to do this to my tits, sorry, *my man tits,* I doubt that a woman would want to do to my man tits what you're doing to them right now man," Daniel spouted breathlessly. "Al-although you never know right man? I mean, I got to tell you, I've dated some freaky women! M-maybe the next woman I date, I'll do this to her tits, yeah!! She'll fucking love it! Gods' man, *I need to cum*!! All this work you've been doing on my goddamned tits has really got me all worked up in my briefs! How about untying my hands and letting me use your facilities huh buddy?"

"Not for a while Daniel," I chuckled. "I want to see just how long I can keep you balanced but teetering on the edge..."

"OH FUCKER!!!" Daniel cried out as I again yanked his meaty nipples forward, stretching them out far. "Well man, I got to tell you, you really know how to fucking balance another dude. Y-you got me balanced and teetering real perilously here bud, but I feel like I'm about to fall off the edge! I feel as though I can fucking fill my damned boxer briefs to overflowing with my sexy mess right about now!"

"Now *that* would be something to see," I laughed, let go of his nipples and stepped in front of my very tortured, much worked up buddy. "If you could cum without touching your cock that truly would be a money maker I would think buddy! And not to mention how the girls would love using these nubs of yours as the control knobs for your cock, ha!"

Looking down I saw that Daniel's cock was truly hard and plumped up in his boxer briefs. He was gyrating real sexy in front of me, his nipples jutted up and real sore looking, but that was okay by me, seeing as those nubs of his had a lot more to endure before this day was out. His white boxer briefs showed a few stains where he had trickled and seeped some pre cum.

"Yeah, that's it Daniel, keep dancing for me," I teased him meanly as he hunched his upper body slightly forward. "Fuck man, I'm not even touching your man tits at the moment and you're dancing as if I was."

"FUCKER man, holy fucking fuck, look at me here, dancing for you to no music playing, fucking fuck fucker, so glad I'm so entertaining to you, but what a game this turned out to be huh?" Daniel asked me, sniveling as he spoke, glancing over at the couch where his discarded suit, tie and shoes were all strewn. "Wh-what do you suppose we should call this game man? Fuck, every game needs a name after all..."

Smiling fiendishly I said, "Let's call it Daniel's Man Tits" and then I reached forward and grabbed the guy's nipples from the front this time.

"OOOOOOOOOO FUCK, g-got my man tits in your clutches again buddy!!" the handsomer than handsome Asian guy ranted. "Fucker you are man, you got me feeling all sensitive and real fucking sexy here in my damned boxer briefs and dressy socks!"

Again he pulled himself to his socked toes as I played his nipples as if they were a musical instrument of some kind.

"C'mon bud, lets see you walk on your toes and play "Daniel's Man Tits" at the same time," I laughed, sounding campy and cruel as I tugged real hard at his nipples, yanking him forward with them. "It's kind of like walking and chewing gum at the same time wouldn't you say?"

"OHHHHHHHHH...wh-what a fucked up way to get a game named after me," Daniel said and plodded along slowly up on his toes. "N-now you really have me balanced real perilously buddy..."

"Just don't fall off the edge Daniel," I chuckled meanly and yanked harder yet on his man tits, forcing him along.

Holding his nipples extremely tight I pulled him forward a bit further and then using them something akin to a leash I turned him in a circular motion, causing him to face in the opposite direction of the room we were in, specifically my living room.

"AAAYYYYYYRRRR easy man, take it easy huh?" Daniel cried. "Th-

that's starting to hurt now…"

"And that's the key word here Daniel boy, *started,* we are just getting started here," I said as he now faced the opposite direction of my spacious living room.

"J-just getting started?" Daniel croaked. "Y-you have got to joking man! We, we, OHHHHRRRRRRR fucking triple fuck; but we've been at this for almost an hour now!"

"Yeah, and that's just the warm-up buddy," I said and this time pointed his nipples downward and rubbed the sides of them vigorously.

"OOOOOOOO man, if, *if* my damned man tits could talk they would ask what the fuck has gotten into me and what the fucking fuck they did to deserve this crazy treatment," Daniel sputtered, sweating a bit now, his goose bumped riddled, smooth fairly muscular body glistening real nice with a sheen of funky smelling man sweat.

"If your man tits could talk *then* we would really make some good money," I said and we both laughed.

I was glad that Daniel was being a good buddy about all this and taking all that I was dishing out on his nipples. I just hoped that he continued in that vain, seeing as I had lots more planned where the handsome Asian stud was concerned. Working his nipples was just the beginning of what I intended to be a long and grueling day for him. Working a handsome guy over in an erotic fashion is one of the things I love most. But if this got to a point where he demanded that I untie his hands and leave his nipples the fuck alone I would of course have to abide by his wishes. All of this was just in good sleazy fun after all and the guy was a buddy, granted, he was a new buddy, but all the same he was a great guy and I didn't want to lose his newly found friendship. And not to mention how I didn't want this to be the first and only time that I got to work him over in this very erotic fashion…

"C-c'mon man, I gotta cum, *at least give me that much buddy,*" Daniel pleaded as I pointed his nipples forward again and tweaked the life out of (into?) them. "Un-untie my hands and let me at my raging tube steak buddy. I mean, just look at that fucking goddamned tent in my sexy boxer briefs man! You gotta let me shoot a load man! I swear, when I'm done cooking my meat I'll let you re-tie my hands again, then you can play "Daniel's Man Tits" some more, *I fucking promise,* I just really, *really* gotta cum! I've never felt so worked up before in all my thirty something years! FUCK, I gotta cum so bad it hurts! Getting a poor fucking guy all worked up the way you have me now and then not letting him have a cum is really crappy bud! So please, just one cum huh?"

The way he was describing his feelings of lust was moving me like I cannot tell you. His pleading and the way he had concluded his tirade I was thinking that he thought he had convinced me to untie his hands…

"Nah, *nah,* not yet Daniel," I said and the look of misery that came over his face was totally sexy and actually heartbreaking in a way.

"OHHHHHHH man, what a shitty ass way to treat a guy you call a buddy, that's all I gotta say," Daniel huffed, swallowed real hard and endured the erotic torture as I squeezed the sides of his nipples, the tips of them jutting up real hardcore at that point.

"Man, look at this shit, your man tits are pulsing," I commented, grinning at the same time.

"Yeah? That is pretty amazing I will admit, seeing as those nubbies of mine never pulsed before! But seeing as they are pulsing let me tell you so is my cock man," Daniel pleaded. "Fucking fuck, wish I had some sweet pussy to bury my big hard guy into at least."

Then, to Daniel's surprise I again let go of his nipples, only this time I did not grab them again (at least not yet) this time I walked away from him, turned a corner in my apartment and proceeded into my kitchen.

"H-hey, what are you doing?" Daniel called out. "*Where the hell are you going?*"

Without thinking Daniel followed me into the kitchen, padding real swiftly on his socked feet...

"C'mon man, you can't just play a guys man tits that way and then leave him all worked up and scorching in his under shorts," Daniel said loudly as he headed toward my kitchen.

He entered the kitchen and as he did so I very quickly stepped in front of him and before he knew what had happened I snapped a pair of sharp teethed tit clamps onto his jutted up nipples, clamping them tightly at the sides.

"AYYYYYYYYYY ohhhhhhh h-holy fucking fucks, holy fucking shit," Daniel grunted, looking down in disbelief at his now clamped nipples, his jaw dropping in shock.

"Double and triple fuck at that Daniel?" I asked him teasingly. "Always adding up and counting your fucking fucks huh buddy?"

"Quadrupled fucking fucks is more like it man!!" the poor Asian guy moaned and slammed his back up against a wall in my kitchen. "OOOOOOOO GODS, y-you got my goddamned man tits in a pair of tit clamps! This ain't sweet buddy, *not sweet at all!*"

He clenched his teeth, squeezed his eyes shut a bit and did his best to endure the erotic agony... I was glad that having his hands tied behind him had been a prerequisite for the game of "Daniel's Man Tits" that I had invented.

"Pl-please man, how much more of "Daniel's Man Tits" are we going to play here?" he asked me, sounding desperate by then.

"Well, seeing as we both left our offices after lunch today and took the rest of the day off I would say we can play till our hearts are content," I laughed and grabbed the thin chain that was attached to the tit clamps. "Maybe after the game is over I'll order some dinner and beer sent in and we can talk about what a great time we had here today, but for the moment I say, onward with the game."

"Yeah, a real great fucking time, fucking fucks man!" Daniel said sarcastically. "God, the fucking pressure on my man tits is awful bud..."

I gave the chain attached to the tit clamps a few twists around my fingers and yanked it gently forward. Daniel's nipples burned and he screeched through his clenched teeth.

"F-F-FUCKER, what a way to dress up a poor sap's man tits," Daniel cried.

"And the clamps are just the first item of attire that will adorn those luscious nips of yours buddy," I chortled meanly and pulled a bit more on the chain.

"OOOOOOOO fuck man, what the hell am I in for here?" Daniel garbled miserably and pressed his back against the wall, looking as though he wanted to somehow escape from me through that wall.

I looked down at his boxer briefs and saw that he had really dribbled a goodly amount of pre cum at that point. At least my new buddy was enjoying all this in a masochistic sort of way...

Then, I let go of the chain attached to the tit clamps, reached into my pocket and brought out a length of rope, squatted in front of Daniel and proceeded to tie his socked feet together in a criss-cross type of fashion.

"H-hey, what are you doing now man?" Daniel asked breathlessly. "GOD almighty, but you really have put the hurt on my poor man tits now bud!!"

"What does it look like I'm doing Daniel?" I asked him and snapped the elastic in his socks against his calves after I was done tying his feet.

"Fucking fucks, it looks like you tied up my goddamned feet! What's the point of all this man?" Daniel squawked as I stood up in front of him, grabbed the chain attached to the tit clamps and gave it a fast tug, sending searing and burning sensations through Daniel's very being.

"AAAYYYYYYYY, SHHHIITTTT!!!" the handsome Asian guy reeled.

I let go of the chain and opened a drawer in my utensil cabinet. I took out four very small egg shaped weights, each of them hooked onto a thin metal chain.

"OH MAN, OH NO," Daniel said after swallowing another big gulp. "Oh come on, I really fucking hope you're not going to do what I think you're going to do, and FUCKING FUCKS FUCKER!"

"These weights weigh about a quarter of a pound each buddy," I said, stepping in front of Daniel and holding up the egg shaped weights. "I'm going to hang them one by one on that chain on your tit clamps."

Poor Daniel pursed his lips together, heaved himself up to his toes and sheer agony showed on his handsome face.

"I gotta cum," he squeaked. "Please man, I'm fucking begging you now, at least give me one goddamned fucking fucked cum..."

Chuckling meanly I responded to Daniel's request by hanging the first of the four metal egg shaped weights on the chain on his tit clamps, dangling it dead center.

"OOOHHHHHRRRR," Daniel panted and heaved himself up higher on his socked toes, pressing his back against the wall, his chest jutted out real nice and invitingly.

"Ready for the second one buddy?" I asked him.

He simply nodded his head and involuntarily thrust his crotch forward; fucking the air it seemed...

I hung the second weight on the left-most end of the chain on his tit clamps.

"OH MAN, oh fuck, oh fucking totally fucks," Daniel seethed, his lips trembling and spittle flying from the sides of his mouth.

The weight in the center of his tit clamp chain pulled down on both of his nipples simultaneously while the one on the left side added agony to his left nipple.

"Now for the right side buddy," I said gleefully, holding up the third weight, swinging it on its chain, taunting the guy even before I set it on the tit clamp chain.

"OOOOOHHHHHH!!!" Daniel cried and now the weights combined were really yanking the poor Wall Street guy's nipples in all directions.

I held up the fourth and final egg shaped weight and set it dangling alongside the other weight that was hanging in the center of Daniel's tit clamp chain.

"There we go, look at that, just look at that shit man, you've got a pound's worth of weights on you along with the tit clamps and their chain," I said, sounding like a proud parent.

"OHHHHHH yeah, fucking bully for me huh?" Daniel asked and un-pursed his lips clenched his pearly white teeth and gyrated again real sexily for me on his socked toes. "FUCKING FUCKS, what an experience, *what a day I'm having!!*"

As the tit clamps hugged and squeezed and bit down on the sides of Daniel's beefy nubbins I marveled at the sight of his nipple tips as they pro-truded large and real pointy through the front section of the clamps. Smiling meanly I took full advantage of that by pressing the pads of my thumbs against the very tips of the guy's nipples.

"AAAHHHHHHHHHH," Daniel heaved still with his teeth clenched. "I just don't get it man, torturing a guy's nipples are real fucked up if you ask me..."

"Totally fucking fucked up huh Daniel?" I asked him and we both laughed as I teased him about the way he swore. "But I beg to disagree, seeing as I think that working a guy's nipples over is great fun. I mean, come on buddy, we're having a great fucking time here today!"

I laughed and yanked the weighted chain on Daniel's nipples slightly forward, getting another good squeal of erotic agony out of him...

"FUCK man, fucking fucks, untie me and let me have one goddamned cum," the young executive pleaded yet again as he pressed himself up against the wall on his tied up socked feet, still balanced up on his toes.

"Nah, like I said, I think you're enjoying this too much Daniel," I replied. "Letting you cum would only put an end to the fun don't you think?"

"Maybe not," the guy croaked and as I looked him over I realized that maybe, somehow, I was falling for this newfound buddy of mine.

Holding the weighted tit clamp chain in my hand I forced the guy to turn himself around on his criss cross tied up socked feet till he was facing the wall, his back to me, giving me a real nice view of his coconut shaped ass globes in his tight sweaty boxer briefs. Moving on his tied up feet was no easy chore for the poor guy but being on his toes helped a bit... And being that I had chosen to tie his feet in a criss cross fashion did allow him some mobility. He was meanly hobbled but he could walk slowly, *very slowly* if I wanted him to. And that seemed to be key here, if I wanted him to, I had the guy in such a way that he had to do anything that *I wanted him to.*

"Wh-what's the point of all this buddy?" Daniel murmured breathlessly, lowered himself to his feet and I sat down at the kitchen table and simply took in the glorious sight of him.

He was beyond sexy, beyond beautiful, and to think that I had met him on the train only less than a month ago at this point. Less than a month now that we had become buddies and luck had really smiled upon me in finding someone so open minded and willing to play my sadistically campy games... I propped my feet up on the table and drank him in, the sight of him, the allure of him, I breathed in the sweaty sexy scent of him, and the overwhelming beauty of him... Trust me on this, the handsome Asian Wall Street stud was not the only one who was plumped up and throbbing in his under shorts at that moment...

"I'll let you stand there and enjoy the pressure on your man tits for fifteen minutes buddy," I said to him. "Then after that we'll resume the game of "Daniel's Man Tits."

"OOOHHHRRRRRR fucking fuck," Daniel squealed and thrust the hardness in his boxer briefs toward the wall he was facing, making his succulent looking ass globes twitch real sexily. "FUCKING fifteen minutes will seem like an eternity for me buddy..."

"Well, from what I read you shouldn't keep a guy's nipples clamped for more than that time," I replied.

"FUCKING FUCKS, you mean to say that you've read up on this shit?" Daniel chirped. "There are books out there on cooking a poor slob's man tits???"

"Yeah, let those man tits of yours really cook for me buddy," I said fiendishly. "I got more plans for them coming up..."

From the side I saw how Daniel's face scrunched up, he clenched his teeth and murmured the words "AAAAYYYYY GOD," in a very high pitched tone of voice...

"Yeah, lots more on the horizon for you and your man tits Daniel boy," I laughed.

My mind wandered to how Daniel and I had first met on a train platform when headed to our jobs in Manhattan...

It was a Monday morning like any other; I had gotten to the Bay Parkway train station (in Brooklyn) exactly ten minutes before my train was scheduled to arrive. I work very early hours at my office job as an inventory supervisor so I always catch the five fifteen AM train, which gets me to my job a half hour before I have to start work. I like those ten minutes on the train station to catch up on whatever current book I am presently reading and to sip my usual cup of coffee that I get at the Dunkin' Donuts which is located just downstairs from the train station. While I stood there reading my book and sipping my coffee that Monday morning I saw the usual crowd of commuters. The guy named Paul who is a religious fanatic and always reading some literature on how to be a better catholic. The young lady who is now thin as a rail but used to weigh at least three hundred pounds, I wonder which diet she used. She could be an inspiration to so many people. The guy named Bill who always eats an apple while waiting for the train and so many of the usual nameless faces that I see every morning, but at that time of the day very few suits and ties on the train. Although my job is an office type of job my company relaxed our dress code years back so like any other day I stood waiting for the train clad in khakis, polo collared shirt and slip-on loafers with black socks, my usual. While I waited for the train I watched the blue collar construction workers standing at their usual spots on the platform while waiting for the train to arrive. The train platform is a bit territorial, with everyone standing in the same spot every morning until the train got there. On that particular Monday morning was when I first saw Daniel, although of course upon first seeing him I didn't know his name. He was clad in a navy blue suit, a white shirt, a light blue taffeta tie and lace-up well shined wingtip shoes. He ascended the stairs of the train station and walked to where I usually stand on the platform after I have finished my coffee. He strode past me and the other people on the platform with a swagger of confidence in his step. He was about five feet ten inches tall with black silky hair and beautiful Asian looking eyes. I guessed that he was Chinese and I guessed his age to be in the mid to upper thirties. I wondered what kind of a job a suit and tie guy could possibly have that he needed to be at work so early in the morning. He carried with him a bottle of Volvic brand mineral water and he sipped it vigorously while waiting for the train. The way the clear plastic bottle was beaded with perspiration I guessed that the water was ice cold, which was good, seeing as it was pretty hot and humid that summer morning, the humidity being what would cause our first chat to happen a few days later. The first few times I saw Daniel on the train we didn't speak to each other, but we did steal glances at each other. I finished my coffee, dropped the empty plastic cup in a trash receptacle and walked down to the front end of the platform, right where Daniel was standing and stood a few feet away from him. He was fiddling with the knot in his tie, sweating in the early morning heat and humidity and a few moments later the "D" train barreled into the station. I and all the other passengers boarded the train and sat down in our usual seats. (I was sure that the handsome Asian suit and tie guy was relieved to sit in the cold air conditioned train.) Like the train platform the train itself is territorial, with commuters sitting in or as near to the same seat as possible every day. As luck would have it Daniel sat down directly across from me and the first thing he did was to put his mineral water bottle down on the seat next to him for a moment while he reached down to pull his socks up. As a foot fetishist (among other fetishes) I always found that to be very erotic for some reason, to see a young handsome guy pull his thin dress socks up right after sitting down. Daniel was wearing thin navy blue dress socks that climbed as high as his calves. (Actually they could be the same socks he was wearing the day we played the new game called "Daniel's Man Tits.") And Daniel wasn't the type of guy who pulled his socks up while gripping the tops of them around his suit pants, no way; Daniel hiked up his socks by reaching under his suit pants, showing off some leg skin and then pulling up those fallen socks. I have to say that when it comes to handsome Asian guys I have always, for some reason enjoyed tickle torturing them. There is something so hot and amusing about hearing a studly Asian guy laugh his head off and sweat while his bare feet are tickled. I guessed Daniel's feet to be around the same size as mine, nine, or perhaps a tad larger, judging from the way his feet filled his shoes. When I saw that he favored thin nylon dress socks the desire to tickle torture the soft bottoms of those feet while he had his socks on (and then off of course) filled my head with gleeful visions. At that moment I didn't for a second entertain thoughts of torturing the guy's nipples, no, that came a bit later. But I would tickle him as well, and spank him, although those stories are for later. While we rode the train I concentrated on the current book I was reading. Daniel disembarked the train at Pacific Street, a pretty normal station for lots of commuters to make connections to local trains, downtown trains and the Long Island Railroad. I wondered if I would see the handsome Asian guy again or if perhaps like so many other people on the trains he was someone I would see only that once. I concentrated on my book for the remainder of my ride to my stop, which would be West Fourth Street in Manhattan.

The next day Daniel was there again, this time clad in a black suit and wearing a lightweight overcoat and carrying an umbrella, seeing as it was raining that morning. Once again he strode past me, walking with that air of confidence about himself that I had noticed the day before. When the train arrived we again sat in the same seats, him taking the seat directly across from me. Like the day before the first thing he did was to reach down and pull his socks up. That day he was wearing black nylon dress socks and like his navy blue socks they climbed as far as his calves. Through the years I have noticed this phenomenon so much that it's uncanny, how when a suit guy sits down the first thing he does is to reach down to pull his thin dress socks up. Even in meetings they do this, it's kind of a ritual I think. And even if their socks are not fallen that far most suit guys will take a moment to hike those stinkers up when they sit down. I think that the manufacturers of calf length dress socks make them with the elastic real thin on purpose, just so the poor guy wearing them will be forced to pull his socks up every time he sits down, that's my theory at least. There's some kind of sadism in that although, granted, not a hardcore one. The thought that went through my head as Daniel pulled up his black socks that day was of his navy blue socks from the day before more than likely all crumpled and bunched up, moist, and sitting in a hamper or laundry bag somewhere waiting for the laundry day, sleazy thoughts indeed. Once again while riding the train Daniel and I stole glances at each other. A few times he stretched his legs out in front of himself and crossed his sexy looking feet at the ankles. His socks were thin enough that I could see the outline of his ankles under them... It was the third time that I saw Daniel that we would begin speaking with each other and a friendship would be born...

The next day I did not see Daniel on the train, seeing as I took the train that came directly after the one that I usually take. I don't recall why I ran a tad late that morning but it really was no big deal, seeing as I still got to work on time. The next day it was miserably hot and very humid. New York City was having one of the worst summers that I could ever remember. I was standing at my usual spot in the front section of the train platform when Daniel strode up the stairs, just as the train was pulling into the station. As on the last two times I had seen the handsome Asian guy we sat directly across from each other. On this day he was wearing a pinstriped navy blue suit with a burgundy silk tie, looking real suave. As he sat down the first thing he did this time, rather than reach down to pull his socks up was to pull his shirt collar away from his neck to alleviate some of the way he was sweating under there. (Nothing is worse for a suit guy on a hot summer day than to be sweating under his shirt and tie collar.) As we looked at each other as he tugged at his shirt collar I saw my opportunity and went for it. I had to get him talking to me if I wanted to know this handsome guy.

"It must be awful to have to wear a suit and tie in this weather," I said to him as he straightened his tie.

"Yeah, the humidity makes it real uncomfortable for me, but this is a summer suit so it's not all that bad," he said and let go of his tie, grabbed his jacket lapels and waved them a bit, trying to cool off his upper body as well.

As he waved his lapels was when I was treated to the sight of his big pointy nipples pressed against his white dress shirt. I quickly stifled a gulp at the sight of those over-sized man nipples and politely told him how my company used to require us to wear a suit and tie everyday as well, but about three years ago upper management had let all us managers and supervisors vote on a relaxed dress code.

"Obviously we all voted in favor of it," I said with a smile as the handsome Asian guy settled comfortably in his seat, not having taken a moment to pull his socks up that day...

"You're lucky that your company did that," he said to me, smiling across at me as he spoke.

"Yeah, it also saves me a lot of money on dry cleaning bills," I said and we both laughed.

At that point he settled his head back and I quickly immersed myself in my book...

As we rode the train I stole glances down at the guy's feet and saw that his socks were a bit slouched down around his calves, real sexy looking navy blue nylon socks with wide ribs in them, definitely not the same navy blue socks that he'd had on the first day I had seen him. Between his very sexy looking feet and those nipples of his the way they pressed against his dress shirt had my mind awhirl with very nasty and very erotic ideas... I imagined that he had to be wearing a white tee shirt under his white dress shirt and if his nipples pressed against both those shirts and were accented in such an obvious fashion they definitely had to be of the oversized nubs that so few men are blessed with...

The next day when I walked to the front end of the train platform Daniel was there before me, which was sort of unusual seeing as I always got there first since I had first seen him. As I strode up next to him he smiled at me and said "Good morning."

"Good morning," I replied as he held his hand out.

I shook his hand and took note of the fact that his palm was kind of cold and moist. In his other hand was his ever-present bottle of Volvic mineral water.

"It's kind of humid again today," he said as he let go of my hand.

"Yeah, it sure is," I replied.

"My name is Daniel," he said to me.

I told him my name was Christopher and that it was very nice to meet him. He replied by saying that it was nice to meet me as well. When the train arrived we sat next to each other this morning rather than across from each other.

"Would you mind holding my water a moment?" he asked me and handed me his bottle of mineral water. "I need to pull my socks up."

"Sure," I said through trembling lips and watched as he pulled his black socks up to his calves, me glorying in seeing that patch of skin on his calf for that moment.

"I honestly think that someday someone is going to invent a pair of socks that don't fall down on us poor guys," Daniel chuckled, looking at me as he sipped his water after I had handed him back his bottle.

"Yeah, I totally agree," I said, not believing what we were talking about.

"I notice that you don't pull your socks up every morning like I have to," he laughed, sounding a bit self conscious.

"I wear OTC socks; that means over the calf," I replied. "They don't seem to fall down as much as calf length socks do."

"Hmm, maybe I should invest in some of those huh?" the guy mused.

"Yeah, maybe you should," I said agreeably.

Daniel then told me that he worked for a bank on Wall Street and the reason that he had to be in so early everyday was that he was a security supervisor and that it was his job to open certain highly secured offices before the bank personnel arrived. I told him that I worked as an inventory control supervisor for a jewelry company and that as the supervisor I also had to be in early before other personnel. The next time Daniel and I saw each other on the train we talked a lot about all the celebrity gossip that was in the news lately. The Kobe Bryant trial, the upcoming Michael Jackson trial, the Martha Stewart sentencing and other very important issues. While Chatting with Daniel I didn't get to read too much but I did get to take in the sight of his beautiful brown eyes while we talked and I also told him how I had recently become a published author. He seemed genuinely impressed by that and asked if writing was something I did for relaxation or because it was challenging or both. I told him that I did it for both reasons. I followed that up by asking him what he did for relaxation and for something challenging. He smiled and said that he liked playing card games, old fashioned Chess and even up to date video games. I saw my next opportunity and did not let it get away. Since becoming a published author I have learned never to let a good opportunity pass me by... I asked Daniel if he would like to meet for a beer some time after work and perhaps we could set up a card game date. I told him that I liked a challenging old fashioned card game of "War" with nasty but fun consequences for the loser of the game.

"Now that sounds like it could be really interesting and something that I can really sink my teeth into," Daniel said, looking at me quizzically. "I never played a card game like that before..."

We set up a night after work where we would meet for a couple of beers so we could get to know each other a bit more and then while having the beers we set up a day when we would both leave work early and head to my place for a card game of "War." Daniel seemed really confident in the fact that he was going to win the game, citing how he planned to make me, as the loser, really pay. Chuckling a bit I asked him what he planned to do to me if I lost the game. He said that he planned on putting me through a heavy-duty regiment of sit-ups, push-ups, and other drawn out sessions of backbreaking exercises. He told me how his dad had been in the army years ago and had told him all about basic training and the horrendous exercise routines that all soldiers are put through. Daniel said how he always wanted an excuse to put someone through a real hardcore exercise routine. When I asked him if he wanted to hear what I had planned for him if he lost the game the handsome Asian stud sipped his beer and said that there was no need for me to tell him because he did not plan on losing the game. Smiling sadistically he leaned back in his seat in the booth we were sitting in and spread his long arms out a bit. He had taken off his suit jacket before we sat down so when he spread his arms out those bulbous nipples of his pressed against his white dress shirt. I hungrily drank in the sight of them and took a hefty swig of my beer...

The Day of the Card Game...

"God damn it, God damn it and fucking fuck," Daniel said as he threw down his last card, having lost the game of "War" inside of only an hour and a half.

It was a Friday afternoon. We had decided on a Friday for the card game, Daniel citing how I would need the weekend to rest up after all the push-ups and sit-ups he intended to force me through once I had lost the card game. We both left our offices at lunch time that day and met at my apartment for the agreed upon game. After a light lunch we began the card game, me allowing Daniel to deal the cards. We sat across from each other at a card table that I had set up in my air conditioned living room. Daniel got comfortable by shucking off his suit jacket, loosening his tie, rolling up his sleeves, and unbuttoning the topmost button of his white dress shirt. When he asked if it would be okay if he took his shoes off I stifled another gulp and told him that it would be fine, adding how my floors were very clean and that his socks would not get dusty at all. Smiling sadistically as he sat across from me at the card table he unlaced his wingtips and got them off his feet.

"Thanks man, I appreciate that," Daniel said. "I always get my shoes off first thing when I get home from work. Now, let's play cards buddy, and I really hope you're in good shape for when I win this little contest..."

And so we played the old fashioned card game called "War."

The rules of the game of "War" are very simple actually. You play by throwing down a card each. The player with the higher value card wins the card toss by taking both cards from the table. If both players throw down a same valued card then a "War" has occurred. When that happens each player must throw down three cards, face down and then toss out one more card each, face up. Which ever player has the higher value card that time wins the first hand that caused the "War", plus they win the cards that were thrown down face down and they win the new cards that they just threw out face up, ending the "War." This happened three times during my card game with Daniel and he lost all three "Wars." At the end of the game the player who achieves the entire deck of cards wins the game. While he played I noticed that he wiggled his toes under his thin socks and pressed his toes against the floor as well, a definite nervous habit I supposed.

"I can't believe I lost that goddamned game," the handsome Asian stud said miserably, leaning back in his chair as I held the entire deck of cards in hand, me being the winner. "I was so sure I had it in the bag!"

"Well, it looks to me my new buddy that what's now in the bag is you," I laughed. "Are you still ready to adhere to the rules of our game?"

"Sure thing man, I am a man of my word, and trust me on this I can do endless fucking push-ups and sit-ups," Daniel said, practically sneering at me.

"Well, push-ups and sit-ups really aren't what I had in mind for you buddy," I said with a sly looking grin on my face.

"Wh-what do you have in mind for me then?" Daniel asked, the sneer slowly leaving his face and being replaced with what looked like some kind of anxious fear.

With that sly looking grin still on my face I folded my arms, leaned back in my chair and said, "Seeing as you just said that you're a man of your word lets start with you getting a bit more comfortable shall we?"

"Sure, I guess," Daniel replied, sounding perplexed.

"Lets pretend we're at the doctor's office and you're about to have a procedure of some kind okay?" I asked him. "What's usually the first thing that you have done in a doctor's office buddy?"

"I, uh, I get weighed usually," Daniel said, obviously wondering where the hell this was going.

"Before that, what happens?" I asked him, starting to sound impatient.

"Well, usually I sit in the waiting room for about a half hour and then the nurse calls me to the examination room where I wait another ten minutes or so for the doctor to get there and..." Daniel gibber jabbered.

"Okay, in between having the nurse call you in and waiting for the doctor to come to the examination room, what happens?" I asked him, sounding very impatient now.

"Well, I usually strip out of my clothes down to my underpants and socks and..." Daniel began and I held up a hand, halting him in mid sentence.

"That's it, you strip down to your underpants and socks," I repeated him.

"*Holy fucking fucks, you want me to strip down right here for you???*"

Daniel squawked in a high pitched tone of voice. "Fucking fuck, you're joking right? Strip down to my goddamned boxer briefs and sexy socks like some sexy male stripper or something?"

"You did say that you're a man of your word Daniel, and you did agree to the rules of the game," I reminded my new buddy as he sat there nervously tugging on his necktie, a look of total dismay etched on his exotically handsome face. "But if you want to back out of it at this point I understand and..."

"Let me ask you this Christopher," Daniel said, him cutting me off in mid sentence now, that look of disbelief on his face growing more intense. "If I had won, would you have agreed to all the push-ups, sit-ups and other intense exercises I was going to put you through?"

"YES!" I replied, my eyes open wide.

"I was planning on working you over in a gym, you would have agreed to that? You would have come with me to the Bally's over here on Nineteenth Avenue and taken all that I would have dished out on you?" Daniel seethed, looking intently at me from across the table.

"YES!" I replied again, my eyes opened wider now.

"And in front of all the people there you would have allowed me to humiliate you that way?" he asked, sounding unsure of himself.

"YES!" I replied again.

"Why man? Why would you have agreed to all that?" Daniel asked me, seeming to be looking for a way out of this mess that he had gotten himself into, sweating in his socks as I would call it.

"Because like you I'm a man of my word," I began in reply. "And I would have agreed to it because I find that I like you a lot and I like being your friend..."

Okay man, *okay,*" Daniel said, standing up and undoing the knot in his necktie. "But please, please man, tell me at least this much, once I'm stripped down to my boxer briefs and socks what are you planning on doing to me then?"

"That is still not for you to know buddy," I laughed meanly, trying to sound as sadistic as possible. "Let's just take one thing at a time shall we?"

"Okay man, just that I really don't have a sweet feeling about all this," Daniel said as he slid his tie off his shirt and dropped it on the couch. "I am definitely not getting a sweet feeling about all this..."

I watched as my buddy unbuttoned his crisp white dress shirt, shucked it off and I saw how his luscious nipples were pressed hard against the white tee shirt he was wearing under his dress shirt. I had been right; his nipples appeared to be of the very over-sized sort that so many men are not blessed with. Daniel on the other hand seemed to be very, very blessed in that area. He placed his dress shirt on the couch where he had put his tie and then shucked off his tee shirt.

"Enjoying yourself so far?" he asked me, looking at me straight ahead, his semi muscular and smooth chest staring me in the face.

His nipples were as pointy as two pencil erasers and just as pink buds. If the guy didn't know it, it amazed me, that his nipples needed some real passionate attention.

"Oh yes, I'm having a great time," I replied, still seated as my new buddy slowly stripped down for me. "And so will you once I get going on you..."

"Yeah, that's what the fucking fuck I'm afraid of," the handsome Asian stud said and undid his belt buckle followed by unbuttoning his suit trousers.

I chuckled a bit meanly as the guy's suit trousers fell down around his ankles. There's something so comical about how most guys look when they are standing with their pants down around their ankles. The sight of the guy with his pants down around his ankles, his socks peeking up out of the pants, his underpants totally on display, a possible erection tenting said underpants, all of it combined is just too humiliating for the poor guy and just too funny for anyone lucky enough to be seeing it...

A few moments later I got up and out of my chair, and stepped over to my buddy as he now stood there clad in just a pair of the sexiest looking white boxer briefs I had ever seen and his navy blue nylon dress socks. A look of utter and total humiliation was all over his handsome face... His cock was semi hard in his boxer briefs already. (It always amazes me how when a guy is feeling fear filled, humiliated, or totally embarrassed for whatever the fuck the reason most of them get totally hard in their underpants. You would think that that cock would shrivel up, but it does seem that most guys out there get off on this kind of being worked over.) Once I got started on Daniel's over-sized man tits that erection of his would be demanding attention...

"Okay man, you satisfied now?" Daniel asked as I drank in the sight of him. "Just like at the doctor's office..."

"Yeah, but with only one difference that I'm about to put on you" I said, reaching into my deep pants pocket.

"What's that buddy?" Daniel asked me, sounding very apprehensive now, obviously feeling very vulnerable as well.

When I brought out the long length of rope from my pocket Daniel's eyes opened wide in shock and his jaw seemed to drop to the floor.

"H-holy fucking fucks, you, you're planning to tie me the fuck up man?" he asked, taking a few involuntarily steps back away from me on his socked feet. "Come on man, you won the game, you got me to strip for you, tying me up is a horse of a totally different goddamned color here buddy!"

"Spoken and said like a true Wall Street bull," I commented slyly and Daniel then saw how I was looking hungrily at his pink fleshy nipples.

At the moment his nipples were real squishy and squashy looking. Once I got started tweaking and squeezing and really working on them they would be as hard and as pointy as two bullets.

"I could have had you strip totally raw for me buddy," I said, holding up the rope. "But I did give you breaks by letting you keep your underpants and socks on..."

"Jeez, some break," Daniel said miserably and his cock engorged to a bit more than semi hard in his boxer briefs.

"So, are you still going to abide by the rules of our game?" I asked him.

"OH fucking fuck, *fuck me,*" Daniel sputtered, pressed his wrists together and held them up in front of his chest. "Go ahead man, do your worst. But I'll tell you, next time we play cards I WILL WIN!"

I was so glad to hear him say that there would be a next time. I smiled and said, "Hands behind you buddy boy..."

His face sank a bit more but again he did as he was told. He took short sounding miserable breaths as I stood behind him roping his crossed wrists behind his back.

"So tell me something here buddy, what was the most kinky thing that a date ever did to you in the bedroom arena?" I asked Daniel as I secured his wrists with double knots each time I looped more rope around and around and around his wrists.

"Well, some feisty chick I dated once or twice asked me if I liked three-somes, and she invited two girlfriends of hers over and those three horned up bitches took turns sucking my cock," Daniel said, sounding real proud of himself. "Fucking fuck man, I purposely took forever to shoot my load that time. I made those bitches really work for my cream soup you know?"

"Yeah, that does sound really intense," I said, finishing tying his hands, but not moving from where I was standing behind him.

The sight of his ass globes was like two coconut shaped melons in his sexy white cotton boxer briefs... When I accidentally on purpose glided a hand over his tight butt cheeks he didn't say one word of protest. So far I was sailing on calm seas it seemed...

"And you fucking fucked all three of those bitches Daniel?" I asked him and swatted his ass cheeks with the back of my hand. "You bad boy, did you fucking fuck all three of them?"

I swatted his ass again...

Daniel simply grinned and said, "Like I said, I really made those bitches work for my soup buddy!"

"Have you ever had a date do this to you?" I asked him and then reached my arms around him from behind, hugged him against me as I crossed my arms over his upper torso and with my thumbs and first two fingers of each hand I grabbed each of his plump nipples, squeezing down hard.

"HUUUUHHHHHH!!!" the handsome Asian stud gasped at the sud-denness of his nipples being grabbed that way.

I rubbed the sides of his nipples in a vigorous fashion, really getting the guy started on his sexy dance for me.

"HUUUUUHHHHH, n-no man, *no date ever squeezed my nipples,"* Daniel panted. *"Holy fucking shit here!!"*

His nipples felt real sweet and all rubbery in my fingers as I squeezed and mashed them up to an erect and hard state...

"I didn't think so, not too many women know how a guy's nipples can be real sensitive and sexy feeling," I commented, increasing the pressure as I worked and worked his nubs.

"F-fucking fuck, *I* didn't know just how sensitive and sexy my god-damned nipples could feel buddy," Daniel grunted and swayed on his socked feet in front of me, me loving the way his sexy butt rubbed against my crotch as I worked and worked his nipples, just getting started actually. "H-holy fucking fucks man, wh-what are you doing to me here?"

"Just having some mean and sleazy fun with you buddy," I replied. "The first time I saw you air out your suit jacket on the train I couldn't help but notice the way your nips were pressed against your dress shirt. It made me really want to get at them, and other parts of you as well, but we'll get to all that later on..."

"Ah, so now the puzzle pieces start falling into place," Daniel laughed, clenched his teeth and endured the ecstasy I was forcing on him. "Fuck, fucking fuck, and double fucks, looks like my nips have become the main attraction here, serves me right for being cursed with such big fucking tits!! (GASP)

"I would call it blessed is more like it buddy," I laughed also, squeezing the sides of his nipples tighter and tighter as the tips of them bubbled up and got hard.

"EEEEEEEHHHHHRRRRR GOD OF GODS!" Daniel seethed through clenched teeth.

I squeezed them tighter yet...

"So, so you noticed the way my big ol' tits pressed against my shirt while we were on the train huh?" Daniel squeaked, gyrating now as I squeezed and teased the fuck out of his man tits, loving the way they seemed to be swelling up between my fingers with each passing second. "That makes me wonder what other parts of me you're planning on getting at, as you so pointed out, *buddy!"*

"Oh, not to worry Daniel, all in good time, all in very good time you will find out," I said chidingly and then tweaked the very tips of his nipples, whirling my fingers over and over and over them. "I see this as good luck Daniel, sort of like its good luck to find a four leafed clover or the way its good luck to dream of a blue cross. I think its good luck to squeeze a nice pair of nipples."

"OH GAWD MAN," Daniel seethed in his part Asian, part New York sounding accent.

With my fingers whirling over Daniel's nipple tips the guy was obviously in a sort of orbit.

"F-fuck man, it feels like you have bionic fingers or something," the Asian stud said breathlessly and at that point his cock was totally erect and tenting his boxer briefs...

So that's how I met Daniel and how I managed to coax the handsome Asian guy into the position he was presently in. What he didn't know at the time that I was working his nipples was that I also had two other tribulations to put him through before the day was over. And seeing as it was only the early afternoon we had plenty of time...

My mind returned to the present moment as I sat glorying in the sight of Daniel standing with his back to me in my kitchen. He was seething and grunting as the tit clamps and the weights I had hung on them tortured him endlessly, tormented him actually in a twisted mixture of pain and seventh heaven.

"So, tell me, are you feeling good buddy?" I asked him about fifteen minutes later, stepping over to him and grabbing his upper arm in my hand as he faced the wall.

"Y-you've asked me that so many damned times now that I think I've lost count," Daniel seethed through clenched teeth, glancing at me and then facing the wall again. "Fucking fucks man; my poor man tits feel like they're on fire and just about ready to explode, and not to mention my seven and a half inch guy too!"

"Ah, so you're a man who measures his manhood and his ecstatic agony by the inch huh Daniel?" I teased him and squeezed his arm tighter. "Okay, once your man tits are really cooked up for me I'll take the tit clamps off them and that should be pretty soon now."

"Th-thank you man, *thank you,*" Daniel spouted, his lips trembling as he spoke.

"Okay, back around and facing me again buddy," I said, gripping his arm tighter and moving him around on his tied up socked feet.

"H-holy fucks man, if you planned on spinning me like a goddamned top why did you tie up my feet?" Daniel ranted, hefted himself again to his toes and almost like a ballet dancer balanced himself and turned facing me as I held his arm tight, keeping him well balanced.

Once he was facing me he leaned himself up against the wall, heaved his crotch forward and his erection was enormous by then. The tit clamps and the weights dangling on them looked torturous to epic proportions by then. The look of sensual agony in his beautiful eyes was heartbreaking and it nearly drove me over the edge. Drinking in the sight of him in his erotic agony I boldly reached forward and with my fingers and thumb I caressed his bulging and chock filled balls in his sexy boxer briefs. The way his underpants were all moist and sweaty made a nice outline of his juicy balls let me tell you. They looked like they were swollen to the size of two kiwis in his sexy underpants. He didn't seem to mind that I was handling his precious family jewels at the moment. I really expected him to tell me to get my hands off his most private of areas. They felt totally hard and tight in his boxer briefs those luscious testicles of his. I rolled them a bit in my fingers. They were obviously beyond chock filled with his Asian man juices.

"OHHHHHH GAWD man, y-you're making more chills eat me up here doing that to my nuts," Daniel reeled and danced real sexy for me against the wall, standing flat on his tied up feet again.

If he didn't mind me playing with his balls I was sure that he would not mind what I was about to do to him next, or perhaps he would mind.

"Fuck man, one cum, one goddamned cum, please man, *please*," Daniel begged and all I did was chuckle as I stopped toying with his balls. "FUCKING FUCKS, I should never have let you get my hands tied behind me man…"

"Okay buddy, I think your man tits are cooked and ready at this point," I said and took the tit clamps along with the weights hanging on the chain of them off the guy's nipples at that point.

"AAAAYYYYYYYYYRRRR GOD!!" Daniel screamed as the blood rushed back into his nipples at what had to have felt like a thousand miles per hour.

"Yeah, I know, it feels worse now that the clamps are off your man tits huh?" I asked him meanly.

"OHHHHHHHRRRR fucking fucks, totally fucked up fucking fucks!!" Daniel squealed and squalled, his eyes squeezed shut, his teeth clenched and his man tits all jutted up and ready for what I had in mind next. "God man, I didn't realize how awful it would feel once you took those devices from hell off me, SSSHHHHIIIIITTTT"

I stepped in real close to him, reached around his lower body, grabbed his coconut shaped ass globes, squeezed them tight and leaned down.

"Wh-what now buddy? What the fucking fuck now???" Daniel asked me as I hefted him a bit upward by holding real tight to his silky and succulent feeling ass cheeks.

I leaned down and with my tongue out slurped one of his jutted up man tits into my mouth…

"OHHHHHHHHH fuck, holy fuck, goddamned fuck," Daniel snorted, looking down at the top of my head, disbelief showing in his beautiful eyes as I sucked, chewed, and slurped his jutted up nipple in my mouth, squeezing his delectable ass globes at the same time. "OH GAWD, it must be lunch time 'cause you're eating my man tit!!"

His nipple felt so hard and durable in my mouth and when I slid the tip of my tongue over the very tip of it Daniel swayed and rocked in my tight grasp. I clenched his ass cheeks tighter and yanked him up higher onto his toes. His nipple in my mouth was jutted up like a pencil eraser and the way Daniel was swaying in my grasp and swooning was sheer ecstasy, for both of us… I felt his cum oozing erection gliding back and forth over my crotch area as I sucked and slurped at his man tit in my mouth.

"OOOOOOHHHHHH fuck, what a buddy you are Christopher, fucking best buddy I've ever met," Daniel spouted breathlessly. "Fucking fuck, stripping me was a bit embarrassing but I can deal with that buddy, tying my hands, well, that was kind of shitty I got to tell you!"

He seemed to be going on and on and reeling in the forced throes of ecstasy that I was heaping on him. I had him practically lifted off the floor by his ass cheeks as I abandoned his nipple that was in my mouth and quickly slurped the other nub into my mouth.

"YYYAAAAAAHHRRRRRRR," the handsome Asian Wall Street guy croaked loudly, looking down at the nipple that I had just finished sucking the fuck out of. "FUCK, just look at my nipple man. I never saw it so sore and pink looking! My poor man tits will never be the same after all this…"

"Oh they will, in a few days they will," I said and quickly swigged his nipple back into my greedy mouth, wrapping my lips around it…

A while later I said, "In a few days they'll be as good as new buddy," laughing meanly as I said it…

"So tell me man, was this what you had in mind for me the first time you saw me on the train platform?" Daniel asked, still kind of breathless.

"This and a few other things," I replied and then stopped kissing his jutted up man tits. "Man, I sure did a hell of a job on these nipples of yours huh buddy?"
"Yeah, you sure as fucking fuck did," Daniel chirped, looking down at his nipples as they were swelling up bigger and bigger it seemed. "God almighty, I have huge nips!"

We both laughed and then in a fast motion I slung the handsome guy up across my shoulders and lugged him toward my bedroom where part two of my day with Daniel was waiting…

"Hey, put me down man!" Daniel hemmed loudly. "What now??? What the fucking fuck now???"

About the Author

Christopher Trevor was born in July 1963 and grew up in New York City. As soon as he was old enough to know how he began writing fiction and has been writing gay erotic/fetish stories for the past ten to twelve years at this point. He became an avid reader as well from the time he knew how and reads everything from fiction, to non-fiction to biographies of interesting and unusual people, people who have made a difference or who have paved the way for others. Christopher attributes his writing artistic inspiration to artists such as Etienne, Tom of Finland, Tagame, The Hun, and most notably Joe T, who Christopher has had the pleasure of speaking with and even meeting over the last few years. Christopher states, "Joe T encouraged me to  write about my fetish because I was embarrassed about it at the time. Joe T said that when we are embarrassed about something that makes it even more enticing somehow." Christopher totally agreed and never stopped writing in this genre. Erotic writers who inspired Christopher Trevor were: Tom Shaw (author of "That Day at the Quarry), C.S. White (author of Big Sur), Larry Townsend (author of countless erotic novels), and Mason Powell (author of the classic story "The Brig.")

Christopher discovered that not only did he enjoy writing erotic tales but that after his first bondage experience he had a genuine flair for it. Writing to erotic oriented magazines about his first bondage experience truly opened the floodgates for Christopher where this style of writing is concerned. Christopher thanks the handsome and muscular "Greg" for that experience way back in time. Christopher took "Creative Writing" courses every semester during his high school years and while other friends of his stopped writing what they loved to write about as time went on Christopher never let a day go by when he didn't write something... "I feel that if I don't write every day I will die," Christopher has said many times over.

Foot fetish stories and all things related; spanking fetish, erotic shaving, muscle bondage, tickle torture, and hardcore stories are just a few of the areas of gay eroticism that Christopher enjoys writing about and inspiring in others as well. As one internet buddy said to Christopher where the black socks fetish is concerned, "Until I started talking with you I never gave a thought to my socks when I got dressed for work in the morning. Now when I pull my dress socks on every morning I get a chill up my spine."

Christopher is proud of the erotic effect he has on people...

Christopher Trevor is also the author of:

The Executive Guide to Foot Fetishism and Office Discipline
1-887895-36-1

Executive Ties That Bind
1-887895-37-X

Don't!! Stop!! That Tickles!!
1-887895-31-0

The Taming of Dominick
1-887895-45-0

Timmy and The Hong Kong Tailor
1-887895-30-2

Love, Torture and Redemption
1-887895-32-9

Timmys Ticklish Trials
978-1-887895-74-3

The Gym Instructor
978-1-887895-44-6

Milked
978-1-887895-66-8

Erotic Street Blues
978-1-887895-97-2

Look for them where you found this book or Goodboner.com.

www.ingramcontent.com/pod-product-compliance
Lightning Source LLC
Chambersburg PA
CBHW071227260626
47162CB00004B/1458